ETA DRACONIS

ABOUT THE AUTHOR

Brendan Ritchie is an early-career novelist and
academic from the south-coast of WA. In 2015 he
published his debut novel *Carousel* and was awarded
a PhD in Creative Writing. *Carousel* was critically
acclaimed and described by the Sydney Morning
Herald as 'the sort of thing that might happen if
Kafka wrote a script for Big Brother.' The sequel,
Beyond Carousel, was released in 2016 and Brendan
has also published poetry and non-fiction in several
notable journals and collections. *Eta Draconis* is his
third book and the winner of the 2022 Dorothy
Hewett Award for an Unpublished Manuscript. In
addition to writing, Brendan works as a lecturer at
Edith Cowan University.

ETA DRACONIS

BRENDAN RITCHIE

UWA PUBLISHING

First published in 2023 by
UWA Publishing
Crawley, Western Australia 6009
www.uwap.uwa.edu.au

UWAP is an imprint of UWA Publishing
a division of The University of Western Australia

THE UNIVERSITY OF
WESTERN
AUSTRALIA

ISBN: 978-1-76080-261-5

A catalogue record for this book is available from the National Library of Australia

The quote on page 113 is kindly reproduced from *The Crucible* by Arthur Miller. First published in the United States of America by Viking Penguin Inc. 1953.

Cover design by Design by Committee
Typeset in 12 point Dante by Lasertype
Printed by Lightning Source

 uwapublishing

FOR
HARRIET

CHAPTER ONE

The radio wavered with static, like it did sometimes when a meteor breached the upper atmosphere.

Elora stirred in the passenger seat, the side of her face warm and numb from sleep. The view outside was too bright to gaze upon immediately, so she kept her eyes on her lap as her senses returned.

A fantasy novel lay on the seat beside her, the story of an elven city besieged by demons. Hoards of these gruesome creatures had been held at bay for centuries by a single, mythical tree. Their horror steeped in folklore and saved for the fireside until the shocking day this tree began to die. One by one, the demons began to manifest in the elven kingdom. Elves died silently and savagely in their homes and gardens. Limbs crushed and twisted.

Faces caught in a primal, ancient horror. Finally, the alarm was sounded and a great war ensued.

Elora had taken the book from her father's shelves on the morning of their departure, burrowing deep into this world as her parents waved from the balcony and she and her sister wound out of their sleepy hometown en route to the distant northern city.

Vivienne was driving, her hands cupped loosely on the steering wheel, her hair up and sunglasses shielding her eyes from the whiteness of the landscape beyond. A tiny, constant frown divided her forehead as if she was straining to glimpse the city still so far beyond them. Her clothes had changed in anticipation of her return to the city: jeans ripped and frayed in careful patterns, a t-shirt bearing the name of an all-girl band from the previous century, tall leather boots that Elora had only ever seen in photos. She seemed calm and focused, no sign of the restlessness that had accompanied her all summer.

Elora wondered if she had slept for only a few minutes, or whether her sister had been frozen in this position for hours. The ocean had disappeared from their mirrors, and a haze now hovered in its wake. Elora had hoped to catch a glimpse of the coastline as the highway swung west, but it looked as though they were too far inland. It would be lost to them now until they reached the city.

She cursed herself and squinted out at the landscape beside them, a dirty-beige patchwork of wheat, barley and land that was too drought-stricken for either. Occasionally there were gullies and creek beds, but many of these had run dry since the last floods. Gravel roads cut long lines through this land to arrive at broken down machinery and abandoned shearing sheds. Everything seemed to be immovable, even in the wind. Elora felt a foreign shudder of loneliness. It was land that belonged not to faces or voices, but to rusted surnames on gates made of steel.

They crested a small rise and caught a vista of the land ahead: more abandoned paddocks, and a highway teasing like a ribbon into an endless series of white-grey corrugations.

The static came again. Longer this time, like the wake of a giant wave.

A car travelling behind them slowed down and pulled off the highway.

'Should we stop?' asked Elora.

Vivienne leaned forward slightly and looked at the sky. It was crystalline and blue. The farmland offered a wide and reassuring view of the horizon to the north and west. No mountains or buildings, just a dull fog behind them from the distant Southern Ocean. 'We're fine,' she said, turning off the radio entirely.

She sounded confident and unworried. Bored, even. Elora might have been reassured by this but for the silence that now surrounded them. It was thick and unnerving. She felt as though she could hear all the way out into space, to the place they had learnt about in school where the atmosphere begins to thin and sounds turn milky and ghostlike. A place called the mesosphere, where their planet raged its silent war with the rocks that come at them over and over.

Elora took a pair of headphones from her bag and put on some music, a pop album that jarred with the landscape and circumstance. She left it playing regardless, trying hard not to think about the hours of driving that lay ahead. Towns with strange names like Ravensthorpe, Newdegate and Dumbleyung, and the gaping spaces between them. Elora had passed through these places as a child, bundled in between suitcases, boxes and bottled water as their parents raced south beneath a heaving meteor shower. Her father had the perfect soundtrack for this moment, as he did for any other: nostalgic and homely folk songs cradled their four lonely souls through the day and the night. Elora feigned sleep, but saw every one of these towns. She remembered their tiny, defiant lights against the black of the land, and cars snaking away from general stores and petrol stations. The feeling of travelling for hours to finally reach a town that stretched no more than a block before heading back into the abyss in search of another.

'How far is the next town?' she asked, taking off the headphones.

'I told you to go before we left,' said Vivienne.

'I don't need to go.'

Vivienne swapped hands on the wheel and sipped some water from a bottle in the console. 'It's an hour away.'

Elora looked back out at the paddocks and wondered whether any of these were the farms of her classmates from school. They were miles from the town now, but students descended from all over to sit in those musty concrete classrooms. She would see them arrive in convoys of buses outside the gymnasium before form, then again at the end of the day, waiting slumped against the faded beige bricks as their friends left for beaches and delis.

'Where were you last night?' asked Vivienne.

'With Frances. Why?'

Vivienne sighed.

'What?'

'Mum made dinner for everyone.'

Elora felt a flicker of guilt. 'She knew I was going out.'

'You couldn't have dinner first?'

'You've barely eaten dinner with us all summer.'

'That's bullshit. Plus, I'm working on my thesis.'

'Don't you have all year for that?'

Vivienne didn't reply.

It had been like this the whole summer. And the one before that. Clipped and strained conversations loaded with the pressure of something larger that neither of them fully understood. Elora was sure things were simpler when she was younger. Or perhaps when both of them were. Vivienne now looked at Elora with a kind of irritated scepticism. As if the act of growing into adulthood was somehow antagonistic. As if there had been other options available to her.

Vivienne turned the radio back on.

Elora riffled around in her bag and took out a map, a forest-green booklet with a black swan on the cover, like all of the free, government-issue roadmaps. She and her friends had grown up

4

imagining the state and country via the simplified graphics of these maps. Towns, roads, lakes and deserts signified by dots, lines and shadings. She traced the long stretch of highway from the coast to the first town ahead of them. Muddled circles marked the raised topography bordering this town. These circles seemed a rare feature of her map. Elora could only find a few others, either to the west of them or a long way to the north.

'Where are the mountains?' asked Elora.

'What mountains?'

'There were mountains. When we drove down with Mum and Dad.'

Vivienne glanced at her. 'You remember that?'

Elora nodded.

'Weren't you, like, four?'

'I was nine.'

Elora waited while Vivienne ran the maths in her head.

'They're west of here. People don't drive that way anymore.'

'Why not?'

'Because the roads are busted.'

Elora studied this area of the map again, hoping it might somehow give a sense of the carnage and destruction she now imagined. She'd just assumed they would be journeying through these fabled mountains on their way to the city. Had even made a playlist to accompany them. It struck her in this moment how little she really knew of the world to the north of their town. How far removed her imagination was from the reality pouring through her window. She folded away the map and sat with her knees pulled to her chest.

Vivienne shifted in the seat beside her. A road train hammered past in the opposite direction, ferrying supplies to the distant southern towns.

'Did they send you an orientation book?'

Elora nodded.

'And information about the student village?'

'I have a building number.'

Vivienne seemed unsatisfied, but let it be.

'Where do you live again?' asked Elora.

'South of the city. Near the river.'

'Near our old house?'

'Not far.'

Elora stared out at the immovable horizon and tried again to filter through her memories of life in this house and city. The things that came to her always felt random and trivial. The glow of fast-food chains. The reek of the river during summer. Waiting in the car as they drove to school or soccer or the supermarket. Vivienne scolding her for staring at the people in the traffic that seemed to engulf them, always. None of these things felt charged with anything in particular. Her life had been severed into two equal sections, city and country. As she finally set out to return to the city, Elora now worried that she lacked a connection to either.

The highway pulsed ahead of them, a crisp white light that made the sun seem oddly vague and mellow.

'Vivienne!'

Elora sat upright and started counting. *One one hundred. Two one hundred. Three one hundred.*

Vivienne took off her sunglasses and checked the mirrors. Two more cars abandoned the highway behind them. They were travelling alone now for as far as they could see. She flicked down both of their sun visors then steadied her hands on the wheel.

'How far is the town?' asked Elora.

'Still an hour,' said Vivienne.

'Further than going back home?'

Vivienne didn't answer. She had increased their speed to above the legal limit. The narrow strip of roadside vegetation blurred into a hedge of dirty green.

Elora continued counting. *Nine one hundred. Ten one hundred.*

In school they had been told that most meteors would explode in the sky rather than become meteorites and make impact. When this happened there would be a noise, sometimes hollow like the pop of a balloon, other times deafening like a jet engine.

Accompanying the noise would be a shockwave. The proximity of the sound to the light determined a person's distance to the explosion, like thunder and lightning. If you saw an explosion then could count to thirty, the shockwave should be gentle or non-existent. When the shockwave arrived before thirty, the government advice was the same as earthquakes. Brace beneath something. Stand clear of trees and buildings. Avoid glass.

Of course, everything changed if the meteorite struck earth.

Fourteen one hundred. Fifteen one hundred.

'Stop doing that,' said Vivienne.

'What?'

'Counting.'

Elora ignored her. She began to notice more cars pulled over by the roadside, some clustered together at rest stops, others solitary and abrupt like breakdowns. There were caravans too. But none of the famed steel fortresses she had seen on television.

'I thought Draconis wasn't striking anymore.'

Vivienne was about to answer when a deep and throaty crackle sounded behind them.

Elora froze. Arms braced and taut against the dash.

'What was that place Dad took us camping?' asked Vivienne.

'What?'

'With the broken jetty.'

'We should stop,' said Elora. She was rigid in her seat. The muscles in her legs, arms, her spine, were contracted in unison. Sunlight glinted on glass all around her.

'Dad thought there would be shops and cabins out there,' Vivienne said, 'but there was nothing.'

'What are you talking about?'

Vivienne ignored this. She was zeroed in on the highway. Eyes down. Hands fastened to the wheel. 'You wanted to camp so bad that we stayed the night in the car. It was freezing and neither of us slept. And we were starving.'

'Dad caught fish for us,' corrected Elora.

'Herring,' said Vivienne. 'Gross.'

They crested a small rise, knifing through the farmland like the ghost of a Shinkansen. Nothing moved in any direction they could see.

'I know what you're doing,' said Elora.

'What?'

'Talking about all of this stuff now.'

'So play along.'

There was another pulse to their left. A giant camera flashing the landscape from above.

Vivienne increased their speed again. Elora dug down further into her seat and started over.

One one hundred. Two one hundred. Three one hundred.

It didn't feel possible that this was happening to them already. Just hours out of home when the strikes were meant to be all but over.

'I remember Dad snoring,' she said, dragging the memory from her brain like an anchor from the sea.

Vivienne nodded, looking pleased.

'And we found some chocolate in the glovebox.'

'Mum's rum and raisin.'

Elora nodded. Vivienne glanced at her, then back to the highway.

Suddenly their speed dropped and the car seemed to buckle downward. As if they had veered into a great headwind.

'Put your hand on the windscreen,' said Vivienne.

'What?' said Elora, abandoning the count.

'Like this. Now,' said Vivienne.

Elora followed her lead and lay her palm flat against the glass.

'Push outwards, but not too hard,' said Vivienne.

Elora tried, but felt the power drain from her muscles like they were melting into liquid. For the first time, Vivienne looked around for somewhere that could shelter them. Thick scrub bordered the highway for as far as she could see. There were no crossroads or sheds. No more cars or caravans.

A small green marker flashed by. Ninety kilometres until the next town.

'What else happened that night?' Vivienne asked.

'I don't know,' said Elora.

'Did we read magazines? Listen to music?'

'I don't know,' repeated Elora.

Her eyes had welled. Everything was blurring now. The landscape. The sunlight burning down upon them. The long arm of her sister, tense and rigid beside her.

'Elora?'

They hurtled forward into the abyss of the graveyard highway. Sky flashing on both sides of them now.

'Kangaroos hopped around the wagon,' said Elora, eventually.

Vivienne tilted her head to listen.

'Late at night. The wind had died and Dad had stopped snoring. I thought you were asleep too, then you rolled over to wake me up. There was this thumping on the ground. Like footsteps or drums. It was cloudy and Draconis wasn't showering much. I couldn't see anything, but it sounded like they were right outside the car. I'd never seen a kangaroo in real life.'

Elora stopped herself. The two of them held a frozen and silent vigil at the windscreen. Somewhere above them the sky creaked and moaned like a door about to be flung wide open.

'You were hoping for a meteor,' said Vivienne.

Elora didn't answer. She slid her hand from the glass and closed her eyes.

Chapter Two

The week before she left for the city, Elora and her friends had taken their final venture into the wilderness east of town. They travelled out in muddled convoys, borrowing cars from parents and siblings and loading them with surfboards, tents and beer. The drive took them inland for a time, past farms and salt lakes, before sweeping back to the south and twisting through a series of ancient rock formations, thick bushland surrounding these towers and the land between them. Kangaroos would emerge from the trees at daybreak to freeze like statues on the highway. At dusk prehistoric insects would breach the deep silence with a calming, rhythmic score. In between these moments, the days were slow and dreamlike. It was Njunga country, at the eastern border of a great pyramid of Noongar land. Ancient beyond all comprehension.

Their campground lay at the foot of a colossal granite headland. Out of endless miles of beach and dune rose sudden swathes of deep-orange rock, running upwards for hundreds of metres, broken only by seams of shadow and hunkered foliage. This headland sheltered the beach and campsites, marking the beginning of a series of national parks that hugged the coastline and ran unbroken into the desert. Elora and her family had camped their way right up and down this coastline during their first few years in the town. Heading east into the abyss seemed to be something that all of the locals did, their four-wheel-drives tessellated with diesel, ice and red meat. The longer and less-travelled the path, the better. For a while Elora didn't understand this pilgrimage: the town was already isolated, and the local beaches were both quiet and spectacular. But as they drove home in the smoky dusk of their first weekend away, and ahead of them the lights of town blipped like a homely beacon amid the darkness of a universe gone wild, Elora no longer felt as though they were living at the edge of the world. The boundary had shifted and, to Elora at least, their town felt different.

It was the tail end of the holidays and the campgrounds still drew scatterings of tourists and locals. They huddled down against the saltbush and banksias in tents and annexes, fishing and swimming through the mornings before taking shelter from the howling south-westerlies. Some of the camping bays had caravans and generators, with a look that spoke of months or years rather than a weekend. Elora's dad had told her of people who had taken to the bush when the rocks first arrived then remained there ever since. Meteorites had as much chance of striking in these isolated national parks as they did in Melbourne or Manhattan, yet somehow these people found solace in the space and the quiet. They were considered spooked or irrational, but Elora wondered if this behaviour was so far removed from that of their own.

For five days they swam, trekked and drank around the fire. Elora and a dozen or so friends from her high school graduating year. Her mother said that parties like this used to be called 'leavers', but Elora was the only one of them going anywhere. Universities were dwindling empires built in cities beset by meteorites. People either attended them on loaded government scholarships to study vital services like medicine, engineering, or communications, like Vivienne, or not at all. Even Elora's English teacher had told her that it was naive to enrol in an arts degree while the world was still on fire.

For most teenagers in the town, the rocks from Eta Draconis brought only monotony and stasis. Their worlds contracted, and they spoke not of years or semesters, but hours, days and weekends. Yet there were jobs in the town, and small lives to be lived amid the surf, bars and house parties. Anything beyond this felt distant, pointless to discuss. Their futures lay suspended somewhere out in the galaxy. Rocks or no rocks. Or worse still, an endless confusion of both. This trip was meant to mark the end of something more than just school, yet a vital ingredient was missing from the air, and each of them could sense its absence. An uncomfortable sameness emanated from all their words and actions, and they worked hard to chase it away with alcohol and revelry.

Their stay was met with broken sunshine, and winds blown in from a cold and messy ocean. Some of them spent the days trekking over dunes and outcrops, cameras looped on necks and hoods pulled over their ears. Others moped by the fire, drinking and sleeping as their boards lay forgotten and dusty with ash. But finally, on their last afternoon in the park, the weather warmed, the wind shifted offshore, and for a golden few hours they swam and surfed like pharaohs beneath the hulking yellow headland.

Serious local surfers didn't bother themselves with this break. It was considered small and irregular, and hours from the popular beaches surrounding the town. However, with a large enough swell from the south, the tranquil waters of the cape would line up with perfect, curling waves for hours on end. They began as distant, rhythmic murmurs at the far edge of the headland, wrapping like wings around its bays and honeyed protrusions.

With the gradual shallowing, these murmurs took a proud and shimmering arch, holding for an age before falling in impossible slow motion, end over end, like curling paper, until they ran aground in the empty sweep of the shore.

Elora spent a frantic hour paddling into anything she could. Her legs jittered with the adrenaline stored, like an electrical charge, in the synapses of a surfer kept on land. Gradually this burned away, and she and the others bobbed serenely past the break, casually picking out waves that held a smaller degree of perfection than the last. People swam and snorkelled in the gentle shore break, taking rests to lay on sand that was so white and so fine that it squeaked beneath each step. An esky and stereo were dragged down from the campsite, and Elora caught herself, mid-wave, while guitar licked out into the dusky, faded surrounds. It felt like a moment to capsule and store away as the defining image of a broken yet perfect adolescence. She thought about this too hard, or for too long, slipping from the board and tumbling like a rag doll through the foam.

When the sky became pale and the headland threw a shadow over the break, they coaxed the last surfers from their boards and trudged back through the dunes to their camp. A punch was made from the remains of their fruit, ice and liquor, while others stoked the fire and wrapped potatoes, sausages and whatever else they could find in alfoil and stacked them amid the coals. Couples drifted off to shower and fool around in the bathrooms by the communal barbecues, returning doe-eyed and smiley as the first of the meteors cut across the night sky.

Of the twenty or so campers, all of which Elora knew well, she was close friends with three. Donnie and Jenna were the fifth-grade couple who had greeted her like a younger cousin on her first day at the strange and insular country school. They were so calming and so present that Elora just assumed they had been tasked by the school with the role of welcoming meteor refugees. But then others arrived, teary and dumbstruck as she had been, yet Donnie and Jenna didn't waver. They had chosen Elora for reasons she still hadn't determined. For a long time she waited to see if these two popular, attractive people might drift away after seeing her house or meeting her parents. She worried that being from the city gave her a novelty that with time would surely wane.

Donnie was a surfer kid with a steady orbit of friends, family and weekend adventures. Through no fault of his own, Donnie had only ever known one place, and he knew it better than most. The dope dealers. The football coaches. The four-street ghetto. Beaches with surf, or snorkelling, or secret car bays. Rumours that were true and others that were fun.

Somehow Donnie seemed fully formed already. And while other kids hovered on the precipice, waiting for the defining event in their adolescence – a car crash, aborted pregnancy, backpacking pilgrimage – Donnie spoke and acted with the certainty of an adult, despite not having experienced any of these things. That he was remaining in town after high school was a surprise to no one, yet Elora did wonder whether the town had enough secrets left for Donnie to uncover.

With her dirty-blonde hair and deep tan, Jenna looked like more of a surfer than Donnie, but actually preferred cars and video games to beaches and sunshine. Jenna was the first one among them to get her licence, then the first to save for a car. She had to be the driver wherever they went, and was often sober, looking at their sloppy expressions with a kind of big-sister amusement as she cruised them through the lonely, shuttered streets in the early hours of the weekend. She was smart without trying, and frustrated one teacher after another with her ambivalence towards her studies. Jenna's father had left her mother and sisters around the time that the meteor showers became serious. Elora had heard people at school say that he had gone into the desert to live underground. The sources weren't reliable, and Jenna never mentioned it, so Elora assumed the truth was something more mundane.

Jenna had an ability to live in the moment that made any talk of the future feel somewhat pointless. It wasn't reckless or extreme, rather an intense form of immersion. When Jenna watched a sunset, or drank a milkshake, or danced to new music, she was *there* and nowhere else. And this radiated from her to those nearby. For Elora, time passed with Jenna in a different way than it did with others.

Donnie and Jenna had remained together for as long as Elora had known them. There were other long-term relationships amid the maelstrom of crushes, cheating and hook-ups within the town's only high school, yet Donnie and Jenna seemed different. They didn't try to mimic adulthood with anniversaries, dates and weekend getaways, nor did they race from one faux catastrophe to the next. To Elora, they just seemed to be living their lives alongside each other. Donnie was Donnie. Jenna, Jenna.

Elora's best friend in the town was Frances O'Neil. She and Frances didn't have a story about their first encounter; rather, theirs was simply a gradual realisation that their interests and personalities were too closely aligned, particularly within the context of a small rural high school, to be ignored. They gravitated together at the front of art class and the back of gym. They put in the same lunch orders, sipped spearmint milks beneath the same trees at the edge of the oval, chose the same creepy movies to rent from the town's solitary video store.

Frances had been medicated for anxiety and depression since the beginning of the showers. She hated this coincidence, and swore to anyone who asked that she didn't give a fuck about Eta Draconis. Unfortunately for Frances there were many others around her who were triggered by the showers, and she was regularly bundled in with this collective, inside of school and out. Her reaction to this was a fully cavalier approach to anything related to meteors: she ignored the news and radio updates, slept in her car, surrounded by glass, almost every weekend, and even kept her window shutters open through the night when the rest of the town – and the country – rolled theirs down and huddled in darkness until morning. Sometimes when Elora crept home late at night, she would see Frances' bedroom from across the suburbs, a tiny frame of light against the dark and shuttered town. It was so fearless and defiant that Elora smiled every time she saw it.

Frances wasn't leaving town for university either. The decision made over a year ago when she quietly switched out of the university stream subjects and started working more hours at her parents' chalet business. Bookings had been strong since the showers started and people stopped flying to places like Broome and Bali. Elora helped out on reception some weekends. Other weekends, if there was a cancellation or vacancy, Wendy and Jim let them stay in a chalet and pretend they were guests. They would lounge about in robes and chug wine from the minibar. The chalets had satellite dishes that sometimes picked up extra TV channels, and occasionally new programs from America. It was on one of these nights that Elora asked Frances whether she would be staying in town. Everyone, including Elora, knew the answer to this already, but she still felt like it was important to ask.

'Mum and Dad need me here,' answered Frances, flicking through the TV channels. 'Plus the doctor says my medication isn't working.'

Elora nodded, dumbly. That wasn't something she knew already.

The punch was too sweet but they finished it anyway, then what was left of the beer and wine. People kept adding food to the coals: marshmallows and chocolate, bananas, sweet potato. Hovering by the fire looking for glints of silver to pull out and unwrap. The stereo kept up for a while before the batteries ran dead and they filled the silence with creepy rumours about strikes and shockwaves from faraway places. Like the school bus in Norway that was found with its windows blown in and the children frozen in their seats, faces glittering with glass and blood in the morning sun. Or the Munich brewhouse full of screaming drinkers holding aloft bloodied hands and shattered steins. Or the cargo liners that left Chile and were swallowed whole by a meteorite tsunami that spread their giant sea containers all along the South Island of New Zealand a year later. Draconis had been a constant presence in their lives, but few of them had ever been touched by her violence. Instead it found a comfortable and distant home in their folklore and gossip.

The stories ran their course, fading into the rumble of the ocean beyond the dunes. The larger circle surrounding the fire splintered into couples and smaller clusters. Donnie and Jenna pulled a rug over to join Frances and Elora as they shared a final bottle of cheap cabernet.

Donnie looked up from the fire, a glint in his eye that all of them had seen before. 'You know there's a crater out here somewhere.'

'I thought all the big strikes were in the north,' said Elora, sitting across from him.

'No, I mean, an old crater. From, like, ages ago.'

'Oh yeah. I've heard that too,' said Jenna.

The four of them looked past each other into the fire. Jenna twirled her hands in the warmth like a mystic.

'It's weird, isn't it?' asked Donnie.

'What?' asked Frances.

'Meteorites before Draconis.'

'Wars before guns,' said Elora.

Her words hung in the air for a moment before Donnie smirked and the rest of them joined him. Elora shook her head, feigning offence.

'Did you guys get the old dinosaur story in school with the meteorite and the dust and everything?' asked Frances.

'Yeah,' smiled Jenna. 'All those cheesy graphics with the hungry T-Rex.'

'You know they don't teach that anymore,' said Frances.

'What do they teach?' asked Elora.

'My cousin's kids are in school, and he says they don't do dinosaurs at all.'

'Why not?'

'So kids don't freak out about meteorites,' said Donnie.

Frances nodded.

'That's stupid,' said Jenna. 'They're going to find out eventually. And kids should freak out about meteorites. They're fucking terrifying.'

'Yeah, but the real story is pretty insane,' said Donnie.

'What's the real story, again?' asked Elora.

Their gazes fell on Frances. This was the kind of information she kept on file. Not school lessons or bus timetables or banking pins. Frances knew album names from the nineties and which brands of cola had the highest caffeine. She would go almost an entire term without offering a word in class, then floor a teacher with a historical account of the art trade during the Second World War. Elora loved these moments, their casual and wicked humour, and the silence that followed.

Frances took a sip of the wine and passed the bottle to Elora. Fire licked at the corners of her wide, brown eyes. 'The meteorite that struck Earth back then was heavy metal, and in retrograde solar orbit.'

The camp was hushed and still under her voice.

'It was big, too, but what people forget is that it's the speed and density that matter. The impact from a rock like that is so powerful that it sets off every volcano on the planet, all at the same time. And it sends millions of tiny fireballs back up into the atmosphere.'

Elora listened, the wine forgotten.

'These fireballs can't deal with the cold of the outer atmosphere, so they melt or explode or something, and every time this happens a tiny burst of heat is let off. Times that by a hundred. Then a thousand. Then a million. Then mix this with all of the volcanos erupting. The whole planet was baked like an oven.'

'How long did it take?' asked Elora.

'A day. Maybe two.'

Elora stared at her. She felt a deep pang of sadness for these ancient creatures. So giant, yet so doomed.

'Fuck,' whispered Donnie.

'That's awful,' said Jenna.

Elora glanced up at the dancing sky above them, suddenly conscious of how long it had been since she actually stopped to take it all in. Above her at this moment she could see a thousand white-hot needles knifing through the darkness. Each one existed for only a second before exploding and being replaced by another. It was chaotic and relentless, like flurried rainfall caught amid an endless gale. Occasionally something larger emerged from this flurry and entered the stratosphere. A light that grew brighter and stole the gaze. It would burn with a pulse that diminished her pupils and drew shadows from the trees surrounding them.

Elora had been through nights that were heavier with meteors, but the bush was vast and black, and had nothing to steal their glow. Draconis was overwhelming at the best of times, but when it stretched out and danced back with this much intensity, a singular life felt trivial in a way that unnerved her.

'Sorry,' said Frances, taking back the wine. 'Buzz kill?'

They smirked, then broke into exhausted laughter.

'I read that when it happened – to the dinos – the rock was so big that it ripped a hole in the atmosphere behind it,' said Donnie.

Jenna looked at him, somewhere between adoration and annoyance.

'So for a few seconds, even if it were daytime, you could see right out into space.'

'That's terrifying,' said Elora, shivering.

'It's also bullshit,' said Frances.

Jenna laughed.

'Whatever. Frances fireballs,' said Donnie.

'Cool band,' said Jenna.

'Your school bus story was better,' said Frances.

'That one's true,' said Donnie.

Elora laughed now too. She felt a sudden and fierce connection to those three faces. Her tiny wolf pack beneath the burning sky.

They'd made plans to stay up until dawn and swim in the light of Draconis, but the park had a way of stimulating the senses to a point of exhaustion. Some of them fell asleep by the fire. Others drifted away to tents to pass out or fool around. Jenna dragged Donnie away from yet another conversation and into their tent. Frances took some water and a torch to her mattress in the back of Jenna's Subaru. She loved to camp, except for the tents, insects and general outdoors.

Elora watched them go, and decided to linger by the fire rather than return to her tent. There were hushed voices within the camp, occasional whispers and laughter, but all was still by the fireside. The wind had turned, now whipping through the dunes in fresh and briny torrents. Elora took off her hood and let them wash over her face.

Camping had always amplified her thoughts and emotions, and again they flooded her in a sea of nostalgia and excitement. She would still be in town for another week, packing, spending time with her parents, trying to remain civil with Vivienne, yet it felt to her like this was her final evening. Her entire adolescence had been housed within this handful of bodies and voices, and now she was moving on, not for escape or for virtue, but rather on a whim that felt more arbitrary every time she looked upward at the heaving, violent sky.

After a while just sitting there, Elora pulled herself up and shuffled over to the Subaru. She slid into the back seat and lay there listening to Frances' breathing in the space behind her.

'Can I sleep in here?' she asked, after a while.

'How did you know I was awake?'

'No snoring.'

'Yet you want to sleep in here.'

The two of them lay in silence for a moment.

'How come you're awake?' asked Elora.

'I'm watching Alpha Centauri.'

Elora propped herself up and peered over the seat. Frances was lying on her stomach with her head raised on her elbows to face the back window.

'As in the meteor shower?' asked Elora.

'Yep.'

'Okay.'

'What? Just because Draconis showed up doesn't mean we have to ignore all of the other showers. Centauri has been around forever.'

Elora pulled herself over the seat to lay beside Frances. She edged across a fraction but remained silent.

'So, where is it?'

'Low down in the south. Just above the horizon.'

Elora followed her gaze out of the window. The sky above the saltbush was pulsing with a rhythmic swell of lights and flashes.

'How do you know it's not just Draconis?'

'The colour and the brightness. Centauri is dust. Just tiny specks of dust drifting around in space. When it hits our atmosphere it dances and sparkles like glitter,' said Frances. 'It's nothing like Draconis.'

Elora glanced sideways at her. 'You okay?' she asked.

'Yeah,' said Frances, after a while. 'Have you packed everything?'

'Nope,' said Elora.

'Anything?'

'Some books, but I might not take them.'

'Vivienne will leave without you.'

'Maybe she already has. She was getting the car ready last week.'

'She's crazy,' said Frances. 'What are you guys going to talk about for two whole days?'

'God. I don't know. I should take the bus.'

'Do you think she will want to hang out once you're in the city?' asked Frances.

'No, I think she'll dump me on campus and I won't see her again until semester break.'

'Sorry.'

'It's fine. It would be weird if we were suddenly best friends.'

'I heard everyone has smartphones in the city,' said Frances. 'The towers are rock-proof or something.'

'Vivienne has one,' said Elora, nodding.

'And the internet is fast. Like before Draconis.'

'Yeah. Vivienne is always going on about it.'

'What does she say?' asked Frances, looking at her.

'Just that it sucks down here. She can't watch movies or do her shopping or whatever.'

The two of them lay in silence, the trees rustling roughly beside them. It was cool for a summer night, the air arriving from somewhere distant and southern.

'I'm glad we were young when this all started,' said Frances quietly.

'Why?'

'Because we don't remember all the stuff that Vivienne remembers. Her whole world flipped upside down. We just lost the cartoons on TV.'

'I miss those,' said Elora. She shivered and curled up away from the window, while Frances kept up her vigil.

'Anyway, thanks for being my friend while you were living here,' said Frances.

'What?' asked Elora, smiling.

Frances was silent, her face turned away.

'Frances. Don't be weird. You totally saved my life in high school.'

'You were hanging out with the O'Brien sisters,' said Frances.

'I know,' said Elora. 'That's what I mean.'

Frances sniffed a little. Elora felt her own eyes welling and fought against it.

'You could have a baby by now,' said Frances.

'Why do they always have to rhyme the names?' asked Elora. 'Ryan. Madeline. Evangeline.'

'Brian.'

'No!' said Elora.

'It's the uncle,' said Frances.

'Brian O'Brien?'

Frances laughed a little, then turned away from the window and sighed, as if in this moment she had fallen into sleep.

'It's weird camping out here with everyone,' whispered Elora.

'Like we're celebrating something, but nobody knows what the fuck it is?' said Frances.

'Totally,' sniffed Elora.

Frances rolled away from her, and her breathing softened.

'Buy a phone when you get there,' she whispered. 'If they fix the tower down here we can message each other about the O'Briens.'

'Okay,' said Elora.

Frances twitched, then fell into a long and rolling snore.

Elora closed her eyes and waited for the flashes of light to dissolve. It took longer these days. Hours, sometimes. They were phosphenes, but since Draconis, people had started calling them phantom streaks. There were all kinds of remedies, involving pitch dark, or blinding lights, or combinations of the two. Normally they didn't bother Elora, but this evening she would have given anything for some respite. She felt paralysed by the energy of Draconis, and worried about what it meant for the people she would be leaving behind. For her mother who would now be without both daughters, thrust into retirement by Draconis and hidden away on the edge of the country. Her father, always so positive, so calm, now trying to fill a void that no partner could negotiate. Donnie, who at eighteen was already too big for the town he would inhabit for the rest of his life. Jenna who hid in the minutiae of life because Draconis had stripped her of the substance.

And Frances. She taunted Draconis in every way possible. Meteorites were a game of chance. Rocks thrown from the depths of the universe into a solar system of spinning, orbiting spheres. Frances' odds were strong – everyone's were – yet she kept playing hand after hand after hand. If Draconis continued, she may be struck and killed, but if it somehow halted and a normal life resumed, Elora worried that Frances' world might collapse entirely.

CHAPTER THREE

Elora felt the flicker of shade across the windscreen, staccato and unexpected. Trees by the roadside. They were spindly and broken, hugging the edge of the highway to escape the engulf of the farmland beyond. She remained motionless, knees held tight to her chest and head burrowed into the ball that was her jacket. The fleeting moments of shade felt calm and nurturing, as if they had already travelled a great journey to a place where sun and sky no longer reigned so fiercely.

She shifted away from the jacket and looked around fully. The farmland had abandoned its barren plateau and was rolling with the mounds and eddies of what looked to be the beginning of a mountain range. There was green ahead of them – not the dark and stubborn green of mallees, but a lighter sweep that etched against the horizon via a series of arcs and whalebacks.

Looking closely at this landscape, Elora could see both paddock and bushland, and in between these the clusters and spurs of an ancient grey stone.

A pulse of adrenaline danced over her skin. There were shadows shifting on the landscape. Her eyes darted upward and her stomach tightened.

Clouds, not meteors.

She exhaled. The weather seemed to be cooling. Perhaps they were already further west than she thought.

Vivienne sat casually in the seat beside her. Her sunglasses were gone, and the sun visors were back on the ceiling. A bottle of water was open and nestled between her legs as she drove.

'Where are we?' Elora asked.

'Almost at Ravensthorpe.'

Elora felt cheated by this. Her dreams had been detailed and epic, yet they'd travelled only an hour.

'Why didn't you stop for those meteors?'

'They were tiny. Barely atmospheric.'

'Everyone else stopped.' Elora shook her head at her sister's faux bravado.

Vivienne shrugged. 'There's no point stopping for a meteor, Elora. They explode where they want. For all we know, those people who pulled over are picking up pieces of their windscreens right now.'

Elora was silent, not buying this cavalier version of her sister, but also in no position to determine the truth of her words. She considered closing her eyes and tunnelling back down into sleep, but something caught her vision in the farmland ahead. A patch of darkness amid the glare. 'Shit,' she whispered.

In the distance, yet immediately huge, were the blackened rims of two impact craters, side by side in a paddock. Two paddocks, actually, as the closest of the craters stretched from one paddock to the next, a fence lying broken and stranded at the edge. The land around was charred and flattened as if by a hurricane. Trees stumped, shrubs still standing but at crazy, untenable angles.

'Don't freak out,' said Vivienne. 'They've been there for ages.'

'How long?'

'I don't know. Years.'

'They're still so black,' said Elora.

Vivienne was silent. Uninterested.

'Are there more?'

'Yes.'

'Can we stop at one?'

'No.'

Elora didn't protest. She wasn't even sure that she wanted to get out of the car and see one of them up close. There was a haze in the air around the craters, as if, even years later, the dust still hovered in shock.

As they drove alongside the craters, Elora saw a vehicle moving nearby: a big, blocky harvester taking in the summer crop. She watched as the machine slowly circled one of the craters, pulling grain from the very edge of the depression. Elora was taken aback by the sight of food being farmed right beside these smouldering gravesites.

The only other crater she'd seen was the tiny hollow just outside of their town. This was a five-metre circle, the vegetation grown back and the warning tape long since blown away. Local kids now used it as a wind break to smoke weed and pretend like hanging around up there was somehow more dangerous than anywhere else in the town.

Elora tried hard to pull her eyes from these new craters, to shrug them off like Vivienne and, she assumed, everyone else in this new world.

Emergency landlines resumed by the roadside within a few kilometres of Ravensthorpe. Three-sided steel boxes that each housed a simple handset and keypad, alongside a list of services including police, ambulance, fire, glass repair, meteorite sightings, news recording and lottery, the whole structure sprayed in blue and maintained by a fleet of government vans. Elora had never used an EL except to mess about with her friends, but she now felt reassured by their familiarity.

The town emerged from the bushland via a power station and abandoned caravan park. More trees followed, then a scattering of houses tracing the final slopes of the ridge. Old fibro buildings with sagging roofs and defeated front lawns. The only things new were the window shutters that clung like braces to the peeling timber facades. Elora stared hard at these houses, trying to imagine the lives being lived within. She saw dogs, cars and play equipment, but never any people.

For a block and a half the houses grew clustered, then gave way to what appeared to be the centre of town. A double-storey hotel rose with some grandeur and peered east to the horizon, meal specials on a chalkboard outside and a sign advertising a house-made ale. Every inch of glass had been covered with timber or iron, like an ark preparing for a flood. Beside the hotel was a war memorial with an empty flag post and a proudly sculpted garden. Signs pointed to public toilets, the police station and a sports oval, none of which she could see. The ghosts of the town's defunct mining operations lingered in a vacated video store, laundromat and café, all of which had been left without shutters. Over time, many of the windows had been blown in by shockwaves.

She saw a mother and daughter leaving a small supermarket, and a farmer parked outside a machinery store. Otherwise the street was empty.

Elora was still taking everything in when it all was suddenly behind her. The houses and buildings ceased, and the town evaporated into road signs, grain silos and another endless highway. She was about to protest when Vivienne slowed and turned them into a service station.

They pulled up behind two other vehicles and idled, waiting. Vivienne took out her fuel card and stretched her neck from side to side.

'Can we get food here?' asked Elora, watching an old attendant speak into the window of a car ahead of them.

'Yeah. But don't use too much of your cash. Hardly anyone will take a card until we get to the city.'

Elora took a purse from her bag and checked her reflection in the mirror. She looked pale in spite of the sun that had followed them since leaving. The kiss of the beach seemed to have left her already, replaced by a colour she couldn't yet determine.

The car in front of them filled and swiped, and Vivienne edged them forward to the bowser, shutting off the engine and passing her card through the window. The attendant was tall and grey, with a stoop that spoke of another job before this. He swiped Vivienne's card, then craned down to peer in the window.

'Full?' he asked.

'Yeah. Thanks,' said Vivienne.

'Won't be much left on the card.'

'That's fine. We have another.'

The man looked past her to Elora. She smiled hello. He nodded.

'The wolves been hunting down by the coast?' he said.

'Not so much,' said Vivienne. She smiled, but in a way that Elora knew spoke of impatience.

He nodded again. 'You drive through that scat?'

'Sorry?' asked Vivienne.

'Those showers out by Munglinup.'

'Oh. Yeah. Nothing much to it.'

The man nodded and coughed, hoarsely. 'Scat ran through a house out here last week. Nothing bigger than a peanut, but still confettied the place. Few of us went up there with some plaster and sheeting on Sunday. Figured we could fill some of the holes, at least. The kids were back from church, using the holes to pass notes to each other while their mother was out carting water from a dam full of dead crows.'

Elora and Vivienne sat in silence, unsure of how to reply.

A car pulled up behind them. The attendant lingered for a moment as if still caught out by the pace of this new world, then straightened and shuffled over to fill up their car.

Vivienne sighed and turned to Elora. 'You can go in now. I'll meet you around the side if this guy is finished before you're done.'

Elora felt oddly anxious. 'Don't you want stuff, too?' she asked.

'Just grab me a Coke.'

Elora hesitated for a moment, then stepped outside. She could feel her sister's eyes on her, and tried hard to look relaxed.

'Don't forget to pee,' called Vivienne, checking her phone for a network.

The air inside the service station was heavy with sweat and over-salted chips. A radio was playing, the reception too poor to make out the song. Window shutters were partially open to allow a view of the bowsers, and their shadow cut across the space inside. Elora veered from the woman tending a bain-marie and found herself in an aisle devoted to meteorite survival supplies: gas masks, fire extinguishers, walkie-talkies, water purifiers, telescopes, canned food, hunting knives, and a whole series of roadmaps. Nothing Elora hadn't seen before, but she was slightly overwhelmed by the sight of it all.

She pretended to browse for a moment, then turned away to the shelves behind her. Rather than food or confectionery, she found racks full of burns treatments and trauma kits – serious, professional-looking equipment that Elora hadn't encountered outside of a hospital.

She left this section and headed straight for the drinks fridge. There was Coke, but otherwise the options were random and limited. Elora reached in for a juice and the label came away in soggy fragments on her fingers. She checked the use-by date; it had expired months earlier. The woman at the counter was shuffling about, and Elora felt under pressure to make a decision, as if her fussiness made a mockery of the world these people lived in. She took a second Coke from the fridge and carried them to the counter.

'Cash?' asked the woman.

'Yes,' said Elora. She looked across at the food in the bain-marie. Everything was coated in a deep orange batter that seemed to glisten in the artificial light. 'Do you have any sandwiches?'

The woman shook her head. 'Veg truck comes through tomorrow.'

'That's fine,' said Elora, smiling politely. She scanned the rest of the counter for something edible, but there only appeared to be gum, peanuts and jerky. She felt itchy and flustered. 'Just the drinks, please.'

The woman punched the items into the register.

Elora took out some cash, then stopped herself. 'Sorry, actually, is card okay?'

The woman didn't reply, but waited.

Elora scrabbled through her purse for the card. She handed it over while the woman took down the number and asked her to sign.

'Is there a toilet here somewhere?'

'Outside and around the back,' said the woman, handing back the card.

'Thanks.'

Elora didn't know how she would carry the drinks and use the toilet, but she was desperate to get out of the shop. She stuffed the cans in her pockets along with the purse and pushed through the heavy reinforced door.

Around the back of the building she found a giant freezer with a back-up generator housed in a thick metal cage. Adjoining this freezer was a toilet cubicle, which was old and smelt of cheap hand soap and wet concrete. Elora stepped through to the ladies and found that only one of the two cubicles was free. She hesitated, but remembered what Vivienne had said. Plus she was close to busting.

She shut the door and sat down. The woman in the cubicle beside her was loud and unsettling, scraping shoes on the floor, sighing and muttering to herself. Elora caught a glimpse of a bag and pillow beneath the cubicle wall and wondered whether this woman might be living in the bathroom. Or sheltering from an imminent meteor shower. People often joked that public toilets were the safest place to be because of the thick concrete and lack of glass.

Elora found herself holding her breath in a way that made her feel panicked and dizzy.

This wasn't how things were meant to be. Draconis was said to be slowly stabilising, her larger rocks having already landed, with just a messy swirl of dust and debris left in their wake. Nothing much left now to breach the atmosphere. The news still contained stories of strikes and shockwaves, but also other stories where people were planning skyscrapers and launching new satellites back into space. Nobody would say it aloud, but people in most places around the globe held a quiet hope for the future. Yet out here, just hours from her home, Elora felt that she had been thrust into a hot zone. People seemed fraught and desperate in the shadow of Draconis, eking out tiny, fractured lives as the rocks rained all around them. She felt duped and immature. Why were people travelling anywhere amid such danger, let alone journeying to cities to begin degrees that stretched away so naively into the future?

Finally the woman flushed and left the cubicle. Elora took a few breaths and tried to calm herself.

She could hear a humming noise coming from outside of the toilets, and voices and the hiss of hydraulics. She remembered that they were travelling on a bus route. The woman was probably just taking a toilet break before getting back on board.

Eventually Elora was able to go, but the tightness in her abdomen remained. She pined for her home in a way that shocked her. She'd expected this feeling to come after weeks or months away, as she sat in classrooms and dormitories, yearning for surf and the cool, salty air of their balcony in the afternoon, but here it was, just hours into their journey. If she wasn't travelling with Vivienne, Elora felt quite certain she would leave on the bus heading back to her home. She didn't care what her parents or friends would think, but there was no way she could allow Vivienne this satisfaction. Her sister's judgement would linger forever, no matter the paths their lives would take.

She washed up and returned to the car with the drinks. Vivienne looked at her curiously, but didn't press. Instead she took her turn in the toilet, then returned via the shop with a pile of food that Elora had somehow overlooked.

They drove out of the town, then turned north, further away from the coast and into the pensive, thrumming heart of the state.

Chapter Four

Elora and her family had driven from the city in darkness, like everyone who fled during the chaotic first wave. Meteors were easier to see at night. Even the smallest rocks would crackle and shimmer against the black void of the state's vast horizons. This didn't mean they could be eluded, but still, people liked to see. Particularly after the strikes in the city.

Elora's mother was on the 22nd floor of her building when the first rock exploded. Her desk was on the 10th, but there was a morning tea that day for a colleague turning 40 and a few of them had taken the lift up to ensure that enough people attended. Janine was happy for the distraction. Elora had been in and out of their bed every night for the past week, and the project she was working on – allocating a new government funding pool to arts organisations – was getting messier by the day. She took a tall cup of coffee with her to the morning tea, joking with a friend about not returning until lunch.

Meteorites had been in the news for some time. It had begun with the discovery two decades earlier that one of the brightest stars in Draco had begun to diminish. Scientists were excited by the prospect that it might be about to supernova – a once-in-a-generation event triggering an explosion so bright that it would draw shadows in the daylight. Yet as the years passed, rather than explode, Eta Draconis simply continued her gradual and sombre wane. Public attention turned elsewhere, but the scientific community remained fixated on this strange phenomenon. Telescopes were redirected in Chile, Hawaii and Spain. NASA pulled data from Voyager 1 while it was still transmitting back to Earth. The Draco Project was launched by a tech billionaire, but it exploded just after lift-off. And right across the globe, in backyards, lookouts and apartments, enthusiasts stood out in the evenings to stare into the dragon and dream of what was taking place in the depths within.

With so much attention on Draco, the meteoroids were detected several years before they reached Earth. A heavy cluster of rocks and debris, fast moving and tightly formed. The volume of the rocks was largely unknown, but their position in a direct line to Eta Draconis suddenly provided a clear explanation as to her dimming, and now also the dimming of the stars around her.

People watched on with fluctuating interest as the rocks made their way steadily through the solar system. They pitched a battle with the ice moon Triton as it spun in retrograde to Neptune, then smashed through the asteroid belt in an event captured in photographs that made the news everywhere. However, it was still expected that any rocks continuing on to Earth would burn up in the planet's heavy atmosphere. People were reassured by the size of the objects – comparisons were made to footballs and pumpkins – and told to expect an impressive lightshow and nothing much more.

Finally, on a clear August evening, Northern Hemisphere skies erupted with a barrage of gold and orange streaks. The internet was immediately awash with photos and video. People ventured to lookouts and mountain ranges for the best view. Children stayed up past their bedtime to see their first ever meteor shower. There was a general sense that the event would be fleeting, something rare and spectacular that was not to be missed. As was predicted, a few meteors made it through the atmosphere and exploded in the sky. Scientists in Canada raced out to find and analyse the debris. Then more meteors descended in places like New Zealand, Uruguay and Northern Ireland. People scurried inside and recounted their experiences to friends and film crews.

Things were exciting and novel, but within hours meteors were breaching in more places than could be counted. Skies pulsed and glass shattered. Ambulances and hospitals were overrun. News stories shifted sharply in tone, then slowly disappeared as more and more satellites were struck and a catastrophic Kessler Syndrome was initiated.

The true composition of the rocks was becoming apparent: high concentrations of the meteoric iron kamacite. They weren't all burning up in the atmosphere.

* * *

Janine and her colleagues were drawn away from their cakes and conversations by a yellow light in the sky. A contrail of sorts, but one that seemed to manifest instantaneously to the north of the city. They gathered at the windows, an excited murmur drifting around as Draconis shifted from their phones and televisions and into the sky right above them. As the contrail billowed outward it looked as though the horizon had been severed into east and west, brilliant blue on either side and a white-hot scar between them. People pointed and took footage with their phones. Janine considered this, but it felt like something she should witness with her full attention. Seeing it now would help her explain the situation to Elora later in the evening.

The sound arrived a millisecond before the shockwave. Just long enough for Janine to inhale and consider reaching for her ears.

One moment they were standing, the next they were knocked to the floor like figurines. People lay in silence for a moment in the stupid shock of it all. Then they screamed. Glass littered the floors, the walls, people's arms, legs and faces. Office chairs were toppled over or clustered like penguins by the far wall. Paper showered down from the walls and ceiling.

Janine had been thrown between a coffee table and a printer. Cupcakes were smeared against her legs and a fan of serviettes trailed away from her face. She tried to move, then just lay there, watching the wind play at their decorative corners. She thought about her daughters playing with their kites on the banks of the river, wind buffeting their hair and dresses, the water shimmering and endless behind them. Beyond the screaming and sirens she could hear seagulls and the hum of her ferry crossing the river below.

* * *

A river of red tail-lights cut a path through the hills and the forests, one car trailing the next in a steady, endless procession. Weeks had passed since the shockwaves in the city and the frantic exodus that saw people hurtle away with little more than cash and suitcases. Petrol stations were overrun and pumped dry. Cars lay flipped and burned by the roadside. Politicians called for calm, but people were convinced that the city was doomed, like Krakow or Jakarta. They fled south, east and north. Some even to the west on boats and cargo liners. There was a frenzied blindness to their flight. No logic but to flee the people, traffic and skyscrapers. And to be moving. People treated Draconis as if she were a flood or fire, wrongly assuming that the safest place to be was in a car heading elsewhere.

The families sharing the road that night had packed up their lives swiftly yet methodically. They towed trailers of fuel and furniture to places where friends awaited. Their houses had been listed for sale, or tenanted. Some had even hosted farewell barbecues and garage sales. It was flight, plain and simple, but conducted with an air of composure that served to reassure not just themselves but also those who remained behind.

This was the first time that Elora had seen the forest. She sat low in her seat behind her mother with a childhood stuffed koala in one hand and an unopened packet of chips in the other. Lines of trees loomed like giant cliff faces on either side of the highway. The forest seemed impossibly dark and thick. She couldn't imagine anyone ever being able to enter such a place, and winced at the thought of what could be inside. Every so often the canopy would break and offer a glimpse of the sky beyond. Elora kept a quiet vigil for these openings to ensure that the forest wasn't hiding an approaching meteorite. Her mother had explained that their father would need to concentrate once they set off, that driving in the country was different to the trips they made to school or the supermarket. Elora worried that he might not get a chance to look beyond the trees to check for meteorites. She was allowed to sleep or eat her chips or do as she liked, but instead she kept her eyes fastened to the sky.

Vivienne was asleep, or pretending to be, on the seat beside her. Headphones trailed from beneath her hood, and her knees were pulled up to her chest, like they were at home watching television. She had stalled their departure at every opportunity, even lingering in her barren bedroom as the removalist truck pulled away and their parents packed the car. When it was impossible to wait any longer, Vivienne emerged from the house wearing headphones and had not offered a glance or word to anyone since.

They drove through the night, and spent the following day checked into a motel with just two television channels and a broken view of a mountain range. Richard collapsed in his clothes behind an eye mask in the farthest of four beds. Janine tried to do the same, but Elora watched as her mother twitched and shuffled, never still for more than a few minutes. Vivienne remained isolated and sullen behind her headphones, obsessively charging her phone as it searched for towers unaffected by Draconis. Elora sat quietly in the midst of it all. She spread sachets of complimentary tea and coffee on her bed and arranged them into shapes and patterns. Watched an old movie interspersed with ads for strange farming equipment. Crept over to the window and peeked through the curtain at the sky and mountains outside.

During the slow tick of the afternoon, Elora went to the bathroom and returned to find that her mother and sister had also fallen into sleep. She stood in the doorway, looking at the three motionless bodies before her, disconcerted to see the reach of her entire life contained in one small room. Just days ago it had stretched out in a way that, to a nine year old, felt complex and infinite. Her parents had assured her that their new life would also contain bedrooms and fairy gardens, best friends and sleepovers. Elora believed them, but had also been caught out by the speed at which everything had evaporated. How a single night of driving could leave her there, watching over her family as they slept in a place with no name.

She climbed into bed with her mother, and when she woke they were back on the road.

They arrived in their new town an hour after sunrise, and Richard drove them not to a house, but a beach. It was nestled beneath two headlands amid a suburb looking south over a wild Southern Ocean. He pulled them into a carpark and shut off the engine. Janine's head fell into her hands with relief and exhaustion. Elora watched as her father rubbed her mother's back and stared calmly out at the sea. It was as if this single vista said everything that they hadn't been able to about the sudden move from the city.

'What are we doing here?' asked Vivienne. 'Where is the house?'

'Behind us,' said Richard. 'Up on the hill.'

Vivienne turned and looked with scepticism at the rows of silent houses spread out and bunkered down against the weather, nothing like the busy suburbs of her home.

'Your mum and I came to this beach twenty years ago, just after we met. We spent a week down here swimming and camping. Said we would come back every summer.'

'Did you?' asked Elora.

'Nope. Not until now,' smiled Richard.

Janine wiped the corners of her eyes and joined him.

Vivienne grumbled something incoherent beside Elora and shoved her headphones back on. Elora shifted in her seat to get a proper look at what lay below. She was unnerved by the drama of the place. The looming headlands cut back to cliffs by what she imagined must have been some kind of immense tidal wave. Reefs jutting out of the water like deadly, jagged sponges. The swell was heavy and broken. It looked as though waves were engulfing the shore from every angle, like it was only a matter of time before it would all be overrun. She wondered who would choose to live on the edge of such wilderness.

'You'll love this beach, Lore,' said Janine, putting a hand upon Elora's.

Elora looked at her.

Richard nodded in the mirror.

Her mother continued. 'On warm days there are lagoons all along the shore. The water is calm and beautiful. And an ice-cream van parks up by the headland.'

Elora believed her, implicitly. She also believed her father when he said that living in a smaller town might be safer than the city. And the both of them when they said that moving was something they were thinking about doing anyway. Yet the more they worked to convince her, the more Elora felt a sickly churn of worry. It wasn't her parents' style to be so outwardly reassuring. Normally she drew comfort from their quiet confidence in life. They didn't seek her approval because their decisions had already been vetted by whatever process adults used to evaluate things like budgets, mortgages or suburbs. Elora didn't like this sudden transparency. The idea that her parents also seemed to be working to reassure themselves.

She tried her best to offer them a smile, before her eyes were stolen again by the sea.

CHAPTER FIVE

They entered country called the Wheatbelt and found it largely dry and barren. Farmland had been creeping south and west for a while now, driven by the relentless heat of a warming planet and the futile pursuit of more rainfall. Left behind were empty sheds, rusted machinery and neatly fenced paddocks of nothingness. Looking upon this land, Elora couldn't help but think that Eta Draconis masked the real crisis gripping her tiny, battered Earth.

Gradually they began passing through minuscule towns with Indigenous names and towering grain silos. Most were desolate outposts, unmoved by the showers nor any other global events before them. The sky ahead cleared to a brilliant blue and there were no further signs of showering above. However, like the onset of rain, the craters in Ravensthorpe gave way to more and more until the entire landscape appeared to be completely scarred by the violence of this foreign invasion. Some were given away by the hovering dust Elora had seen earlier. Older or smaller craters were less obvious, particularly within a landscape devoid of significant vegetation. The ground would sometimes just shift in shades of brown before something darker and circular became apparent. Built structures became rarer, but Elora did see a silo that had been struck by a meteorite some time ago. One of three, it was severed at the waist, laying open to the sky. The remaining concrete was stained black by the strike and white by the birds that had arrived to feast on the grain within.

She was surprised that the highway remained untouched amid so many strikes, but as they travelled further Elora remembered that they were traversing a single ribbon upon this giant, reaching landscape. She found reassurance within this. It brought odds and fate into play in a way that she could somewhat reconcile.

Vivienne cycled through songs on her stereo, and for the most part Elora was happy to listen. Their tastes weren't totally aligned – Vivienne would only listen to new music, which could be hard to access with the showers – and tended towards pop, whereas Elora had grown to love the folk singers dominating her parents' collection. Still, the music was enough of a distraction for Elora to gather herself and find some others. She ate some of the snacks that Vivienne had bought from the station, wrote descriptions in her diary of the towns they passed though, read some more of the fantasy novel. Her sister was right beside her, heading to the same city and university as her, but the divide between them felt as large as it had ever been. Vivienne was chasing down cars to pass while Elora fought off a homesickness that burrowed deep into her bones.

She also took the time to reread some of the material the university had posted out to her upon confirming her enrolment. The booklets were thick and glossy, full of students lounging on outdoor beanbags or laughing around tables at study groups. The campus itself looked cubist and imposing in spite of the gardens, banners and sunshine. It wouldn't have been Elora's first choice, but Vivienne would be based there for one more year, and nowhere else ran a course on drama.

The pages about her course were full of dynamic images of rehearsal, stage decoration and captivated audiences. *Students will engage with historical, contemporary and experimental approaches to drama at theoretical, practical and pedagogical levels. Units in this course will cover a breadth of topics including playwriting, improvisation, Aristotelian narrative theory, reimagining Hollywood, producing, set design, and Russian method acting. Possible career paths for graduates include teacher, playwright, actor, director.*

Elora stared at the words and images as the country blurred in her window. She waited to feel something akin to the excitement these things once triggered, but all she could find was a faint and constant nausea.

Vivienne kept them going at a rapid speed. They were stopping overnight – with road closures and rerouting, the city was no longer reachable within a day – but still she powered them forward. This journey was a hiatus from her life, and Vivienne clearly wanted it over with. She had barely unpacked for her stay at home when the talk shifted to their drive back to the city. As always, their parents did their best to entertain her, coming off like tour guides with their suggestions of cafes, beaches and shopping. Elora knew, as did they, that Vivienne's head was in a thousand other places. Nobody mentioned it, yet there was an unspoken sentiment that Vivienne's trips home for Christmas, Easter and winter holidays could cease as soon as the following year. Elora wondered whether Vivienne would have even opted out earlier were it not for her also starting university.

Early into the afternoon, Elora began to notice other cars joining them in their journey north. The highway became dotted with movement both ahead of them and behind. As Vivienne began passing more and more of these travellers, Elora realised that they were students. They drove faded hatchbacks and family sedans passed down from parents and siblings, P-plates stuck haphazardly to windscreens, windows down against the heat of the day. Some of these cars had three or four people inside, laughing and talking as Vivienne rounded them up and then chased down the next.

'Are all of these people going to the party tonight?' asked Elora.

'Halfers? Yeah, probably.'

Elora had counted more than thirty cars already. 'Where are they coming from?'

Vivienne shrugged. 'Towns on the coast.'

Elora looked in the mirror at the cars trailing behind them, then took out her map and tried to get a sense of their position.

'The halfway thing isn't literal,' said Vivienne. 'It's halfway between home and the city for us, but for most students it's way less than that. Or a total detour.'

'So why does everyone stop there?'

Vivienne shrugged. 'It just started one summer, then people kept going. You have to stop somewhere, so you may as well party.'

'What's the town like?'

'At Halfers? Boring.'

'Really?'

'Yeah. But that's the point.'

'Why?'

'If enough people go, the location is irrelevant.'

'Like Burning Man.'

Vivienne looked at her, a hint of accusation in her gaze. 'What do you know about Burning Man?'

'It's a festival I read about. People come from all over America to meet in some desert.'

'Nevada,' said Vivienne.

'What?'

'It's held in the Black Rock Desert, Nevada.'

Elora glanced at Vivienne, trying to gauge her sister's take on this new topic. 'I read that it's a huge party where they burn a man. A wooden man,' Elora added, cautiously.

'Not just a man. They burn all kinds of things.'

'Like what?'

Vivienne lowered the volume on the stereo. 'Every year there's a temple. Something massive and symbolic that you can see right across the desert. People write messages on the temple to mourn the loss of someone in their lives. A friend or family. Someone they loved. Even a pet. Then it's set alight on the last night of the festival and everyone gathers around to watch it burn.'

Elora thought back to the article she had found in her father's magazine. The photos of people wearing goggles and jumpsuits. 'What else do they do there?' she asked.

'Camp out. Listen to music. Party.' Vivienne glanced at Elora, seemingly considering how much to share. 'There's art, too. Exhibitions all over the place. People creating stuff during the festival.'

'Theatre?' asked Elora.

'Of course.'

'It sounds awesome.'

'Yeah, but you gotta look after yourself. There's no shops or toilets or anything. It's just you and the desert. And it's hot out there. Like forty degrees, with dust storms and nights that drop below zero,' said Vivienne.

Elora tried her best to picture this strange dystopia.

'Radical self-reliance,' said Vivienne.

'What?'

'It's one of the Burning Man principles.'

'Radical self-reliance,' repeated Elora. 'Do you know the others?'

Vivienne smiled slightly and shook her head. 'There are lots.'

'Does it still happen?'

'What?'

'Burning Man?'

'Yes,' said Vivienne, as if it were a given. 'The temple last year was Draco.'

'The constellation?'

Vivienne nodded. 'They built a model of the whole system.'

'That's so cool. Are you going to go one year?' asked Elora, playfully.

'Yes,' said Vivienne, blunt and definite.

They sat in silence for a moment, Elora not knowing whether she should continue on with the topic or let it be.

'Anyway,' Vivienne said, 'Halfers was, like, three hundred people when I started going. But there's been way less lately. Hopefully there'll be fifty or sixty tonight,' said Vivienne. 'It's awkward otherwise.'

Elora considered this for a moment. 'Do you think people will stop going to university soon?'

'No,' said Vivienne. 'What is everyone going to do? Fix roads and work emergency? Plus, soon Draconis will stop showering and people will have their whole lives to live.'

Elora smiled to herself. Vivienne had a relentless confidence about the future. It had germinated in high school when she developed a strong, almost antagonistic desire to live out the life dangled just ahead of her before the start of the showers. Boyfriends, parties, university, career, travel – all of it. During her first year of university, Vivienne joined the guild, the social club, the soccer team, the orientation committee. She thrust herself into the middle of a flagging university scene and squeezed from it whatever she could. On weekends she went to dance clubs, house parties, shopping malls, and on road trips up and down the coast. She worked in a bar, then a clothing store, then volunteered for a communications company in preparation for her future career. They heard about all of these things during a weekly phone call, a flurry of news so removed from their lives that the three of them often sat in stupor in the aftermath. During all of this, for Vivienne the rocks hurtling down from Draconis were an irrelevant sidenote.

Elora wondered how much her own decisions were marked by this. In a way, university seemed obvious and logical, yet she didn't feel a desperate need to leave town or make a mark on the world. Studying at university – and studying drama – at a time of such crisis and uncertainty felt defiant in a way that Elora couldn't channel. She wasn't drawn to this defiance like Vivienne was. Drama whispered to her in quiet and mysterious ways. It was a voice she wanted to hear more of for her own, selfish reasons. Vivienne would never understand this, though not once had she judged Elora for her choices. For Vivienne, theatre would be a part of the future as much as any other thing.

Elora sat in silence, caught out by this sudden burst of conversation between them. She wanted it to continue, but also felt a pressure to say something worthy of this moment.

They passed another car, a red hatchback with a sticker on the back of a whale and a headland.

'We're still a couple of hours away,' said Vivienne, turning the music back up. 'You should get some rest. People don't sleep much at this thing.'

Elora slumped down in her chair and turned away to the passenger window. She felt a strange exhaustion that she hadn't been able to shake. It agitated her that Vivienne had picked up on this. She had missed huge chunks of Elora's adolescence, but still assumed she could return home and read her thoughts and moods with ease.

Elora hid her eyes behind sunglasses and straightened her posture. Somehow the land outside seemed to flatten further. Even the gentle undulations melted away into the landscape. In the distance there was now only whiteness and glare. *Salt lakes*, she thought as she tunnelled downward into sleep once more.

CHAPTER SIX

Their first few weeks in the new town were spent like a long summer holiday. The removalist was delayed due to backlogs and craters on the southern highways, so they lived out of suitcases, eating take-away food and sleeping in bunkbeds that had been left inside the dusty beachside rental. A house that Janine found for them, built tightly into the eastern side of a headland and peering quietly over the town and bay. The rambling and unusual layout included window seats, balconies and a reading loft. It felt a million miles from their modern house in the city, and Elora kept remembering, with silent spikes of glee, that this was where she lived now.

Her new home felt small, yet mysterious. The ocean was beset by more islands than Elora could count. She tried on several occasions, but the pyramids of granite seemed to shift about and disappear with the weather; sometimes they were hazy and distant in the wind and the drizzle, and other days they loomed up upon the town and its people like an invading armada. Surrounding these islands was a dark and ominous ocean that switched as it shallowed to the clearest tropical blue that Elora had ever seen. One side of the headland was battered by constant southern swells, while the other lay static and tranquil within a deep, sweeping bay. It was this bay that they looked upon over breakfast, and again with iced tea on the balcony in the afternoons, then at night as they cleared away dinner and watched as the long and broken jetty began to flash its strange signals into the surrounding abyss.

Norfolk pines engulfed the town centre, and from above looked like sentinels guarding against the barren expanses that surrounded them. Beneath these pines lay supermarkets, gift stores and weathered hotels. Buildings were painted blue, their signs all beachy typography or graphics with waves, sun and umbrellas. The air smelt of salt, and the bay could be seen from anywhere with an elevation, but still the town shouted *beach!* with every other breath. Elora tried out the mini-golf, the go-kart circuit and the burger van selling milkshakes by the jetty. She and her mother trekked around the headland, and her father took her to the museum, which housed pieces of an old fallen space station. They watched together as brilliant white sailboats appeared in the bay on weekends, traversing the waters like kites in the sky. A heatwave struck and a howling desert wind sent them sheltering inside with icy poles and movie marathons while fire trucks screamed out to the surrounding bushland. Elora was at a never-ending summer camp, and woke each morning with a tingle in her stomach. The whole thing felt exciting and adventurous, as if fate had delivered her a free pass from the monotony of school and childhood, instead offering up something dramatic and movie-like.

The meteors had also held their bargain with the town since they arrived. They had been spared any major strikes, and the shockwaves had been regular but gentle. This was pure anomaly, yet the longer it continued the more it began to grow in the psyche. People began to attribute the lack of strikes to things such as prevailing winds, the thickness of the ozone, local topography, and the Earth's axis. Then to astrology, religion or the supernatural. All over the country people were swarming to these places as they did to newsagents that happened to sell a winning lottery ticket. It was all fate and superstition, but it became harder to argue against such things in the midst of an unparalleled cosmic event.

Only occasionally would Elora sense the magnitude of what was happening to their planet. A photo or headline would catch her eye from the newspaper her father was reading, or they would pass a truck ferrying pristine new cars to the smash repairers, windows shattered and glinting like crystals in the sun. A ship would limp into the port and float there for days while repairs were carried out and stories circulated through the town of meteorites pounding the Southern Ocean.

One evening she left bed for a drink of water and found her parents huddled around the television as reports filtered through of a strike in some faraway city.

'Where is that?'

They turned to find her standing in the doorway, cup in hand and hair tousled madly from sleep.

'A city in Europe,' said her father.

'Do you want me to tuck you in?' said her mother, walking over and taking her hand.

'Was it a meteorite?'

Janine nodded. 'A long way from here.'

'Was there a shockwave, like in your building?'

'We don't know, sweetheart. Your father was just about to switch it off.'

Richard did so. 'Night, Lore,' he said, smiling kindly.

'Night,' she replied, trailing after her mother back down the hall.

Elora hadn't seen any windows in the pictures. Just fire and rubble, people huddled together on the street, and bodies covered in plastic.

Rather than tuck her in, Janine climbed straight into bed beside her. Elora nestled back into the warmth and the smell of her mother's creams and balms. Sleep cradled her swiftly, and when the morning arrived everything continued.

* * *

While Elora immersed herself in the novelty of their situation, Vivienne flatly refused to accept this new life. She sheltered in her bedroom, swinging from days of sullen silence into deep and powerful rages. Elora would listen to her scream at their parents about being dragged from the city. How they were selfish and irrational. How nothing bad had happened to her friends, nor anyone else they knew. To Elora these rages seemed shocking and irreconcilable. How could someone profess such hatred of their life and parents and not follow through by leaving them both? The episodes would usually end with Vivienne and her mother hugging some hours later. Vivienne still voicing her argument, but in tired and defeated tones.

Worried that her sister may actually leave them, Elora took to spying on Vivienne during the fleeting moments when she emerged from her room. Vivienne divided this time evenly between the couch and bathroom, only briefly visiting the kitchen, and never joining them for meals on the balcony. She kept her phone with her always, even as the town's network went down for days at a time, maintaining her rapid and secret messaging with her friends in the city. Only once did Elora see Vivienne leave the house during those initial weeks. She caught a lift with their father into town and returned on foot several hours later. Elora and Janine watched on with interest as Vivienne emerged through the door carrying a milkshake and shopping bags from an electrical outlet and clothing store. They waited for her news: where she'd been, what she'd bought, an appraisal of the town – anything, but Vivienne just took a snack from the kitchen and returned to her room without any further insight.

Elora did learn from Vivienne's search history that she was assessing university and accommodation options in the city. She was quietly stunned by this discovery. Not the idea that Vivienne was planning further study, but that she would consider doing so away from her family and in the place from which they had just fled. Elora hadn't assumed that their shift to the country would be permanent, but thought that any future movements would be some time away and eventually made together. Her fear of Draconis was rationalised by the pure assumption that anything they faced would be done so as a family. If they had to shift again, or sell all of their possessions, or flee in a caravan or boat somewhere, Elora felt that she would be okay as long as Vivienne and her parents were with her. The idea that Draconis could trigger not just disturbance, but separation, sent a chill through Elora stronger than anything she had experienced from the rocks exploding above them.

Her parents did their best to placate Vivienne and create a sense of routine and structure within the household. With Janine off work and without school until the new year, it was a challenge they were unlikely to win. Elora also noticed small changes in her parents' behaviour that added to the household's sense of quiet disarray. Her mother began speaking of her work and career in past tense, as if they had occurred many years ago and would not be resumed. Rather than turn her attention to another job, Janine took up interests such as indoor gardening and crochet with a commitment that went well beyond her normal approach to such things. Elora was unnerved to see her mother ageing before her eyes and seemingly happy to be doing so. It felt like only days ago that she was rushing off to work long days in the hum of the city. Talk of new projects, promotion and the foreign cycle of office politics.

On the surface, her father seemed largely unaltered by their circumstances. Even when he started the new job at the rural insurance company, donning the awful polo and staying up at night to read and edit the company's giant policy documents,

Richard still operated at the same methodical pace. Still rubbed her mother's shoulders while she was at the sink. Still made them all breakfast in the morning, as if pouring cereal into bowls were both a skill and favour.

Outside of work Richard took to preparing their house for the interruptions in power and supplies that people were experiencing all over. He would arrive back at the house with a carload of cans, rice, legumes and other foods they didn't normally eat, and Elora would help him unload it into a storeroom beside their garage at the base of the house. Every few days she would see her father add things to this room. Gas bottles. Torches. Camping equipment. Sometimes at night he would wander down on his own and shuffle about listening to music while she drifted off to sleep. The stockpiling made sense to Elora – she had seen stories on the news of other families doing the same – yet she had noticed other things among the food and camping equipment. One shelf seemed to be reserved for old photography equipment her father had begun to gather. Film cameras. Tripods. Lens kits of varying shapes and sizes. Beyond this she also noticed a cocktail-making set that had not existed in their previous house. Elora hadn't heard of her father making cocktails or practicing photography since before she was born. She watched for signs that he may be about to take them up again, but the collections remained in storage and grew steadily with every week that passed.

* * *

Not long after their arrival her mother also had the windows fitted with thick steel shutters. Elora watched a team of two tradesmen install them. Matted hair and eyes that were bright against a deep orange tan. *Surfers*, she deduced. Elora eyed them curiously as they paused to check the wind and occasionally left on a whim, not returning until the following day. They also stopped to take call after call for other jobs all across the town. Business was booming, yet still the surf came before all else. When Elora asked her father where they were one afternoon, he took her out onto the balcony with a pair of binoculars. They traced the sweep of the bay all the way around to the boat harbour on the eastern end. The ocean smoothed as it reached the harbour, then Elora saw puffs of brilliant white spray shooting up from the water.

'What are they?' she asked, eyes glued to the binoculars.

'Waves breaking in the wind,' said Richard. 'When it blows from the shore it smooths over the waves and makes them better to ride on. The spray you can see is the top of each wave being blown back by the wind as it breaks.'

Elora watched some more.

'Are the window shutter guys over there?'

'Maybe. Or maybe somewhere else. There are a lot of breaks here.'

'Why don't you surf anymore?' She looked at him seriously. An accusation as much as a question.

'Well, there isn't much surf in the city.'

'So you will now that we live here?'

'Maybe,' he said, following her gaze out across the bay.

Elora put the binoculars aside and glanced back at the house.

'Why are you storing cameras and cocktail stuff with the food in the garage?'

Richard hesitated, not to stall, rather to arrive at an adequate answer.

'I guess it's just my way of processing all of this.'

Elora glanced at him.

'Pretty weird, hey?' said Richard.

'Yep,' said Elora.

Richard smiled. They watched the water, waiting for the next set of waves to arrive.

'They said on the news that a debris field was overwhelming the Earth's satellites,' said Elora.

'That's true,' said Richard, impressed.

'So what will happen when they're all gone?'

'I don't know. I guess we won't know much about the weather for a while.'

'For a while?'

'Until the meteors finish.'

'So they will finish?'

Richard inhaled some of the thick, salted air and looked at her squarely.

'Well, I don't know that for sure,' he replied. 'But most things finish, eventually.'

Elora held his gaze, probing and fierce, then looked back out at the bay. 'Will you teach me to surf?'

'Sure, if you want.'

Elora returned to the binoculars. A set arrived in the bay, sparkles of white to rival the fizzing sky above them.

Chapter Seven

Vivienne and Elora arrived at Lake Grace with the sun still high, then watched as the motel gradually filled with other travelling students. Voices and laughter drifted past their window as they lay eating potato chips and staring at an old American sitcom. One by one, cars pulled up outside the neighbouring rooms, music thumping then vanishing as engines were shut off and bags unpacked. Beyond these noises lay the slow, deep quiet of a rural outpost at dusk. The Earth exhaled against the heat of the day, and insects prepared to ascend from wherever they lay hidden. Somewhere in the distance there were waterbirds.

Vivienne seemed nonchalant about the activity outside. Aside from hanging a jacket in the cupboard, she had done nothing in preparation for a party. Instead she used her phone and the town's fleeting network to make a series of calls, the first about her job in the city, the second possibly social but it was difficult to tell with Vivienne. The final call she made was to the government information line on road closures and infrastructure damage. Vivienne listened for a while, a frown on the forehead and her eyes fixed on the floor. She didn't mention anything afterward, so Elora assumed the way ahead would be fine when they set off tomorrow. With these tasks out of the way, Vivienne simply lay down and watched the television. It was the closest to relaxed that Elora had seen her sister in weeks and an abrupt change from the urgency of their drive.

Elora tried to follow her lead, but found herself with a jitter in her stomach that stole away the lethargy she had felt up until now. She unpacked her bag. Peered out the window at the gathering cars. Poked around the ageing, box-like room for souvenirs or information. There wasn't much to see, just a pair of stark single beds running toward a television that rested on a dusty buffet. The cupboards inside the buffet were bare but for a kettle, two cups and a scattering of sachets. The bar fridge was similarly empty. Beyond this room was a bathroom with a small, frosted window and towels that were stiff and musty with age. Elora searched hopefully for bottled lotion or shampoo, but realised quickly that this wasn't the type of place that would offer either.

Vivienne tolerated her shuffling for a while, but eventually cracked. 'Do you want to go and get us some drinks for later?' She handed Elora her purse.

'From where?'

'The bottle shop. There's only one.'

Elora lingered, hating the adrenaline that had immediately spread throughout her body. 'What do you want?'

Vivienne shrugged. 'Something with vodka.'

'How much should I get?'

'Whatever you think.'

Elora looked at her, then took her jacket from the bed.

'Take a key,' said Vivienne.

'Why?' asked Elora, alarmed.

'Because I might have a shower,' said Vivienne, glancing at her strangely.

Elora pulled on some sneakers and pocketed both her own purse and Vivienne's. She took a key from the buffet, trying to act casual about the whole thing.

'Town is two streets down, but you can cut across the oval,' said Vivienne, her attention back on the television.

Elora nodded and slipped out into the fading daylight.

Their room was one of twelve grey-brick buildings, all with common walls. Sitting opposite were twelve identical rooms, each with a single window and a cream-coloured door. Every ten feet or so a spindly TV antenna reached hopefully skyward from the roof beside a static and rusted vent. None of the rooms had shutters attached, and Elora could understand why. It was the type of morbid, lonely accommodation she imagined would normally remain empty but for the occasional truck driver or road crew who may be willing to bed down, but only after a night drinking at the local hotel.

Between the buildings ran a gravel car park lined with the sedans and hatchbacks they had passed along the way. Even beneath a layer of highway dirt and insects these cars popped with colour against the sun-bleached surrounds. Beyond the final pair of rooms Elora saw another row of cars, with several tents pitched haphazardly among them. Here she found a student unloading a bag and esky from his car. He was tall and thin, wearing board shorts and a cap from a local football team. She watched as he shuffled around emptying the car into a messy pile at the foot of his tent. A high school backpack. Portable stereo. Pillow with a blue-striped cover. Elora found herself wondering what had driven him to university in the midst of Draconis. The sight of him out there – all of them out there – alone and preparing to party against the backdrop of such emptiness felt both tragic and defiant. The last of a dying breed.

Other than this student, everyone else seemed to be shut away in their rooms or tents. It seemed odd to Elora that most people had arrived yet were waiting to meet at a designated time. It gave a gravity to the party that made her nervous, as if she were waiting for some kind of scheduled indoctrination. She moved quickly, worried that if she hesitated or absorbed too much then her thoughts would again be overrun.

From the motel grounds she rounded the back of the service station that had held their key upon arrival. It was closed now, and lights were on in the adjoining house. Elora couldn't see anyone, but caught the smell of burning meat drifting out from within.

The highway was quiet beyond these buildings. Elora walked beside it for a block until she reached the football oval Vivienne had mentioned. Goal posts still rose from the ground at either end, yet the grass had disappeared except for circles of green around the hidden sprinklers. Elora stepped over a steel railing and cut across the oval in the direction of some trees and buildings in the distance. She felt exposed in the open space and found herself glancing cautiously skyward. Draconis was murmuring softly and Elora only caught a few small needles in the sky above. A pale, waning moon had replaced the sun, looking fragile and diminished. The tides had been fluctuating for months now, disrupting the shipping in and out of the archipelago and sometimes leaving cars stranded on beaches along the coast. Elora had heard people speak of the state of the moon, questioning whether the showering had shifted its orbit or altered its composition. She shuddered to think of a place with no atmosphere to protect against Draconis, her rocks arriving at will to dig crater upon crater. It seemed a miracle that the moon still existed, let alone continued its work pulling and tugging at their lakes and oceans.

Elora crossed a footpath and rounded a corner onto the main street of the town. It was smaller than Ravensthorpe, and appeared less affected by Draconis. She passed a chemist with a noticeboard advertising sheep manure, dust masks and a litter of puppies. The supermarket was closed, but the shutters were up as the staff prepared the shelves for the following day. Next door was an op shop and then an insurance outlet for the company her father worked for. The buildings ceased at a neat and manicured park that housed a picnic area and some play equipment. An elderly woman stood alone in this park while her dog sniffed the base of a tree.

Elora smiled a hello as the dog finished and the woman continued on.

'I'm glad you have that jacket on,' the woman said, shuffling by.

'Oh. Thanks,' said Elora.

She watched as the woman and dog crossed the street without pause and made their way to a row of houses beneath the shadows of an old water tower.

Beyond the park were large signs pointing north to the city. They would be there tomorrow, the rambling concrete jungle where Elora had been born and lived until they fled. It didn't seem possible after all these years. Even the lettering on the sign looked fraudulent and historical, like it referred to a place that once existed but surely now did not. Elora shivered and turned back to the town.

A faint hum of voices greeted her from the double-storey hotel sitting opposite the supermarket. They were gruff and male, but the sound was reassuring nonetheless. Elora headed over and walked beneath the balcony, close enough to glance through the tall windows. A handful of men dressed in t-shirts and hi-vis hovered by the bar. There were tables for dining and a television screen glowing green with a rerun of a sporting fixture from before Draconis.

A drive-through bottle shop was attached to the side of the building. Two students emerged from the shop as she hovered outside, girls her sister's age wearing tight, torn jeans and chunky hiking boots. They carried a box of beer cans and large bags full of crushed ice.

'Hey,' said one of the two girls, pausing her conversation for a moment before resuming.

Elora smiled and gave a stilted wave, then continued on inside. A heavyset man gave her a brief glance from behind the counter before resuming his business with a racing card. Elora took out her ID in readiness and looked around for the premix vodkas. The inside of the store was small, just a wall of fridges and a muddled shelf housing wines, spirits, nuts and jerky. Elora was taken by the uniformity of the fridge before realising that it only held cans. Not a glimmer of glass for sale in the whole enclosure.

She found the worst flavour vodka drinks available for Vivienne and bought herself some rum and colas. The man at the counter didn't ask her for ID, just whether she wanted ice like the rest of them. Elora shook her head, confused, and paid him for the drinks with cash from Vivienne's purse.

Outside, the street seemed to have grown dark in a matter of minutes, and Elora hustled back towards the oval. There were beautiful arching lamp posts above her, but none of them had yet timed on. Her father had spoken of some towns that were on restricted power in the wake of showering, and others that had been taken off-grid entirely and now ran intermittently on solar or generators. Elora cursed herself for not considering this, and Vivienne for not telling her. Ragged clouds were gathering in the sky, and it felt a long way back to the motel.

She came upon the oval and found it swallowed by darkness.
Shit.

It was a clear path across the ground, but she didn't have a torch, nor a spare hand to hold one. Instead she turned down the side street that ran between the highway and town. The streetlights were off here too, but the concrete was pale enough to hold on to a hint of the daylight still in the sky to the west. Elora hugged the drinks to her chest and strode back as fast as she was able. The sidewalk was broken and rough; she swallowed down an increasing urgency to run.

Eventually a glow began to emanate from the highway ahead of her. The streetlights were on, and in their luminance she saw the silhouettes of other students. Some were heading back to the motel with drinks of their own, others walking in her direction for the town. Elora slowed and caught her breath. She felt flighty and younger than everybody else in this world. How could one month mark the reign of an entire school and town, and the next one find her so small and so lost? She felt a desperate need to ring her father and tell him all of the things that she had seen. For her whole life he'd asked about her day and she'd had nothing to tell. Now, suddenly, everything.

People began passing her, and Elora hid from their gazes for fear of crying. The motel was just ahead now, but she didn't want to arrive back looking and feeling like she did. Instead, she made her way to a bus stop by the service station. She sat on the empty bench and sipped on a rum while her feet dangled in the dry evening air.

At home her parents would be drinking now, too. A bottle of red wine already open from the night before. Her father chopping up a salad with his eyes on the television, her mother hovering between the stove and pantry as she added to her shopping list for the weekend. The mail and the local newspaper would be lying on the bench beside the fresh bottle of wine that her father had bought on his drive home from work. He would have taken the coast road, idling in car bays to watch surfers dive beneath the heavy southern swell. Her mother would have started on the wine before he arrived, ushering a glass around the rambling terrace of their garden as she watered, weeded and looked upon the neighbours. After dinner they would linger at the table to read the paper and joke about the stories within. Her father would share the gossip he had garnered from the golf club while her mother wiped the benches and ran a bath. Eventually she would disappear with a novel while her father dropped the window shutters then searched the television for a documentary that would ferry him to sleep. Outside the town would blink away quietly, forgotten to the world amid the chaos and light.

Elora placed the empty can back with the others. She felt the comforting numb of alcohol dance along her cheekbones and considered drinking another can right there. Doors were opening and voices gathering in the space behind her. The idea of a party out here seemed absurd, and Elora willed for a bus to emerge and take her south. She no longer cared what Vivienne or any others would think. This was their world, not hers, and she hated herself for ever thinking otherwise.

Chapter Eight

The Halfers party was staged in an abandoned car park behind the motel. It was flat and empty land, arbitrary besides its proximity to the accommodation. There were no fences or borders indicating where the party began or ended, just a clustering of silhouettes talking and drinking against the milky darkness of a clouded rural sky. Within these clusters were two giant firepits. The flames of one licked skyward, high and angry at the night, while the other had been left to burn down and was now covered in an array of grills and hotplates. Food was transferred haphazardly between this fire and a series of trestle tables off to the side where people milled, eating hotdogs and potatoes glinting in foil. Occasionally someone would return from the fire with a tray of something that drew a small crowd until the food inside was gone.

A trough divided the fires, and stood as a focal point for many of the students. It was thick concrete, and built low to allow animals – Elora guessed cows – to drink when the droughts took a hold. What it was doing behind a service station, or how it had arrived, was uncertain, and never could its owner have imagined such a fate. The entire length was brimming with cans and bottles caught in a frozen river of ice. At several points along the trough there were purpose-built bridges housing candles and food. Hovering above the structure was a metal frame decorated with lights, bunting, and paper planes made from high school certificates that were now pegged to the wire and blown ragged in the wind. Benches, milk crates and other random seats were gathered either side of the trough, taken up by people drinking and talking above the music.

Elora sat within a muddled semi-circle of milk crates on the side of the trough closest to the food. Vivienne was somewhere over the other side where some speakers and a mixing desk stood in the light of the larger fire. When they arrived Elora had hovered by her side for longer than either of them wanted, Vivienne looking at her oddly as Elora followed her to the drinks, then the food. Then to some people Vivienne knew by the mixing desk. She didn't tell Elora to leave, but neither did she include her in any significant way. Elora felt like a shadow, and hated herself for it, yet she had no tools for the strange new anxiety that had grown in her ever since they left the coast. Drinking helped to a small degree, but she may have remained by Vivienne's side or retreated back to their room had it not been for the girl who asked about her plane.

'Which one is yours?' asked the girl.

'Sorry?' asked Elora.

'Which plane?'

Elora was fishing around for one of her drinks and one for Vivienne. She stopped and wiped the freezing droplets of water from her hands, then buried them back in her pockets. The girl was standing beside her, holding a can of her own and looking up at the bunting and planes above them.

'Oh. I don't have one,' said Elora.

'Are you second-year?'

'No.'

The girl looked at her with an expression that Elora couldn't place. 'I'm sorry. I just assumed that everyone here graduated.'

'Oh no, I did. I just didn't know about the planes. Or the ice,' said Elora. 'Or anything, really.'

The girl seemed to relax a little. She was shorter than Elora, with hair that melded into the night's blackness and small, mouse-like features.

'We didn't know much either until we arrived this afternoon,' she said, looking around. 'The people next to us at the motel are in their final year of medicine, so they told us about the party. I guess it's like the ones we have at home. Except for this ice thing.'

Elora smiled. 'It's hard to find your drinks,' she said, digging around in the ice once more.

'Yeah,' said the girl, looking at the can in her own hand. 'I've never even had this before.'

Elora glanced at her and laughed, then stopped her searching and instead took the closest can. 'I'm Elora.'

'Annabel,' she replied.

Elora drank some of the sweet, lemony premix she had found.

'Do you know many people here?' asked Annabel.

'Just my sister.'

'You're here together? That's cool.'

Elora shrugged and tried a smile. 'What about you?'

'Three of us drove up from Albany.'

Elora nodded.

'Where are you from?' Annabel asked.

'Esperance.'

'It's just you and your sister from down there?'

'There are others, but I haven't seen them here,' said Elora. 'Maybe not everyone stops for the party anymore.'

Annabel took a sip of her drink and looked around again. 'Did you think it would be bigger than this?'

Elora followed her gaze into the crowd. It was busy all around them, but not far beyond the bodies and voices stood an inky void of empty bushland. They were just an ember of light in the darkness.

'Yeah. Only because people talk about it so much,' said Elora. 'But Vivienne did tell me it was getting smaller.'

'Because people aren't going to uni?'

'I guess.'

'Our teachers wouldn't even talk to us about uni unless we were doing comms or medicine.'

'Which one are you doing?'

'Medicine,' said Annabel. 'You?'

'Drama,' said Elora, laughing as she said this.

Annabel looked at her in bewilderment. 'I don't know anyone doing that,' she said.

'Me neither,' said Elora.

They both laughed at this. Elora drank some more of the can and looked across at the party. She realised for the first time since leaving home that she didn't know where her sister was. The people near her were strangers, and those by the food tables were too dark to see. Elora looked beyond them to the larger fire and eventually caught a glimpse of Vivienne dancing with some others. She was twirling in circles while her hands drew patterns in the embers spiralling above. Everything about Vivienne was familiar in this image. Her hair. Her neck. The straightness of her spine. The way she seemed at home within a crowd but somehow also stood apart. It was a mirror version of their mother from the pictures on their mantle, yet Elora found herself staring at this free and mysterious figure, not knowing the first thing about her.

'Have you ever been to the city?' asked Annabel.

Elora drew her eyes from her sister. 'We used to live there.'

'Really? What's it like?' asked Annabel rapidly.

'It was ages ago. I was pretty young.'

Annabel looked at her, waiting for more.

Elora felt a reluctance to elaborate that she didn't anticipate. She shook this off and tried hard to think of something else to say. 'I remember it was really hot all of the time. Like one of our hottest summer days in Esperance, but over and over again. We used to catch a train to a beach that had cafes and pine trees right next to the water. I remember the shopping centre we used to go to with gardens inside. And the huge park right next to the city that was burned by Draconis a few years ago.'

'When did you move?'

'Mum's work was hit by a shockwave during the first showers. We shifted pretty much straight after.'

'Was she okay?'

'Yeah. Mostly.'

Annabel seemed caught out by this information. A flaw in her vision of the place she had been dreaming about for all these years.

'Have there been many strikes in Albany?' asked Elora.

'Two,' said Annabel. 'Both in the same year, and both in the ocean.'

'Is that good or bad?'

'Bad, mostly. The surge washed away houses all around the bay. Then again when they were halfway through rebuilding. It's weird down there now. All these empty mansions.' Annabel smirked. 'Kids climb up onto the balconies and sit there smoking dope like millionaires.'

'So weird,' said Elora, smiling.

They stood in silence for a moment, a bubble amid the noise and movement.

'I heard the university has buildings with glass that doesn't shatter,' said Annabel abruptly.

'I read that, too.'

'And the campus internet is super-fast.'

Elora smiled. There was a sparkle in Annabel's eyes that spoke of an excitement she remembered feeling some time ago.

71

'And the student village has a pool,' said Annabel. 'Are you and your sister going to be living there?'

'I am. She has a share house.'

'So we could be housemates?' said Annabel.

There was a holler from across the trough where someone was balancing unopened beer cans on their forehead.

'Or we could be living with that guy,' said Elora.

Annabel laughed, and Elora felt a whisper of herself return.

'Do you want to come sit with us?' asked Annabel.

Annabel's friends were talkative and inquisitive like she was, quickly drawing Elora into the group they'd formed with students from all over the south. Everyone seemed taken aback by her choice of drama as a major, but it felt to Elora as though this was out of genuine curiosity rather than any kind of judgement. She deflected the attention and instead asked them questions about their hometowns. The beaches where they lived. The mountains to the north of them. These conversations felt different to those she'd had around another campfire just a week ago. People here were new to each other and eager to display the maturity that had seen them all leave home that morning. When they spoke of Draconis, the fatalism Elora was accustomed to was replaced by long discussions about planetary orbits, floating phone towers and glassless cars. Elora knew little of these things, and lost herself in the conversations bouncing around her. It felt like something other than denial or naivety. Nobody here assumed that Draconis would spare them – it just wasn't something of interest to them. As a story it didn't offer them any agency, so they chose not to discuss it any further. Elora felt a pang of treachery at how much more connected she already felt to these people than those she'd left behind. Her friends at home seemed consumed by Draconis and its melancholy, their humour black and their plans full of escapes that never stretched further than the night or weekend.

They each made trips to the food tables, filling their stomachs in whatever way they could. Elora lost people in the hustle and movement, but others emerged out of the darkness. Strange faces turned familiar in the space of a few rambling hours. The clouds above them blew away east during this time, and Draconis held court with a sea of shimmering darts.

At one point there was a cheer that rose above the crowd, and Elora turned to see a girl take her paper plane from above the trough and glide it majestically above the crowd, until it descended like a dive bomber into the fire. This started a procession of other students doing the same, until almost every first-year had unpinned their certificate and sent it skyward for its doomed maiden voyage. Annabel appeared beside Elora in the midst of this commotion with a pair of fresh drinks. Elora wasn't devastated about not having a plane of her own, but she appreciated Annabel's solidarity regardless. They tried each other's drinks, and laughed about the awful taste and their freezing hands.

'There was one other strike in our town,' said Annabel after a while, breaking the small pocket of silence between them.

Elora pulled her eyes from the fire.

'It was a tiny rock. They said just the size of a melon.'

'Where did it land?'

'A few blocks from our house, actually,' said Annabel. 'We live on the west side of town. Across the bay in a suburb called Little Grove.'

'Was everyone okay?'

'Yeah, we were lucky. It missed the houses and landed on a beach. There's this weird rock pool there now from the crater. Heaps of fish too, but nobody will eat them.' Annabel laughed a little.

'Was there a shockwave?' asked Elora, strangely nervous about the ending to this story that had concluded so long ago.

Annabel nodded. 'My dad's a nurse. He helped bandage people while we waited for the ambulances.' She paused. 'A couple of minutes after the shockwave they just started turning up on our doorstep. We set up a triage at the dining table and I sat beside Dad, handing him gauze and antiseptic as he pulled splinters of glass and wood from people we'd never met before. The sky was crazy with showers; nobody knew whether there were more rocks coming. My mum bakes when she's stressed, so she made all kinds of cakes for everyone. We kept going all night, cheering every time we could see an ambulance flashing our way from across the water.'

Elora smiled. 'That's when you decided to become a doctor?'

'That's what Mum and Dad tell people,' said Annabel. 'Mostly I just kept acing chemistry, and I really wanted to see the city.'

Elora laughed, and urged Annabel to burn her plane in the fire with the others. Annabel hesitated for a moment, then handed Elora her drink and skipped over to unpin the last remaining plane. There was a crowd of people between her and the fire, so she stacked up some milk crates and stood, now a head taller than everyone, and sent her plane swooping down into the flames. Elora cheered, and Annabel feigned triumph like an Olympian.

She hoped, quite desperately now, that they would be roommates.

Inevitably the fires began to wane, and people clustered together for warmth amid the sharp, arid air. Elora also noticed figures setting forth into the bushland beyond the car park.

'Where are they going?' she asked the people beside her at the fire.

'The lake,' came a reply.

'Lake Grace?' she asked.

'No, a salt lake,' said Annabel, emerging beside her. 'A few kilometres west of here. They go there every year to watch Draconis.'

Elora didn't understand what she meant, but before she could ask any more questions the people beside her began to follow. Suddenly the party was stirring and mobilising. People pulled on jackets and fished unopened drinks from the depths of the trough. They took whatever lights they could find and headed out into the darkness like a rambling circus troupe. Elora put her drink down and fell in beside a couple of Annabel's friends. She didn't have a light, but the sky was fizzing above them and there were silhouettes all around her. She didn't know whether Vivienne was among them or back at the party. It was late, so she may have even gone back to sleep to ready herself for the drive in the morning. The idea of this – of anything else – felt a million miles away from Elora. The party and the darkness had consumed her in a way she hadn't expected.

The ground beneath them turned from sand and broken gravel to something softer. Elora felt weeds and shrubs brushing past her jeans like small, furry animals scurrying by in the night. The music of the party still pulsed behind them, but she could hear insects and frogs now also, their song rhythmic and steady, unperturbed or too many in number to be silenced by the night's strange visitors. A bark of laughter sounded ahead of them as somebody fell and was helped back to their feet. Elora's eyes had adjusted to the darkness; she could make out most things around her, but still couldn't see a path of any kind. Whoever was leading them through this messy scrubland seemed to know where they were headed.

Gradually the trees began to thin, and the ground beneath them firmed once more. It was different to gravel. Elora's boots found hard, chalky footfalls amid the foliage. Their pace slowed even as the way became clear and she felt the bush opening ahead of them.

Suddenly there was space. Wide and alluring, like the ocean.

The trees evaporated and people began to fan out. The air smelt damp and briny, but without the stories of the sea.

All at once people were whooping and hollering. Elora lifted her gaze and saw Draconis filling the sky with a million tiny fires. Out there in the lonely heart of the state, where lights were few and the darkness pure, it was an awesome, frightening sight.

Still, Elora didn't understand their journey away from the party until she lowered her gaze and found the water ahead of them.

The lake was vast and overwhelming, banks running left and right in a curve too wide to see where they returned to meet again. Salt stretched in the distance for a time before giving way to a sheen of water so still that it reflected every glimmering detail of Draconis right back up at her.

Elora's head swam with dizziness. She had seen Draconis reflected in the dull haze of the ocean. In the windscreens of the cars they passed in town. Even in their drinks as they sat outside for long summer barbecues – but never anything like this.

People were moving out through the salt to the edge of the water. Elora followed these figures, now silhouettes against the brilliant, burning lake. The shore had no lap or eddy; water simply gave way to salt in silent whisper. Elora looked at it cautiously as she entered. She had spent so many hours in the thrust and violence of the ocean shore that it was difficult to compute such a gentle agreement.

Stepping out into the water felt like entering Draconis proper. She was within the chaos now. Lights zipped across her legs and torso. Fires burned along her forehead and cheekbones. The movement was rapid. Cellular. It felt like creation as much as it did destruction. Elora stretched out her arms and swam her fingers through the thickness of it all, and realised that others were doing the same beside her. She turned and looked back at the shore. People were staring upward. Spinning in circles. Making out. Passing drinks and dope back and forth between them. Some were laying down in the salt and laughing hysterically as they tried to make angels. Others crouched taking photos of the point where the sky and lake merged into an orchestra of light and movement.

Halfers made sense to her in this moment. This lonely, barren town was no less arbitrary than the entire universe was in the path of Draconis. Meeting here was like stepping through a gateway to a life lived in spite of it all. Or perhaps not in spite, for they were all now struck by its wonder, but willingly beneath this falling sky. To study wasn't to assume a future, nor was it to deny the fate pelting down from above. It wasn't even about graduating or leaving a legacy in this new world. They were in this place because it was halfway to understanding more about something. Elora wondered whether it even mattered what this something was. As long as this journey continued for some, then their existence as a race could be reconciled. And if they were to become extinct, it seemed important to leave in the manner with which they had arrived. To be looking. Thinking. Reaching.

Finally, Elora found Vivienne's profile across from her. She hadn't returned to the motel, instead she was standing still on the shoreline, her head tilted upright to the horizon, a calmness resonating from her that Elora hadn't seen before. Even as the people around her danced and stumbled, Vivienne floated serenely between the lake and sky. A moment passed, and she turned to meet Elora's gaze as if she already knew – as always – of her younger sister's whereabouts. Elora smiled, wide and dumb. She couldn't help herself. Vivienne smiled back, knowingly, as if this one exchange somehow reconciled their entire failed relationship. For once, though, Elora didn't care. She was headed to university.

CHAPTER NINE

Elora woke to the noise of car doors shutting and tyres crunching over gravel. She turned away from the sounds, eyes still closed against the red light of the morning. Her bed was warm, and she hoped for a moment that sleep might pull her back into oblivion, but another noise reached at her, this time from somewhere nearer.

Vivienne was talking in clipped sentences on the phone about insurance or excess or something that Elora couldn't make any sense of. Elora kept still and tried to listen. There were long pauses where her sister waited, then offered a curt yes or no. Occasionally she provided an address or date. It seemed like she wanted to ask a question or say something further, yet the recording didn't allow it.

Elora was awake now. The beige wall beside her bed appeared rough and flaky in the morning light, as if the paint was barely clinging to the plaster beneath. She stared at it for a while and tried to register whether she had any kind of nausea. There was a tightness in her stomach, but it felt more like anxiety or hunger than the legacy of drinking. She sat up and turned to take in the rest of the room. Vivienne's bed was made, her bag packed on top. Beyond this the curtain was partially drawn on a vacated car bay and a bright and blustery morning.

Vivienne glanced over momentarily, then turned away from her and continued the call. Elora shuffled into the bathroom and sat on the toilet, staring at another wall, then washed her hands and face under frigid water at the basin. Her reflection appeared marked by the solitary night away from home: shadowy hollows stole the sharpness of her freckles, and her hair seemed darker with the grease of a day's travel. Elora wasn't concerned by these changes, just intrigued. She assessed her face, hair and body for several long minutes. All the while Vivienne continued to talk on the phone.

Now properly awake and curious, Elora left the bathroom and pulled on her jeans from the night before. Vivienne was listening again, and writing something down on a notepad. Elora skirted around her and the second bed, then slipped out onto the verandah. She squinted against the glare, shifting back a step to where there was still some shade. Just a scattering of cars remained by the motel. One of these, a station wagon, was being loaded with bags a few doors down from her. Elora watched as the students hustled their stuff into the back and did a final check of the room. Their car engine rattled awake, and the driver waited for her final passenger before reversing out and heading away with some urgency. Only then did Elora realise that it was no longer early.

She turned her gaze in the other direction and found Vivienne's car, parked and lonely, from the night before. The windscreen was fractured into a web of glistening diamonds.

A shiver rippled along her neck and her eyes darted to the sky. It was clear, and too bright to see much anyway. Elora turned and noticed that the window of their motel room was intact. She quickly realised that this was the case for all of the rooms she could see, and the few remaining cars. Returning to Vivienne's car, she edged closer and saw a stray and unopened can of beer laying by the driver's wheel.

The door opened behind her.

'Can you get the manual?' asked Vivienne, hovering by the door.

Elora turned. 'When did this happen?' she asked.

'Last night,' said Vivienne. 'It's in the glovebox.'

'Was it a shockwave?'

'It was drunk kids throwing beer around.'

Elora turned back to the car, then moved over to find the manual. 'What are we going to do?' she asked, carrying it back to Vivienne.

'Get it fixed,' said Vivienne, holding out her hand.

'Today?'

Vivienne took the manual and disappeared back inside without answering.

Elora lingered on the verandah. The only other remaining cars were idling beside each other, passengers talking and testing two-way radios with their windows down. Elora looked over hopefully to see if it were Annabel or any of her friends from Albany. The last time she had seen them they were huddled together by a dying fire, eating marshmallows that they couldn't be bothered melting, the party spluttering out chaotically around them. Elora didn't recall farewelling these people or heading back to the motel, just the heavy smell of smoke as her hair fell across her face and into the pillow.

Annabel had told Elora about the red hatchback she'd inherited from her mother – the same one Elora and Vivienne had passed on the road from Ravensthorpe. The cars across from her now were both white, and the people inside looked older and unfamiliar. Elora watched them talk and laugh until eventually they were satisfied with the radios and edged away from the motel in a lonely convoy. Watching them leave brought on a numbness, as if too many emotions were being triggered all at once, leaving each one to be cancelled out by the next. She stayed out there until her legs began to prickle from the sunlight, then returned inside for a long and lukewarm shower.

When she surfaced from the bathroom Vivienne was laying on her bed watching the television with a bag of chips. Elora put her towel down on the other bed and looked at her sister. It was a scene transported from some distant, teenage past. 'What did they say?' she asked.

'Tomorrow afternoon,' said Vivienne.

'Isn't there someone in town that can do it now?'

'Not in this town.'

'Will I miss orientation?' asked Elora, slightly panicked.

'I can show you around,' said Vivienne, studying the kids' cartoon on the television with the same concentration she used for study or driving.

Elora lingered for a moment, then sat on the side of her bed. She pictured the convoy striding out ahead of them, unaware that one of their number had been left behind in this barren nowhereland.

'Did you tell Mum and Dad?'

'I thought you might want to call them,' said Vivienne.

Elora felt a strange and sudden urge to avoid doing so. 'Maybe later,' she said and climbed back into her own bed.

Vivienne glanced sideways at her for a moment, then returned to the television.

They stayed there on the beds, eating snacks from the car and watching one of two channels until late in the afternoon. Elora found it strange being around this calm and static version of her sister. She kept expecting Vivienne to leap up and bundle them into the broken car, or pace the room thinking of ways they could get to the city. Vivienne's sudden apathy made Elora feel edgy, as if now that she herself finally felt some sense of trajectory, Vivienne had decided to stand in her way. Elora knew this was ridiculous, yet she felt a resentment at Vivienne's apparent lack of concern for their situation. The snacks and soft drink spread out across her bed. The remote dangling loosely from one hand while she tapped away at her phone with the other. Even the lines on her forehead seemed to have melted away. She seemed more at peace now, in this random place, than she had been all summer.

When the sun lowered enough to find its way into the room, Vivienne finally pulled herself up and padded over to the bathroom. Elora watched, waiting to see whether this was a hiatus or something more substantial.

'The service station will close in half an hour. What do you want for dinner?' asked Vivienne, back in the room and pulling on her shoes.

'From the service station?'

'Yeah, Elora. There's no McDonald's here.'

Elora was silent, uable to think of anything.

'Or you can come over with me?'

'No. I'll just have whatever looks decent.'

Vivienne nodded, and put on her sunglasses in preparation for the glare outside.

'I have to pay them for another night, so I might be a while.' She lingered for a moment. 'So feel free to call Mum and Dad.'

Elora looked at her and nodded dismissively. Vivienne seemed to consider saying something further, then simply sighed and wheeled around out of the room. For a moment Elora was draped in sunlight as the door swung open, then left alone in the quiet and shadowy room.

She turned onto her side and looked at the landline across from her. There was a game show on the television, contestants buzzing in to answer history questions from an over-tanned host. Elora watched on for a moment, trying to immerse herself in the false drama, then she got up and checked the fridge. It was empty but for an eye mask and some flat lemonade from the car when they arrived. She sat back at the foot of the bed and picked up the phone across from her. The receiver purred steadily in her ear, the thrum of wires running deep beneath the earth and rock.

Elora dialled. The line rang a lazy five times.

'Jetty Hotel. Frances speaking.'

'Do you have any rooms?' said Elora, comically baritone.

'Holy shit,' said Frances, chewing on something. 'Are you in the city?'

'Nope,' said Elora. 'Not even close.'

'Serious? Why? Is Vivienne too wasted to drive?'

Elora smiled. 'She actually parties pretty hard.'

'Vivienne?'

'I know.'

'Does she, like, dance, or drink?'

'Both.'

'That's weird,' said Frances.

Elora smiled. 'What are you eating?'

'Chips from the vending machine.'

'Aren't they five dollars?'

'Six,' said Frances.

'You could buy two packets twice the size at Coles.'

'Yeah, but they're right here in the foyer.'

Elora laughed. 'Is it busy there?'

'No. I'm bored out of my mind. Can you please tell me some stories?' said Frances. 'Why aren't you in the city?'

'Some dude threw a beer at Vivienne's car last night and smashed the windscreen. We're stuck here until it's fixed.'

'Holy shit,' said Frances. 'Sounds pretty wild.'

'It was kind of tame, actually,' said Elora. 'Well, maybe not tame. Just … different.'

Frances waited for Elora to elaborate, but she couldn't find the words. 'Is Vivienne mad?' asked Frances.

'She was a little mad this morning. Since then she's been kind of relaxed.'

'Weird,' said Frances, licking salt from her fingers. 'Where is she now?'

'Getting dinner at the servo.'

'Joy.'

'Yep.'

'Is anyone else still around?'

'I actually think we might be the only two people in the entire town.'

Frances sniggered, her mouth closed, and the sound coming out of her nose. 'Your mum must be freaking out.'

'I haven't called them yet,' said Elora.

'How come?'

'Because I needed to book a room at the Jetty hotel.'

'That's funny, but your mum will kill you.'

'I know, I know. I'll call them in a sec.' Elora looked at the door as if it might reveal how long she had before Vivienne returned.

'You okay?' asked Frances.

'Yeah,' said Elora. 'It's just weird out here.'

'Are there craters everywhere and meteorites raining down?'

She was joking, yet Elora felt a cold shudder run from one shoulder to the next. 'Big time,' she managed, after a moment.

Elora heard Frances scrunch up the empty chip packet and sip on something from a straw. A television had been playing in the hotel foyer when they started talking, but it was now switched off. Frances sounded strange in the quiet.

'How are *you*?' asked Elora, more serious than she intended.

'Elora, it's been, like, two days. I'm pretty similar.'

'Sorry,' said Elora. 'It feels way longer.'

'Tell me something about the party,' said Frances, changing the topic.

'Like what?'

'I don't know, anything. What drinks did they have?'

'Just cans.'

'Okay,' sighed Frances.

'No, I mean there are literally no glass bottles in the whole of the Wheatbelt. Everything is in a can.'

'Kinda paranoid,' said Frances.

'I know.'

'Oh, and everyone dumps their drinks in this giant animal trough. It's too dark to see, so you just end up drinking whatever you pull out.'

'Not bourbon, I hope.'

'Oh, god. I can still smell my vomit in Jenna's car every time she picks us up. I haven't said anything because I feel bad, but it's so gross.'

'Elora, I think she knows,' said Frances, laughing.

Elora groaned, embarrassed.

'What else?'

'Some of the people were okay,' said Elora. 'I met some medical students from Albany that will be living on campus. Mainly talked to a girl named Annabel. She had some good stories about Albany. Her parents' house is right on the beach across from the city. It sounds awesome there.' Elora caught herself, surprised at how uncomfortable she felt.

'Cool,' said Frances, monotone. 'So you were just hanging out drinking the whole time?'

'Pretty much. The motel is right next door, so people were going back and forth. Hooking up and getting more drinks. There was a DJ that was supposed to be good, but I don't really remember what she was playing.'

'Probably because you were loaded,' said Frances dryly.

'Probably.' There was a moment of silence. Elora thought she could hear the wash of the bay in the background. 'The lake was cool,' she added as an afterthought.

'You guys went to a lake?'

'Yeah. Apparently they do it every year. Not that Vivienne told me.'

'Do what?'

'Walk out to this salt lake to stand in Draconis.'

'What do you mean "stand in Draconis"?' asked Frances, her tone shifting slightly.

'The lake is a total glass-off,' said Elora. 'When Draconis is firing at night the whole sky is reflected in the water like a mirror.

It's super shallow, so you can walk out for ages, and it kind of feels like Draconis is flying at you from the sky and the ground and everywhere. Pretty terrifying now that I think of it.'

Frances gave a soft murmur. She sounded lost in thought, and Elora suddenly felt a great distance between the two of them, like a decade of familiarity had evaporated in a matter of days and now they were strangers once more.

'I should probably let you go,' said Elora after a moment.

'True. There's a family in the foyer who've been staring at me this whole time.'

'Shut up,' said Elora, smiling.

'They probably want to check in or something annoying like that.'

'Your parents should fire you.'

'Hopefully one day.'

Elora smiled. She heard footsteps outside. Vivienne was returning with their meals.

'You should call yours,' said Frances.

'I will,' said Elora.

'Okay, bye,' said Frances.

'Okay, bye,' said Elora.

They lingered a beat longer than normal before Frances hung up.

Elora kept the phone to her ear. It was hot against her skin yet she felt a reluctance to pull it away. She yearned to see Frances' window beaming out across her hometown once more, and hoped that this light was not going unseen. That her complicated and fragile best friend might somehow become a touchstone for others in that dark and lonely town.

Vivienne was outside, fiddling for her key. Elora stared at the door, strangely frozen by the phone. As Vivienne entered she finally hung up and went straight to the bathroom. Vivienne watched her go but didn't say anything. Instead she dumped some bags on the table, and from the bathroom Elora again heard the drone of the television.

★ ★ ★

They spent the evening in the same way as the day, stretched out like patients on the long single beds. The television cycled through game shows, news, soaps, then reality shows, and back again to the news. Elora felt the murky edges of a hangover, and was grateful for the salty food delivered by her sister. They didn't speak other than to share the food or comment on the television, yet the silence felt more natural than during their time on the road. Vivienne hadn't asked about Elora's phone call, and Elora hadn't brought it up. She felt a tinge of guilt about not yet calling her parents, but also hated the fact that her sister assumed she needed to. Part of her wished that Vivienne had returned to the room while she and Frances were joking about the party or Jenna's car, that Vivienne had seen how easily she had taken to leaving home and all that had followed.

At some point Elora fell asleep, then woke to find her sister sleeping also. The television was still flickering, and a lamp was glowing beside her. She slid quietly from her bed and found the remote next to Vivienne. She switched off the television and stood for a moment in the silence of the room. It was expansive – not a whisper of noise inside or out.

Elora was struck by their transience in this giant, static land. Just a night ago she had felt the fullness of the world encircling her, loud and chaotic and speaking of so many things she had yet to experience. Now they were alone in a place so quiet that it seemed somehow removed from time. Staying on in this town felt dangerous. Not because of Draconis, but because it felt like this place might swallow them with its silence and oblivion. Elora's thoughts drifted to the dinosaurs, frozen and pensive in the rock beneath them. What would they make of the people scattered across the land they once roamed? And of the sky, threatening and fickle above once more?

Elora shivered and climbed back into bed. Before switching off her lamp she turned the television back on. The news was playing from earlier in the evening. Strikezones and shockwaves. Religious holidays. Basketball highlights. Food being farmed from craters. She muted the sound but left the images flickering above them. The world was in flux, but at least it still existed.

* * *

Late in the night Elora sat up from a broken sleep and noticed faint blue streaks sliding across the motel walls. She watched them for a few moments, trying to elicit an appropriate reaction from a brain that lacked both sleep and hydration. The television signal was out, the screen caught in a dull, looping grey, and nothing else in the room was capable of emitting this kind of light. The wall opposite her was surging with a constant, shifting blue, not unlike the ocean. For a moment Elora wondered whether she may be dreaming of home, but the silence she'd experienced earlier was now broken by a humming noise, choral and electric. Millions of things all acting in unison.

Meteors.

She rose from her bed and walked over to the window. The edges of the curtains were alive and pulsing with blue. Elora's heart began to thump, and the feeling disappeared from her legs. Her fingers traced the curtains until they found an opening.

'Wait!'

Elora jumped at the noise.

Vivienne was suddenly beside her at the window. She pulled Elora back a step and eyed the curtains warily. 'What did you see?' asked Vivienne.

'Nothing. Just the blue light, and that humming noise.'

'How long have you been awake?'

'I don't know. A few minutes. What does it matter?'

'Because sometimes people wake up without knowing why. Then they head to a window to see what's going on just in time for a shockwave.'

Elora stared at her, horrified. 'You think a shockwave is coming?'

Vivienne looked back at the window for a moment, then pulled the curtains aside.

Elora flinched.

'No,' said Vivienne, peering out.

Elora followed her gaze and found the sky alive with neon blue. Meteors were streaking and blipping on top of each other in frantic clusters of light and movement. They swarmed like insects, one after another, across the entire northern sky. From where they stood it was like a giant, falling river of chaos.

'What is that?' she asked.

'Draconis. Somewhere to the north.'

'Why is it so blue?'

Vivienne was silent for a moment, her eyes scanning the sky as if it might suddenly spit out an answer.

'I don't know,' she said.

'That's the way to the city, isn't it?'

'Yeah,' said Vivienne. 'But there's more to the south.' She nodded to the space behind them.

Elora turned and noticed the small bathroom window glowing in the same way as the others.

'That's home,' she said, alarmed.

'We're a long way from the coast, Elora.'

Elora stared at the window. She couldn't tell whether she was being naive or placated. 'I'm calling Mum and Dad,' she said, pacing over to the motel phone and picking up the handset.

The receiver was silent. An echo where the dial tone should be.

'No tone?' asked Vivienne, tapping away at her mobile.

Elora shook her head. 'What about your phone?'

'Nope,' said Vivienne, sighing.

Elora felt a thick lump of dread rising up from her stomach. She reassured herself that the disruption would only be temporary, the line to her parents not severed forever. She replaced the phone and moved back over to the window. Rather than standing by the glass, she sat on the edge of Vivienne's bed, feet dangling and still without feeling. She was exhausted, but doubted that she would be able to return to sleep.

Vivienne had also returned to sit on the bed. The two of them there with their faces drenched in blue.

'What should we do?' asked Elora.

'Wait it out,' said Vivienne. 'Not that we have a choice.'

They sat without talking for a while, the night engulfed by the hum of Draconis. It felt warm and frantic, like the crowded chambers of a bee hive.

'Maybe it's finally ending,' said Elora.

Vivienne eyed the window with scepticism, but didn't respond. Eventually she pulled her gaze away, slumping back on her bed and drinking some water from a bottle by her bedside. 'What did you think of the party?' she asked.

Elora glanced at her momentarily, then back out the window. 'It was fine.'

'I saw you talking to some people.'

'Med students from Albany.'

'Then they'll be in the village with you.'

Elora nodded. She stared at the reflection of her sister in the window, calm against the torrent of movement in the sky. 'Why didn't you tell me about the ice?'

Vivienne shrugged.

'Or the planes? Or the lake?'

'Did it matter?'

'Yes. I didn't have any ice to put in the trough. Or a certificate to burn.'

'That one was new to me.'

'What about the lake?'

Vivienne sighed. 'Nobody told me about Halfers before my first semester.'

Elora felt small and manipulated. She put her hands beneath her thighs for warmth and practiced contracting the muscles in her calves to bring some feeling back to her feet.

'But you had a good time?' asked Vivienne.

Elora shrugged.

Vivienne studied her for a moment, then returned to her phone.

'Why do you still come home every Christmas?' asked Elora.

'What the fuck, Elora?'

'You don't seem to like it. So why not just call on the phone or something?'

'At Christmas?'

'Yeah. It's not like we're religious or anything.'

Vivienne shook her head and smiled in spite of herself. 'Nobody likes being home for Christmas, Elora. It doesn't mean you don't go.'

'That's stupid.'

'Yeah, well, things might change now you're living away from home.'

Elora wasn't convinced. 'Did you always like the city more than the country?'

'Yeah.'

'Why?'

'I grew up there.'

'So did I.'

Vivienne didn't respond. Both of them knew that it wasn't the same for Elora.

'What do you miss so much about back then?'

'Before Draconis?'

Elora nodded.

'Aeroplanes. Proper internet. Shopping. A million things.'

'But why? What do you miss about them?'

'I don't know,' said Vivienne, standing up and pulling the curtains closed. 'There's too much fate in the world now. Everyone just fumbles around waiting to see what will happen.'

Elora watched her sister, waiting for her to continue, but Vivienne slid back beneath the covers and was silent. Draconis seeped in at the edges of the curtain while Elora remained seated at the foot of the bed.

'What did that old guy mean by wolves hunting by the coast?' asked Elora in the darkness.

Vivienne turned over in her bed. Elora couldn't see her sister, but she could feel a gaze upon her.

'Eta is binary. She has a sister in Draco.'

'I know,' said Elora.

'Did you know that there's a third star in between them?'

Elora was silent. Blue light traversing her skin like rain.

'Alruba,' said Vivienne, just above a whisper. 'It's small. Faint.'

Elora waited.

'A while ago, before any of this started, Arabic tribes used to talk of a battle in Draco. Explosions and flashes of light. They said that Eta and her sister were up there stalking and hunting Alruba,' said Vivienne. 'That she was a foal, and they were wolves closing in on their kill.'

Elora stared at her in the darkness, everything hidden but her eyes with their flicker of blue. Long seconds passed without a word between them.

'Why did you ask me about that night we went camping?' she asked.

'To distract you,' said Vivienne as if it were obvious.

'Yeah, but why that story?'

Vivienne hesitated for a moment as if there was something she might say, then rolled back over, away from Elora. 'We should try to sleep,' she murmured. Her breathing flattened and she didn't say anything further.

For a while Elora sat frozen at the end of the bed. The strange blue light licked at them like tentacles, and to turn her eyes from it felt fraught and dangerous. If she were with anyone but Vivienne she may have remained there and kept a vigil, but instead she climbed into bed and burrowed deep beneath her blankets. Her body craving darkness in a world where it had long been forgotten.

Chapter Ten

Nobody arrived to fix the windscreen the following day. Nor the day after.

Draconis had softened during that first morning and been simmering wickedly ever since. Phone connections and internet in the town were completely severed, and the weak mobile network had disappeared, so Vivienne had no way of reaching her insurer or the repair company. They went into town to see if anyone knew of another repairer. People were friendly, but their eyes told of a silent resignation; the services they still had were few, and shrank further with every rainless winter. Elora felt uneasy about probing these people for a way to escape their home. She bought food she didn't need from their stores and tried to think of pleasant things to say about the town. Vivienne glared at her in these moments as a child might at their senile parent.

The television remained out, but the radio reported heavy showering in all kinds of locations across the state. They hovered closely during these broadcasts, trying to catch a mention of the city, highways or home. Confirmed strikes were few in number, but this was often the case as authorities grappled with thousands of sightings and outages. There was every chance that their windscreen repair had been delayed, redirected to somewhere more urgent.

Orientation had come and gone at the university, and Elora now feared she would miss the start of semester. She imagined Annabel and her friends already entrenched within the campus and village, already forging lifelong friendships that she would never be able to penetrate. The momentary connection she'd made to this life and these people now felt distant and imagined. She spiralled, worrying that the door to university was closing forever. Perhaps Annabel and her friends would end up being the last of the graduates, hopelessly trying to guide the masses as the wolves of Draconis hounded from above. Elora began to feel that it was right for her to be removed from this group, that her presence had been a mistake from the very beginning. She yearned for the repairer to arrive, not so they could be on their way to the city but so she could somehow convince Vivienne to drive them back to the coast.

The hiatus Elora had witnessed in her sister at Halfers had evaporated with the arrival of the blue showers. The frown returned to her eyebrows, as did a restlessness to her legs. Vivienne now refused to talk or think beyond the next moment, the next plan. She went door to door in the town, seeking out news on the roads and nearby services. Bought duct tape from the supermarket to try securing the shattered windscreen enough for travel to a neighbouring town. Checked in with the monotone strike reports and road conditions on the radio every hour. They had already stayed two extra nights, yet Vivienne's bag remained packed and ready by the door. The only thing left out was a roadmap spread wide across her bed.

Neither of them had been able to reach their parents, and Elora quietly festered over the stupidity of not calling them when she had the chance. Vivienne hadn't asked her directly, but Elora was clear on her sister's assumptions: Vivienne thought that she had been on the phone to her parents when she returned with dinner, that Elora had cut the call short and sheltered in the bathroom to hide her homesickness or fragility. Elora felt paralysed to correct this. Her decision to call Frances now seemed immature and reckless, rather than a sign of her new independence. She also sensed that Vivienne felt guilty for not calling their parents since their departure, as if she had broken a promise to their mother, and the only solace to be taken now was that at least Elora had been in touch. She pictured Vivienne giving their mother all kinds of assurances in the days before their departure, reining in a woman teetering on the edge of a breakdown that she had fought so hard and long to avoid.

Guilt hounded Elora throughout the slow tick of each hour. She hoped desperately for the phones to return so she could call home and struggle out from beneath its reach.

★ ★ ★

After a restless night's sleep and another cold breakfast, Elora crossed the oval with empty shopping bags and a list from Vivienne.

The town seemed busier than normal. Utes she hadn't seen before pulled up at the service station and agricultural supplier. A road crew were hovering tiredly by their truck, eating breakfast from the bakery and awaiting instructions on the two-way.

Inside the supermarket, Elora had to wait at the checkout behind a woman with a convoy of loaded trolleys and more cash than she had seen in her life. She hurried back to the motel with her shopping, keen to share the meagre news with Vivienne.

The dew had burned from the oval when she crossed back over. It was warm already, the sky bleached and yellow. Elora stopped as she approached their motel room, a dry desert breeze rippling at her t-shirt and fluttering the edges of her shopping bags.

There was a car beside Vivienne's, new and glaring-white in the morning sun.

She moved forward into the shade of the verandah as Vivienne emerged with their suitcases. Elora watched her roll them over to the hatchback.

'Whose car is that?' she asked.

'Hire company's,' said Vivienne.

'You hired a car?'

Vivienne gave a brief and impatient nod, then loaded their bags inside.

'What are you going to do about yours?'

'I don't know yet. The repairer will make it here eventually. And it's pretty easy to find.'

'We're just going to leave it here?'

'For now, yeah.'

Vivienne took the shopping from her and loaded it into the back. Elora felt stupid for not guessing why she had been sent away with such a long shopping list.

'Where are we going?' she asked.

Vivienne glanced at her. 'To the city, Elora.'

'What about Mum and Dad?'

'Hopefully we'll be able to call them once we get out of this town.'

'We don't even know if they're okay,' said Elora, catching herself.

Vivienne stopped and looked at her curiously. 'You heard the news. Heavy showering in the Eucla. More east of the city. I'm sure they're still fine.'

Elora was taken aback by the speed at which this was happening. She felt a strange reluctance to leave their motel in this small and ghostly town. 'When are we leaving?'

'Now,' said Vivienne. 'If the roads are clear we can get to the city by dark.' Vivienne stopped and looked at her sister standing rigid and pensive between the cars. 'We can't wait around here forever. Your classes will start, and I have stuff I can't miss.'

Elora couldn't arrive at a counter-argument. Esperance was a big town, and any major strikes would have certainly made it to the news. Her parents were likely fine, though worried sick about their daughters who hadn't been in contact for days. The best thing they could do in this moment was probably make it to a functional phone, irrespective of the direction they were travelling.

'We're stopping in every town to try the phone,' said Elora.

'Sure,' said Vivienne, as if this were obvious, then disappeared inside for the rest of their things.

Elora remained where she was. Sand and dust swept by her ankles, then fanned out, hiding the last of the tyre marks and footprints in the carpark. She felt certain then that she would never return to this place. Halfers had emerged from nothing, and vanished in the same sudden way, choosing her and Vivienne as its final patrons. She could see the charcoal and ash of the fires beyond the motel, a sombre and lonely sight amid the empty land. Not how she pictured the climactic end to Burning Man.

The wind whipped at her from the east, and Elora felt as though she was being tossed about in a giant, fickle storm. Important things were happening all around and she couldn't get a handle on any of them. She turned and strode over to the driver's seat of the hire car. Vivienne would fight her for it, but she no longer cared.

* * *

The highway north was deserted but for lonely farming utes and the sagging bodies of kangaroo roadkill. Elora did her best to relax as she drove, but she felt a hint of anticipation as they crested each small rise and caught a glimpse of the landscape ahead of them. Draconis had rained down somewhere within this wide and silent land.

For a while the landscape was dominated by a massive salt lake, many times bigger than the one they'd all ventured to during the party. The highway pierced through its eastern flank, offering an ocean of blinding whiteness until they were clear and rising back up into the gnarly, broken farmland. The further they penetrated into this land the more it seemed to have been left behind. Not during Draconis, but in the droughts and fires that had raged in the years before. Elora had only ever considered what it was like to have a contented existence interrupted by Draconis. Passing the weed-filled paddocks and boarded up farmhouses drew her thoughts to those who had already been struggling when the meteors arrived. Did these people curse their gods and flee further into the abyss? Or was Draconis met by resignation and a mocking, bittersweet laughter? Elora tried to hone in on the rare drivers that passed them by. All but one were men. All middle-aged or older. Many would raise a single index finger from their steering wheel in acknowledgment of their passing. Elora took to doing the same in reply, drawing nothing further from the farmers, but she was taken by the idea that maybe it offered something small and novel amid the crushing monotony.

Twice they stopped to try the pay phone in tiny farming outposts. Neither gave a dial tone. Elora tried not to think of home, instead focusing on the highway and ticking off the signs that counted down the kilometres to the next town – the next phone. Vivienne seemed less anxious now that they were moving north again. Her gaze was steady and her legs had ceased their jitter. She kept her phone charged and ready for the networks she was convinced lay just ahead of them.

Early in the afternoon Elora realised that it had been a long time, perhaps more than an hour, since she remembered seeing another car either passing them by or trailing behind. She turned to mention this to Vivienne, who was hidden behind glasses beside her, when the surface of the highway seemed to alter. It was suddenly rougher beneath their tyres. The car took on a slight vibration, as though they were travelling over stone or gravel.

Rather than subside, the vibrating intensified to a full-scale shudder.

Elora decelerated.

'Did you hit something?' asked Vivienne.

'No. When?'

Vivienne didn't answer, instead sitting upright and taking off her glasses. She seemed angry at herself for relaxing in the passenger seat.

'Should I stop?'

'Just drive slowly. Maybe they've been working on the road.'

Elora took them down to sixty and held the wheel in both hands. 'We haven't passed a car in ages.'

Vivienne was focused on the horizon ahead of them.

'Vivienne?'

Vivienne ignored the plea, squinting hard into the distance. 'There's a crater in the highway. Fuck.'

'What?' replied Elora, braking hard.

They doubled forward, shopping toppling over on the seat behind them.

'Easy,' said Vivienne, putting a hand on the wheel. 'It's further up. On the bend.'

Elora brought them to a stop and followed Vivienne's gaze to a curve in the road a few hundred metres away. Smoke hovered above the ground, caught in the sunlight like a murky halo. Beneath this Elora saw the slight inclination of an impact crater, earth shoved upward like paper then careening around in a sickly, perfect circle. It devoured the highway and a wide patch of the surrounding ground. Following the edges, Elora found a cluster of other smouldering craters stretching away on either side of the highway.

'You better reverse back. We were driving over the impact debris,' said Vivienne.

Elora glanced at her, confused.

'It can be hot,' said Vivienne. 'The tyres might blow.'

Elora edged them carefully back down the highway until the road became smooth once more. They idled there in silence.

'Why isn't it roped off or anything?' asked Elora.

Vivienne was rustling through her bag for something. 'We don't know when it hit.'

Elora was shocked by these words.

'The road crews might be stuck on the other side. There are bigger towns that way.'

Elora stared out at the craters. They were like a series of cauterised lakes. An element of the volcanic about them all, as if the Earth's crust were rising up to assess these strange new arrivals.

Vivienne tried her mobile for a signal – more out of habit than expectation. After a moment she switched it for a roadmap and studied a square of the large, yellow booklet. 'We'll have to go back south for a while,' she said, after a moment.

'To Lake Grace?' asked Elora, oddly comforted by the idea of this.

'No. We'll turn west before the lakes. I'll drive.'

Vivienne had already unbuckled and was stepping out of the car. Elora didn't argue. She kept the engine running and shuffled across to the passenger seat.

Being in the vicinity of the craters felt fraught, as if they were trespassing somewhere gaseous and interplanetary. A place where humans shouldn't venture. They U-turned across the empty highway and Vivienne accelerated back the way they came.

Before long they reached a smaller road cutting south and west through broken farmland. Vivienne turned them onto this new path without any discussion and increased their speed back up to the limit. The sun had peaked and was now arching over their shoulders in search of the ocean. Time ceased the slow irrelevance that had pervaded their time by the salt lakes. Draconis had sent a charge into the air. Certain things were in action, and it no longer felt safe to be static.

They saw craters smouldering in distant hills, and the deepening sky was again alive with streaking, but this new road remained clear.

The country to the south shifted between shades of brown, yellow and green with the rise and fall of low-lying ridges. Eventually the road ended and they were able to circle back to the north via another. Elora traced their progress on the map, looking ahead to the point where they could rejoin the highway. The detour had added a full two hours to their journey, but the highway could still deliver them to the city in the evening.

A car rocketed past, a blur of white travelling fast in the other direction. Elora watched it tailing away in the mirror until it was swallowed by the landscape.

Two more cars flashed by. Vivienne swore.

'What?'

She didn't answer.

More cars passed and Vivienne decelerated reluctantly. There were flashes on the road ahead. A fire utility was parked lengthways across the bitumen, traffic cones running away into the scrub on either side.

Vivienne pulled up on the shoulder of the road and turned them around.

'Shouldn't we find out what's happening?' said Elora, trying to look past the utility.

'It's more craters,' said Vivienne.

'I didn't see any.'

'They'll be further along.'

Elora looked at her map once more. There was a shudder in her hand that spread like a vibration through the translucent paper. 'We'll have to go a long way south before the next crossroad.'

Vivienne didn't respond; she seemed to know this already, had already shifted ahead to formulating her next plan.

'Does your map have unsealed roads?' asked Vivienne.

Elora studied the lines and dots in front of her.

'They'll be broken lines. Maybe grey instead of black.'

'Yes,' said Elora.

'Any that can get us back to the highway?'

'Maybe.'

'So can you direct me?'

Elora was silent. The shudder in her hand was making it difficult to focus on the map.

'Just tell me when to look out for a turn,' said Vivienne. 'I'll slow down so it's easier.'

Elora nodded and picked out a long and straight road cutting northwest through an empty section of the map. There were other options prior to this but they were winding or broken. Elora kept them to herself, and counted the number of turns before the road she had chosen.

After half an hour of heading back the way they had come, Elora found what she thought was the road, and they turned west into the lowering sun. It was just above their eyeline and seemed to bounce up off the farmland as if it were water. Elora didn't like it. They couldn't see Draconis through the glare, and by the time this was gone it would be nightfall. She wanted to be back in the motel room or headed south to the ocean.

The map told them nothing about this land but for the road. Out her window Elora saw paddocks swaying with rolling crops next to others that were dusty and abandoned. Beyond these to the south there were mountains etched against the horizon like ships returning from an ancient voyage. She wondered whether they could be the mountains from her memory of their drive all those years ago. Circled by their detour and still so distant.

'Is there a town at the end of this road?' asked Vivienne, breaking the silence. 'Or just highway?'

'Highway,' said Elora.

'And then how far to a town?'

Elora looked at the map. 'Maybe fifty kilometres.'

Vivienne didn't respond. Instead she seemed to be searching the farmland beside them.

'Do we have enough petrol?' asked Elora.

Vivienne paused. 'No.'

Elora looked at her. 'Are you serious?'

'This car has different consumption to mine. I didn't adjust my calculations.'

'What are we going to do?'

'We need to find a farmhouse,' said Vivienne, still scanning the paddocks.

'Why?'

'They'll have fuel storage. The government allow it because of the machinery they use.'

Elora felt a rumble of panic. They hadn't seen another vehicle or service road since taking this new path. Her map told of nothing but space and rolling terrain. This road had been cut from the land for a reason, but many things may have passed since that day.

The sun made a final stand above some clouds at the horizon before sinking behind them and morphing their colour from grey to a sickly orange.

Vivienne took off her sunglasses and rubbed her eyes. She looked pale and weathered. Elora was struck by the rawness of this image and had to pull her gaze away. She couldn't remember ever seeing her sister tired.

The landscape flattened and Draconis seemed to manifest instantly in the skies to the north, fizzing darts of white and blue. Vivienne switched on their headlights and slowed down to conserve the remaining fuel. It felt like they were crawling compared to her normal, frantic speed.

Long minutes passed in the steady, mindless rumble of their tyres over gravel. The land turned to ink and lost any sense of shape or undulation. Elora fastened her gaze on the sky, trying to keep a vigil as she had done for their father as a child. Occasionally Draconis glimmered brightly enough to offer a sweep of the landscape. Each time it looked barren and endless.

Elora was rapidly wavering, close to sleep and hating herself for the ease at which it was happening. Her blinking slowed, eyes stealing extra seconds of a warm darkness that she knew would soon be permanent.

Somewhere out of this stupor came a clear and yellow light. Several yellow lights. All moving in unison along a ridge in the distance.

'Vivienne,' said Elora, urgently.

Her sister's head whipped around. 'Shit.'

They braked hard, hands bracing on the dash. Lights continuing towards them.

One one hundred. Two one hundred.

Elora slunk down low in her chair. Caged by glass and still so far from any home she had known.

Three one hundred. Four one hundred.

Insects disappeared from the night and the air around them seemed to inhale in readiness for an explosion. The blinding moment when galaxies would finally collide. Vivienne remained upright, staring hard at the lights. Inexplicably she turned from the road and accelerated towards them.

CHAPTER ELEVEN

High school arrived and Elora and her friends were funnelled into its stooping grey buildings alongside the rest of the town's adolescents. One school for the whole of the district and the giant reach of farmland that spread north, east and west to the horizon. Each morning a convoy of buses descended upon these rambling school grounds, some from the headland where Elora and her parents had made their home, others from the eastern reaches of the town, others from a suburb known as Castletown, where tents once stood that housed prospectors on their way to the goldmines in the north. Others still from the grain stations dotted throughout the region with names like Jerdi and Cascades, huge silos and truck bays acting as drop-off points for both wheat and children. Elora became used to the rhythm of these things, and gradually found her place within it.

She and Frances hovered happily on the fringe of a small group of popular students, teenagers too absorbed in their weekends and evenings to be able to take their schooling seriously. On weekends they hosted house parties and bonfires at hidden beaches. Many had older brothers or sisters in final year who could drive them places in cars or buy them alcohol. Some of them were surfers or football players, and others had jobs at take-away shops and video stores where their friends would meet and loiter in the evenings. Elora's parents were quietly amazed by the activity these kids drew from a sleepy coastal town.

While Donnie and Jenna existed at the centre of these things, Elora and Frances drifted in and out at their whim. There were subjects and teachers they liked at school, and neither gained much of a spark from classroom rebellion or the minor acts of delinquency carried out on weekends. Sometimes while Donnie and the others were sneaking into MA films or out setting off fireworks from the jetty, Elora and Frances would say they had to study, but instead take over their parents' lounge rooms and hold video marathons with microwave popcorn and giant affogatos. Neither had boyfriends, but both had made out with boys from their year and spoke often of whether they wanted to do so again. It felt as though there was plenty of time for this, and rebellion, and everything else in their lives.

Vivienne had left for the city and university during the summer, as had been her plan from the moment they arrived in the town. Two years of study and recluse had seen her top the school in both physics and mathematics. She received offers from all five universities, and spent a week touring the campuses with a handful of other students, landing on an institution that was pivoting into meteorite-resistant communication technologies. Beyond this there would be post-graduate study, then a job at one of the multinationals she would engage with during student placements. Everything mapped and now finally underway.

While her initial hatred of the town had mellowed, Vivienne left without a note of nostalgia or sadness. On her final night the family went out for dinner together at a Chinese restaurant, Richard toasting awkwardly above plates of sizzling noodles and Janine apologising for tearing up more than once. Elora watched the indifference in her sister and felt a sadness at the distance that already existed between them. She hated Draconis in this moment, but also knew that much of it went beyond the meteorites and shockwaves. Vivienne now phoned home every Sunday evening, as requested by their mother, sharing her news and listening patiently as Richard provided theirs.

In contrast, Elora's relationship with her parents had been fortified by Draconis, and only grew stronger in the wake of Vivienne's departure. When Draconis took down satellites, mobile phone towers, plane travel, and, for a while, most of the internet, it collapsed time in a way that meshed generations together. Just as Elora was about to embark into an adolescence her parents could never truly understand, it was whisked away and replaced by a warped mirror-version of their own. Elora grew up listening to compact discs and reading fantasy novels from the town's only bookstore. She spoke to her friends via the family landline, fighting for time and privacy like in a sitcom from another century. Weekends away from home were spent camping or at carefully orchestrated sleepovers.

Most of the time, though, heading home from school on a Friday meant two days living the lives of her parents. She and her father would rise early to buy croissants and drive along the coast past the surf breaks before returning home for breakfast and coffee with her mother. In summer this would be followed by the beach; in winter, the shops or garden. At night they would visit a local restaurant, or one of them would experiment with an elaborate dinner. Elora became obsessed with pasta, finding a hand roller at the hardware store and making long strands while her parents watched and drank wine at the kitchen bench. Then there was time to themselves, framed around the idea that Elora needed this for homework. A lot of the time she did, but often she just sat in her bedroom rearranging books and looking through her clothes. Later in the afternoon on a Sunday they would drift back to the kitchen and make a dinner together, something warm and nostalgic to ferry them gently towards the week ahead. They would eat this in front of the news and whatever came next. Elora liked the ageing dramas set in countries like Ireland and Norway. They would watch these together, sombre yet strangely reassured by the thought that there were rocks showering on the people in these faraway places too.

Elora's interest in drama had emerged quietly and somewhat mysteriously during primary school. In classroom activities her reluctance to speak out or put herself at the front of the line would strangely evaporate. Teachers and classmates watched on in surprise as Elora performed for them uninhibited. Pretending to be an animal or a season. Conveying the emotions associated with a series of words and images. The others played along too, but Elora found herself immersed in these activities in a way that she didn't experience elsewhere. At first there were gold stars and certificates, then proper drama classes and roles in the end-of-year plays and productions.

By Year Nine she'd acted in every one of the school's annual theatre productions, small roles with a line or two of dialogue she would chant in her bedroom like a mantra. Then in Year Ten she was given the lead role in *Grease*, beating out the three other girls auditioning. Her hair was bleached blonde from the surf and had grown out to shoulder length before the play was announced. Janine teased it up for the audition, and they found tights and a leather jacket in one of the local thrift stores. The teachers still held the audition, but when Elora stepped on stage with her beaming smile and oversized heels, the competition was over.

Productions weren't broadly attended in a school and town fixated on sports, agriculture and the ocean. Audiences consisted of parents and friends of the students in the cast and occasional members of the fledgling theatre company. Still, as the show premiered to a scattering of faces turned expectantly her way, Elora felt an electricity in her fingers that seemed to hijack her thoughts and movements, delivering a performance that was entirely removed from herself, but also somehow she felt more at home than she had ever been. At the end of the show she was transported back to herself by the hollering of her friends, sheepishly taking a second bow as her applause rolled on and on like rain.

A year on and Elora looked back on the experience as hokey and immature. She and Frances were now obsessed with horror movies, manga and grunge music from another era. Things that, to her mind, were sophisticated and mature, and a world away from the saccharine and patriarchal universe of *Grease*. Against her teacher's wishes, Elora opted out of the auditions for the upcoming reproduction of *The Crucible*, instead volunteering to direct the play, a role not normally assigned to anyone at the school, student or otherwise. Drama teachers facilitated rehearsals and art teachers cajoled students into building sets and making costumes, and on the night, everyone helped backstage and in the box office. Their goal was to ensure that the play ran rather than impart any kind of artistic vision. Yet Elora was granted her wish, and plunged herself into the production while her teachers watched on, impressed, but also with a degree of apprehension. She enlisted Frances as her art director, and the pair of them built a giant mood board in the school's humble drama space. It was full of gothic imagery and portraits of old Hollywood actors. Teachers looked upon it with judgement, some turning it to face the wall or removing it altogether when younger students arrived for their classes. Elora and Frances developed playlists of contemporary songs to close out scenes and to introduce others. The music jarred during rehearsals, but Elora liked the contrast between old and new. She also convinced Donnie and Jenna to take on lead roles in the production, which was a major coup as far as the teachers were concerned. Engagement by popular students in anything extracurricular was extremely rare, and seen as not only a way to reach these students but an opportunity to steer future students toward a mindset more civic. It gave Elora some freedom and autonomy with the production, and she intended to use this fully.

As the term continued, time ran away from them and the mood board turned out to be more impressive than the set or costumes themselves. By the day of the premiere they had only managed a stark and basic stage, just a house and a courtroom draped with some broomsticks and strange-looking ghouls that Frances had created. The cast were dressed in an eclectic array of period clothing from local op shops: slacks and bonnets, gowns that were overly dark and ornate. Elora had forgotten about lighting altogether, so the stage would be illuminated by a dimmed-down version of the house lights. It left faces in shadow and the set looking flat and one-dimensional. Elora had a feeling that her teachers decided not to remedy this as a lesson to her about diligence or humility.

The cast and crew milled excitedly backstage while creepy folk music filled the theatre and people took their seats. Donnie and Jenna had been relatively committed during rehearsals, but still weren't entirely off book. Donnie appeared an odd choice for farmer John Proctor, slumped and casual in his delivery, often appearing on the edge of laughter while significant drama was taking place around him. Elora encouraged Donnie to run with this, telling him that his character knew something that the others did not. Jenna, as Proctor's secret lover Abigail, appeared more aloof and sinister during rehearsals than smitten. Elora had initially described the role to her as a secret witch, and Jenna seemed to have kept a hold of this ever since.

The play would premiere in less than half an hour, and the two of them sat backstage in their costumes, chatting and laughing as if they were at home on the couch.

'How are you feeling?' Elora's mum asked her as they met beside the stage just minutes before the start.

'Fine,' said Elora.

'Cool music,' her dad said.

Elora smiled, and they all lingered for a moment. There was a tension in the air that spoke of something other than the nervous excitement of the previous school plays.

'I wish your sister could be here,' said Janine.

Elora tried a smile. The idea of this brought a whisper of anxiety that she had so far avoided. 'I better go.'

They hugged her and wished her good luck, then took their place in the centre of the ageing theatre.

The first two acts went by smoothly. Donnie kept to the script and Jenna cut a brooding and magnetic figure as Abigail, often pacing and muttering words that the audience craned to hear. The Year Eight student cast as Betty drew laughter rather than horror with her scream, and the music came in too abruptly between scenes, but Elora saw moments of intrigue on the faces of her audience, and the theatre remained mostly quiet between dialogue, with just the creak of floorboards and the shuffle of Norfolks outside. As the play moved into the final act, something seemed to shift within the audience. The novelty of the event appeared to diminish, and a genuine engagement took hold. People were no longer watching out for their classmates or children – they were invested in the scenes unfolding before them. In the world Elora had created. Her pulse started thumping as the play reached its climactic scene.

'I have given you my soul, leave me my name!' growled Donnie as he tore up his confession.

A hokey gallows was pushed onto the stage by a crouching Frances. Donnie stepped up and noosed himself. There was a pause, long and beautiful, where the audience were wide-eyed, waiting for the final action. The lights dimmed further, hiding the stage from view. A murmur from the crowd. People stretched their legs assuming it was over.

Suddenly there was music and pulses of electric light from a torch held by Frances. Then a gasp from an older lady and laughter from Richard as the stage was alight once more and swarming with hideous witches. Donnie's eyes were wide and wicked in the noose as Jenna, costume transformed into gothic rags and midnight makeup, emerged from the madness and glared at the audience.

'He who hunts for witches hath be prepared to find them,' she shrieked.

Elora caught the gaze of her teachers, shocked and nervous at the arrival of this secret appendix.

'Stretch our necks by day, but take heed of those whose reign begins in the night!' screeched Jenna, and whipped her arm in the direction of Donnie.

The rope above him whooshed into flame. People gasped and a child started wailing. Donnie pocketed his lighter and sprang about in a haunting jig, smiling and laughing as the flames grew much taller than anyone predicted. Elora looked around for Frances, and their eyes met, sparkling like never before. Elora gestured for her to draw the curtains as Jenna and the other witches circled and circled, knocking down props and bumping into each other in a frenzied mania. The curtains closed to a smattering of stunned applause and Elora ripped a fire extinguisher from the wall and covered a hysterical Donnie in foam.

The immediate aftermath of the play was a blur of hugs and laughter. The cast were jacked-up and hyper – not only had they performed in front of their friends and family, but they had been a part of something dramatic and rebellious. The building's fire alarm had sounded, and two of their teachers engaged in a full-scale argument at the side of stage while the audience were still leaving. Elora had been hauled off for reprimand, following the teacher while riding a stray broomstick and smiling back at the crew with a deviousness that shocked even herself. It was the makings of high school folklore, and something many of her classmates would never forget.

Elora's admonishment was brief, delivered by the teacher whom Elora had predicted would defend her. The teacher spoke about occupational health and safety, and Elora's responsibility for the crew and the building. At the end of it all were some positive notes about the play, and even a compliment passed on from the director of the theatre company. Elora had never really been in trouble before, and felt a silent thrill that it was happening, and in full view of her parents and friends. It felt like she had arrived somewhere mature and sophisticated. She thought again of what her mother had said about Vivienne, and this time Elora did actually wish she had been there.

Eventually she emerged into the foyer to a whoop from Donnie and an extended, prideful embrace from both of her parents. The crowd had diminished but a cluster of students and parents still remained. They were buzzing from the play and needed a space to decompress before heading back beneath the shutters of their homes and bedrooms. Elora drifted around and thanked the cast, receiving several compliments from various parents as she did so. Only one sought to question her on the ending, and Elora felt more for their mortified young daughter than any kind of remorse. When she arrived back to her parents, Frances, Jenna and Donnie were all gathered together with them, talking and laughing in a way that made Elora's heart swell more than she would admit to any of them.

They chatted for a while longer, congratulating each other and humbling her parents with answers to their many questions, before Donnie became restless and they funnelled outside to say their goodbyes beneath the hulk of a Norfolk. Elora knew that her mother was uncomfortable in spite of her casual front, so she waved off her friends and the family piled back into the car.

Her parents talked about the play all the way back to their house, reliving certain moments and discussing the themes as if they were back in high school. Elora was happy just to listen and melt down into the comfort of the car and the evening. As they edged past the final sweep of shops and rose up into the headland, she felt a bursting gratitude for this small and weathered town. For the arms that had embraced them all those years ago. For what it had done for her mother, now heading out at night and saying the types of things she always used to. For the job it had delivered her father and the house that came with it, a house that Elora now adored for its quirks and strangeness. And for the people it had thrust into her life. So utterly random, yet so perfect.

In this moment, Elora also realised without any flicker of doubt that one day she would leave this town. That no matter the depths of her roots, her future lay elsewhere.

Chapter Twelve

The early evening air was dense with the churn of generators and the bitter smell of burning diesel. Dogs danced and skittered by the heels of workers returning to the homestead and others setting out, two-ways and thermoses in hand to begin their night shifts. Men and women wearing safety glasses and driving utes with no windscreens, like a series of travelling puppet shows, one arriving after the other.

The house itself was large, its two wings running away from a tall, bullnose frontage. A verandah ran the length of the horseshoe structure, and was lined with boots, eskies and heavy wooden benches. Any light from inside was blanketed by thick iron shutters, but noises still escaped out into the night: the clank of plates and kitchen utensils, pipes thudding on and off with water, measured voices that occasionally broke into a laughter that rippled through the building like a breeze skirting the very tops of trees.

A road train was idling and hissing somewhere beyond the homestead, blinks of red light marking the beginning and end of each carriage as the driver assessed their load before setting out for the coast on whatever highway they could find. Past this there were a series of large sheds, silent grey squares against the black of the night, then the abyss of paddocks filled with wheat and other things. They had caught glimpses of these crops by the roadside as they shadowed the boy's car to the homestead, but neither paid much attention, instead locking onto the taillights as they wound deeper and deeper into the farmland, further from the city and any sense that the world was still working as it should be.

The boy had been harvesting since midday with a flock of others, spread out across the gaping property. Draconis had sent these people into a panic with her latest strikes. Several of their crops had been flattened into carpets by the shockwaves, others scorched by brushfires sent racing across the ridgeline from the impact craters. What was left had tripled in value almost overnight, but it had to be brought in now while the trucks could still find a way through to the coast where a handful of shipping companies were still brave enough to send their cargo liners out into the sea.

Elora and Vivienne had listened, jittery in the car, while the boy rattled off this information and more beneath the giant, glowing frame of the harvester, as if he was the one who needed to explain himself and not the girls flashing their lights in a frenzy by the roadside. Eventually he stopped and asked them whether they needed fuel. It was blunt and forthright: this had happened to others before them.

Now Elora waited, alone in the car, as Vivienne negotiated a cash figure for the precious petrol they had pulled from the holding's reserves. She had taken both of their wallets, and had been talking with a woman on the verandah for almost a half hour. The conversation had appeared tense at first, the boy hovering to the side like a cat bringing home something spoiled and forbidden. Elora had heard from her father how paranoid people became about petrol during the first wave. Prices had never recovered from this, but the government regulations and fuel cards meant that buying through official channels was now civil enough. Cash exchanges such as this were technically illegal, but not uncommon.

Eventually the woman flashed a tired smile and the boy disappeared across the lawn towards the far wing of the building. Elora watched him go, tall and upright in spite of his nervousness, as if his teenage body had somehow leapt ahead of the rest of him and a confusion remained as to whether he should catch it up or reel it in.

Vivienne turned and headed back to the car. She walked slowly, some of the urgency gone from her movements. Rather than sit back in the driver's seat, she continued on and opened the back door.

'They're offering us a room for the night,' she said, taking a bag from the small mountain of others in the back.

'You don't want to keep driving?'

'Of course I do,' said Vivienne.

Elora looked at her sister. The tiredness had taken a hold in her shoulders, yet her eyes were clear and focused. Vivienne was formulating, even now.

'There's a crater across the highway near Wagin,' said Vivienne. 'Nobody can get through until the road is fixed.'

'So we can't get to the city?'

'Not this way.'

'Are we going home?'

Vivienne glanced at her for a moment, then shook her head and closed the door without elaborating.

Elora stepped out of the car and walked around to where she had assembled both of their bags. 'Vivienne. What are we going to do?'

'Stay here the night.'

'Then what?'

'I don't know yet.'

She handed Elora a bag and locked the car, orange lights pulsing into the dimming surrounds. It was night now, but Draconis was cloaked by a mat of heavy cloud. A breeze danced around the homestead, fleeting and cold for February. Before they set off across the lawn, Elora watched Vivienne pause to check that the car was secure.

They had been given a room in the worker' quarters. Squat and simple, with a bunk bed, wardrobe and wash basin. There were a dozen more of these in a wing running off the main homestead. All of them were shuttered against Draconis, offering no sense of whether they were empty or inhabited. Another wing housed the living quarters for the landholders, and in the buildings connecting them were some large and somewhat ornate common areas such as a dining hall and kitchen. Lights ran the length of verandah and walkways, making up for the lack of anything escaping from the building.

Vivienne dropped her bag on the lower bunk and spent a while washing her hands and face in the basin. She took out hair ties and bottles and worked through a practiced routine. Elora sat and watched for a while, the homestead murmuring around them with a steady thrum of voices, doors and footfalls. It reminded her of school camp in the long halls of a beachside hostel. She never liked these camps, even when Frances was allowed to go along and sleep in the bunk above her.

A bell sounded and she glanced at Vivienne.

'That's the dinner bell she was talking about,' Vivienne. 'Wash up and we'll go and eat something.'

Ten minutes later they entered a wide and homely dining hall to a few sideways glances, but mostly the workers seemed occupied with their food and conversation. Men and women, older than Vivienne but weathered in a way that may have clouded the true figure. They wore faded blue workwear and woollen socks, having left their boots in a pile by the door. Some were seated at a series of long trestle tables, others milled by a window through to the kitchen. Food trays and plates sat atop a bench beneath this window, alongside a giant urn heating water. Away from the dining area stood a pool table and a pair of ageing couches. A television was glowing without a signal on the wall above.

The sisters lingered by the door for a moment until they caught the eye of the woman Vivienne had conversed with outside. She waved them in without fuss and gestured to the kitchen window. They smiled in response and shuffled over to the food.

A small queue was filing past the window. Vivienne led them to the end and they waited for their turn.

'Do we pay somewhere first?' whispered Elora.

Vivienne shook her head. 'I gave them some extra when I paid for the fuel.'

'What about the room?'

'Don't worry about it, Elora.' Vivienne shook her head and passed her a plate.

They took their turn at the counter. Chops and gravy. Bread rolls. Trays of roast vegetables. Elora was starving, but tried not to overload her plate; she already felt like an awkward guest in the house of a stranger.

As they were finishing serving themselves the woman emerged behind them. 'You find your room okay?' she asked.

Elora turned around but couldn't word a reply.

'Yep. Thanks again for the offer,' said Vivienne. 'And for the food. We've been living out of service stations since we left the coast.'

'Chose the wrong day to drive to the city,' said the woman, refilling her mug with strong instant coffee.

'I'm Vicky,' she said to Elora, who was hovering awkwardly with her food.

'Hi,' she said in response.

'She's Elora,' said Vivienne, sharing a smile with Vicky.

'You're heading to university too?'

Elora nodded.

'Smart family,' said Vicky. 'Enjoy your dinner.'

'Thanks,' said Elora fleetingly as Vicky left them for the kitchen.

The two of them found an empty table to sit with their food and ate in silence, both hungrier than they realised. Vivienne paused halfway through her meal and went and fetched them two cups from the urn. Elora sipped the milky tea and felt a warm comfort in the food and surroundings. It whispered to her of home, but she swiftly shut the door on these feelings.

The crowd began to thin around them, workers heading off to sleep or continue the harvest.

Just as they were eating the last of their food, the boy from the harvester padded over to their table. 'Mum says I should come and say hello,' he said, his voice low and gravelly in spite of his youth.

Elora smiled but couldn't bring herself to say anything. Vivienne glanced at her, then the boy.

'I'm Vivienne. This is Elora.'

'Hayden,' he replied, still standing.

'Do you want to sit down?' asked Vivienne.

'Yeah. Thanks.'

Vivienne put their plates aside and Hayden took a seat at the end of the table.

'Is Vicky your mum?' asked Vivienne.

Hayden nodded and took a sip of something in his mug.

'But you work here?' asked Vivienne.

'Yeah. I just finished school. But I work here too.'

Vivienne nodded and looked at the awkward pairing across from her with a flicker of impatience. Elora was sipping her tea and trying hard to think of something to say.

'Do you run internet out here?' asked Vivienne.

'Normally. Draconis knocked it out a few nights ago.'

'Those blue showers?' asked Elora.

Hayden looked at her and nodded. Their eyes caught for a moment before he looked away.

'Do you know where the strikes were?' asked Elora.

'Not really. One of our drivers says all over.'

'In Esperance?'

'He didn't say. Is that where you're from?'

'It's where our parents live,' said Vivienne.

Hayden seemed to burrow down into his memory for something. His features were young but serious, framed by hair that was roughly cut and the colour of the scorched wheat they'd seen growing all over. 'The craters we've had here have been small,' he said. 'Heaps of them, but nothing bigger than a car. Maybe it's the same in other places.'

'Are there many road teams out here?' asked Vivienne.

'Yeah. My cousins work in one.'

'So they'll get that highway open soon?'

'That hole is pretty big, I think,' said Hayden.

Vivienne looked at him, pensive. They sat in the stillness of the room for a few moments. It was only eight, but it felt as though they had already stayed awake long into the night.

'Holdings like this have a satellite phone,' said Vivienne, a statement rather than a question.

Hayden nodded. 'We have two.'

'Which satellite do you talk to?'

'It's always changing. I don't think there's many left up there.'

Vivienne offered a brief smile and finished her tea.

'Is the phone working right now?' asked Elora.

Hayden shrugged, doubtful.

'We can't use it, Elora,' Vivienne said. 'They cost, like, a thousand dollars a minute.'

Elora was sheepish, and Hayden looked apologetic.

'We went camping in Esperance once,' he said, after a moment.

'Whereabouts?' asked Elora, brightening a little.

'I can't remember the name. There were kangaroos on the beach.'

'Lucky Bay?' said Elora.

'Yeah,' said Hayden.

They shared a smile.

'Did you surf?' asked Elora.

'I don't really know how, but we swam in the waves a lot. It's windy there in the afternoon.'

'You need to get out early in most places.'

Hayden nodded.

Abruptly Vivienne stood up and took their plates. Elora glared at her, assuming that she was meant to follow.

'I'm going to bed,' Vivienne said. 'Is there a bathroom some-where near the dorms, Hayden?'

'Yeah, at the end of the wing. Just keep walking around the corner and a light will come on.'

'Great. My hair is disgusting. Can you thank your mum again for us?'

Hayden nodded.

Vivienne took Elora's empty cup and stacked it on the plates with her own. 'Don't stay up too late.'

Elora felt an urge to follow her sister, but she also wanted to keep talking to Hayden.

Vivienne took a few steps away from them, then stopped and turned back to the table. 'Where was that truck going?' she asked.

'Which one?' asked Hayden.

'It was idling by the shed when we arrived.'

'Albany,' said Hayden. 'That's where most of our grain goes now.'

Vivienne nodded and continued on her way. Elora still didn't know whether or not to follow her back to the room. Before she could decide, Vivienne had dropped the plates in the kitchen and was gone.

Elora and Hayden sat in silence for a moment. The dining room was empty now and lights were dimmed in the kitchen.

'Do you want a Milo?' asked Hayden. 'There's a tin in the kitchen.'

'Sure,' said Elora, smiling.

She followed him into the kitchen and watched as he navi-gated the industrial-sized cupboards, taking out the Milo, two large mugs and a jar of biscuits. Elora realised then that this was Hayden's family kitchen.

'Where is the school near here?' asked Elora.

'Wagin.'

'Do you take a bus?'

Hayden shook his head. 'I drive. Or used to.'

He took their mugs from the microwave and passed one to Elora.

'Thanks,' she said, holding the sides for warmth.

It felt strange to go back out and sit in the empty dining area, so instead they remained in the kitchen, leaning against the long timber bench.

'What stream did you do in school?' asked Elora.

'ATAR.'

'Are you going to uni?' asked Elora, surprised.

Hayden shook his head. 'It's just what they put me in.'

'Right.'

'What are you studying?' asked Hayden.

'Art. Major in Drama.'

Hayden sipped his Milo and seemed unsure of what to say.

'It used to be a big course before Draconis,' added Elora. 'Actually, way before that. When universities first started. Now there's only one uni in the city that runs a major. But you can get a job as a teacher or in the theatre. Or film.'

'It's what you're into,' said Hayden.

Elora stopped and glanced at him, struck by the simplicity of these words. She nodded and looked back down into her cup. 'Were you always going to work here after school?' she asked.

'Everything we grow is worth so much money now,' said Hayden.

She nodded.

'Without satellites, farmers can't predict the weather anymore,' said Hayden. 'A lot of people get caught out by rain or no rain. Don't know when to seed or harvest. Even a small crop now is a big deal.'

Elora smiled. 'It's cool that there's work here. We don't have much at home.'

'Are there farms in Esperance?'

'Yeah. But I don't think they get enough rain anymore.'

Hayden nodded and they stood looking around at the long country kitchen. Red-and-green plaid tea towels. Framed photos of livestock being ushered across a bridge. A calendar on the fridge branded by a tractor company.

'Most of my mates from school are working in the Kimberley now. There's an American company up there mining craters,' said Hayden.

'Really?'

'There's something in the rocks from Draconis. It's different to the ores we have on Earth. Stronger, or lighter. Or both, maybe.'

'It's so crazy,' murmured Elora.

'What?' asked Hayden.

'I don't know. Just that someone saw a crater and that's where their mind went.'

Hayden thought about this seriously. Still and tall against the bench.

'What are you into?' asked Elora, after a while.

'What do you mean?'

'Like how I'm into drama.'

Hayden shrugged. 'I like dinosaurs.'

Elora smiled. 'My friend Frances is obsessed with dinosaurs.'

'We have fossils here,' said Hayden.

'Dinosaur fossils?'

'You want to see?'

* * *

It was quiet and still on the verandah of the homestead. As they pulled on their shoes Elora had to remind herself that they weren't heading out in the deep of the night. It was still early and the workers had only surrendered to bed because another shift loomed with the rising of the sun. A rolling race to whisk their wheat from beneath the falling sky.

Hayden took a torch from his pocket and led them out onto the driveway and around the southern wing of the building. Their shoes crunched on the dirt and gravel, silencing the insects that ticked loud like creaking bones in the grasses and trees. Draconis feinted and flickered above them behind a bank of heavy cloud.

The ground began to incline as they passed the fuel tanks where the truck had been idling earlier. Elora assumed that they were headed for one of the sheds beyond this, but Hayden turned them off the road and through a gate that led out into a wide expanse that appeared to offer nothing but a thin line of the horizon ahead of them. Looking harder, she saw the glow of a solar light hovering by a door cut into the ground.

Hayden guided them towards it, pausing as they neared. 'Sorry. I should have asked if you were claustrophobic.'

'What is this, like, a bunker?' asked Elora, looking at the door.

'Yeah. For bushfires. And Draconis now, I guess.'

Elora nodded, hesitating.

'I can just go grab a fragment,' said Hayden.

'It's fine. Can we leave the door open?'

'Sure.' Hayden slid the timber across on a heavy steel frame and reached inside. A light leapt out of the ground like a giant projector.

Elora shielded her eyes, then carefully followed him down a dusty ladder.

The light was actually quite dim inside; once her eyes had adjusted, Elora had to focus to make out the details of the room. It looked to her like a hallway that didn't lead anywhere. One side was lined with shelves, cupboards and a wash basin, the other had a long bench seat and a pair of old bunk beds. Elora saw cans, books, gas bottles, and water. At a table by the bench was an abandoned card game beside a couple of empty beer bottles.

'I used to hang out down here with my mates. Something to do,' he shrugged.

Elora smiled and looked over the random assembly of cans. Baked beans. Chicken soup. Peaches in syrup.

'I don't think it's deep enough for a big strike, but we loaded it up when Draconis started,' said Hayden. 'Sometimes I feel like there's better stuff down here than there is in our kitchen.'

'My dad is the same. We're always having to go down to the garage when we run out of things in the house.'

Hayden propped his torch on one of the shelves and shifted some gas bottles and water jugs aside. Elora watched him, curious, until he stood back a step and gestured her over. The empty shelf exposed a craggy and grey patch of earth acting as the wall of the bunker. It sat higher than the earth around it, and had been left alone while the rest of the wall was cut smooth. Elora looked at it blankly until Hayden traced the outline of something with his torch. A lighter shade amid the grey. The rough shape of a broken axe.

'I think it's a jawbone. Or part of a jawbone.'

Elora inhaled. 'Wow.'

Hayden passed her the torch. She leant in closer and surveyed the ivory curve of this ancient creature, caught so proud and elegant in its moment of extinction. She went to speak but the words stuck in her throat, and she found herself oddly on the edge of tears.

'You okay?' asked Hayden, taking the torch from her as she sniffed into her sleeve.

'Yeah, sorry. I'm just tired,' said Elora, looking away and cursing herself. 'Do you know what kind of dinosaur it is?'

'Not really. A theropod maybe. Dad's worried that they'll come and dig up his paddock if we tell any scientists.'

Elora nodded and smiled. 'It's really cool.'

She helped Hayden restock the shelf, then the two of them made their way silently back over to the ladder. The trapdoor above offered a small frame of the night, blue light from Draconis in contrast to the murky yellow that surrounded them.

Elora put her hand on the ladder, but hesitated. 'That highway won't be fixed for ages, will it?' she asked.

'A few weeks, maybe,' said Hayden.

They looked at each other, then up at the sky.

'Have you guys seen showers like this before?'

Hayden shook his head. 'Some people are saying it's the end of Draconis. Just small rocks now, and the dust that's turned everything blue.'

'What are other people saying?' asked Elora.

'That it's the start of something bigger.'

Elora shuddered, and suddenly wanted to be back with her sister.

'What will you guys do?' asked Hayden.

'Go home. I hope.'

'You don't want to go to the city?'

'I don't know,' said Elora. 'I didn't realise what it was like out here. What Draconis had been doing to everything.'

Hayden looked down, searching for the appropriate words or answers, as he seemed to do often. Elora fought a sudden urge to press herself up against him. To lift his chin and feel a pressure moving back against her. For the universe to feel less vast, even if only for a moment.

'Sometimes I think the dinosaurs were lucky,' she said,.

Hayden glanced back at the walls of the bunker. He nodded, then led them back to the homestead.

CHAPTER THIRTEEN

Vivienne was asleep when Elora returned in the night, and gone when she awoke the following morning. The room was empty and still. For a while Elora lay listening for sounds that might reveal something about the state of the world outside, but this proved futile. A dense and constant wind filled the air, drowning all noise and shuddering by the homestead like a breaching river.

Elora had no sense of the time, nor how long she had been alone in the room. Slivers of daylight crept past the window shutter and the room was starting to warm. Her stomach felt tight and empty, as if she had been entire days without food. She sat up, wondering suddenly whether it may already be afternoon. She pulled on her jeans from the evening and stepped down from the bunk. Vivienne's bags lay packed and ready by the door as they had since their arrival. Elora felt a sweep of relief to see them there, to know that her sister hadn't finally abandoned her for the city.

She spent a while by the basin just washing her face and thinking about the previous evening. Their journey had taken on a dream-like state where everything felt normal in spite of its fortuity. That they were stranded in a foreign homestead with Draconis turning blue seemed oddly inconsequential in comparison to smaller things, such as the possibility of a warm breakfast or another conversation with Hayden. Elora found little comfort in this stupor or the severe rushes of panic that flooded back in the moments when it cleared. They were here among strangers, had no path to the city, knew nothing of their parents' situation. And Draconis was simmering – festering – above them. This was their reality, so she compelled herself to find a way to stay within it.

Outside, the sky was grey, but the wind warm and dry against her skin. Elora's eyes couldn't handle the shift from their dull room to this endless, arching sky; for a while she just stood by the door with her hand on her forehead. A crow tried to call, but trailed off. Somewhere distant an engine was idling.

Eventually She moved along the verandah to the communal bathrooms and found them empty. She was relieved by this, and used the toilet in solitude. Towels hung on hooks from those who had risen earlier, Vivienne's among them. Elora considered taking a shower, but felt uneasy about the quietness of the homestead and Vivienne's whereabouts, so instead she washed her face again then headed across the lawn to try to find her sister in the dining room.

The room had hosted breakfast and now lay dormant amid the faint smell of burnt toast and coffee. Elora walked over to the serving bench and peered through into the kitchen. A dishwasher groaned and slushed by the fridges, but otherwise the room was quiet and empty. There was still food out on the serving bench. Bread for toasting. A bowl of bananas. Some jams, and a small glass ramekin with a cube of butter. The urn was cycling on and off with a low rumble. Elora resented Vivienne for again saying nothing about her plans or whereabouts. She wanted to find her and see was going on, but her hunger won out, so she toasted some bread and filled a mug with water and two teaspoons each of sugar and coffee. There was no milk that she could find, so she added another sugar and drank the coffee black. She ate the first piece of toast just standing by the bench, then took her second over to a table with the rest of the coffee.

The door opened and Vivienne entered just as she finished. Elora watched as she strode over, a sharpness to her expression and walk as if it was she who had been searching for her younger sister all morning.

'Did you eat something?' asked Vivienne, hovering by the table.

'Why did you let me sleep so long?' asked Elora.

'Weren't you up late?'

The question was loaded, but more with impatience rather than any kind of judgement. Elora ignored her regardless. The night before felt both distant and vivid, and she didn't yet know how she felt about any of it. Vivienne watched as she finished her coffee and placed the cup on her empty plate.

'What have you been doing?' asked Elora.

'Talking to people. Working out a plan.'

'Hayden says the highway will take weeks to fix.'

'I know.'

'So we're going home?'

Vivienne didn't say anything right away.

'Vivienne?'

'I'm not doing that, Elora. Why do you keep bringing it up?'

'Because we don't have a choice anymore.'

'Of course we do.'

'What? Hang around here and wait?'

Vivienne gave a tiny shudder and shook her head.

'Then what?'

'The southern highway is still clear. We just need to find our way over to it.'

'That's crazy. This whole thing is crazy.' Elora stood up and took her dishes through to the kitchen. She stood washing them in the sink while her sister waited in the dining room. A million counterarguments swirled through Elora's head, but she couldn't bring any of them to the surface.

'We can go through the mountains,' said Vivienne calmly when Elora finally returned.

Elora stopped and looked at her. She felt a murmur of excitement that she knew was both fraught and naive. 'You said the roads were busted.'

'I spoke to one of the truck drivers. They bypass the mountains on their way to the coast, but he said they see four-wheel-drives moving through there all the time. Especially since the last showers.'

'Why especially since the last showers?'

'I don't know,' said Vivienne, impatiently. 'Anyway, we should get moving soon so we're not out there at night again.'

'We don't have a four-wheel-drive.'

'Vicky said we can borrow one of theirs.'

'What about the hire car? We're just going to dump that now too?'

Vivienne sighed as if she were reasoning with a child.

Elora stared at her. 'What's going on with you?'

'Sorry?'

'Why do you need to be back in the city so badly?'

'I live there, Elora.'

'Bullshit.'

'What?'

'You're totally frantic.'

Vivienne pushed in Elora's chair as if she might leave.

'You've driven us through a shockwave,' Elora continued. 'Dumped your car. Taken us out into the middle of nowhere. And now the mountains?'

They stood in silence for a moment. The dishwasher had stopped; now it was only the wind that spoke of anything outside of the room and homestead.

'I don't want to get cut off,' said Vivienne.

'From the city?' asked Elora.

Vivienne nodded coldly and stared across the room.

Elora watched her. Saw her mother in the sharp profile and the gaze that would lock onto something but only so her thoughts could continue racing onwards. Her sister was penned-in and desperate – this time not by their home or the long summer holidays, but by fate and the universe that threatened to block her way forward.

'I'm not going,' said Elora, surprised at her certainty. 'I need to speak to Mum and Dad.'

Vivienne exhaled slightly and met her gaze. 'They know we were stuck in Lake Grace when all of this started. They know the phone lines are a mess. I told Mum that if anything happened we would call them when we could. Moving on is still the best way to do that.'

'They don't know we were stuck in Lake Grace,' said Elora.

'You called them from the Lake Grace motel.'

Elora shook her head. She felt a strange mix of righteousness and fear. 'No, I didn't.'

Vivienne rubbed her temples. 'I heard you on the phone when I came back with dinner.'

'To Frances.' Elora wandered over to the adjoining table, pretending to take an interest in a stray coaster.

'Are you serious?' asked Vivienne.

Elora nodded.

'You didn't call Mum and Dad?'

'I was going to,' said Elora. 'I didn't know we would be dodging meteorites this whole time.'

'Great. So they have no idea what's happened to us.'

'Which is why we should go home.'

Vivienne stood frozen in the hall while Elora fiddled nervously with the coasters.

'I'm going through the mountains to find a phone,' said Vivienne. 'Then I'm going to drive to the city.'

Elora shrugged and kept her eyes away from her sister. Vivienne lingered for only a second longer, then left her for the brightness outside.

The dining hall was quiet in her wake, as quiet as any place Elora had been. She collected the rest of the stray coasters and stacked them in a perfect pile on the table beside her, a circle of fiery red against the dull brown veneer. Elora felt a deep swell of panic in her limbs. They shook with a violent and foreign energy. She ran from the hall, just making it to the bathroom before crying into her sweaty, trembling hands.

* * *

The wind blew itself out in the afternoon and gradually the sounds of the homestead emerged. Utes pulling up then driving away again. Voices, muffled and clipped in passing. Steel and machinery echoing from somewhere beyond the ridge. Elora sat on her bed, reading the fantasy novel and listening to this foreign soundscape. She hadn't moved since breakfast, and had no plans to go any further than the bathrooms.

Vivienne's bags had been gone when she arrived back from the shower, and Elora assumed that her sister was now making her way to the city alone. For some reason Elora felt that Vivienne's journey would be smooth now that she was free of her kid sister. She knew Vivienne best as a fragment, distant and unreachable, but constant in her trajectory. Part of her world for a few brief moments on the phone each week, then back into a void that no one in their family thought to question. There was a comfort and clarity in this distance that had become muddled by their recent proximity. It highlighted the detachment between them, and asked an awkward question as to whether either had the desire to bridge this space. People had said this to them all summer, how it would be nice to be close to your sister. Elora nodded along, unconvinced, and realised now that Vivienne had probably felt the same.

Late in the afternoon there was a soft knock on the door and Elora rose to find Hayden standing outside. He was dressed in his work clothes and covered in a fine dusting of dirt.

'Hi,' said Hayden.

'Hi,' replied Elora.

She felt sheepish for still being on the property, and hadn't yet figured out what to say or do about Vivienne leaving without her.

'The phone has connection to a satellite. Do you want to try your parents?'

Elora's breath caught in her throat. Immediately she felt her eyes welling.

'I asked your sister. But she said you should go first.'

'She's still here?' asked Elora.

Hayden nodded, confused. 'Aren't you leaving tomorrow?'

Elora sniffed and nodded. 'Sorry, I'm half asleep,' she lied. 'Shall we call them now?'

'Yeah. The signal will drop if Draconis flares again.'

Elora pulled on a jacket and followed Hayden out of the building and across the lawn. She wanted to talk to him, ask him about his day and Draconis and all kinds of things, but felt too nervous about the phone call. *Would the line be connected? Would her parents be okay? How would she explain everything about Vivienne?* As they moved through the dining area, Elora caught sight of her sister at the other end of the room. Vivienne was consumed by her laptop, but obviously aware of their presence in the hall. *Why had she waited for her?* Elora hesitated for a moment but Vivienne didn't turn from the screen.

At the opposite end to the kitchen, Elora and Hayden entered a hallway leading past a series of bedrooms. Her eyes wandered into each. She had seen the faces and heard the voices of the people in this land, but still had no real sense of their lives outside of work, the things that happened behind these doors, the dreams and nightmares that swirled around them. One of the bedrooms was messier than the others, clothes on the floor and video games stacked in piles by a television. Hayden glanced inside and increased his pace ahead of her.

They turned down another smaller hallway and entered a wide office space with several computers. The room smelt of people and coffee, and Elora worried that it had been cleared out just for her. One of the shutters was open, offering a vista of the farmland to the east: paddocks cut low from the harvest, tree lines sweeping south along the ridge, the clouds persisting above but now holding a hue of swampy purple.

Hayden rolled a chair across to a desk housing a bulky grey phone. 'It dials like normal, but takes a while to connect sometimes.'

Elora hesitated, caught out by how quickly this had all come about.

'It doesn't really cost that much,' said Hayden. 'Plus Dad is loaded these days.'

Elora smiled and steadied herself.

'I can shut the door if you want?' asked Hayden.

'Okay. Thanks.'

Hayden gave a brief smile then closed the door and left her alone in the room.

Elora sat on the chair by the phone. The view from her desk was framed like a painting. Time felt slow and gentle, like she could feel the long stretch of each season. Each harvest. Eventually she looked down at the phone. A small icon was glowing with a signal from a beleaguered satellite somewhere above them all. Elora watched as it wavered from one bar to two, then back again. She sat there, playing with the zip at the bottom of her jacket. A crow dipped in and out of view. Clouds hung static in the sky.

She picked up the phone and dialled. There was a pause, but only for a moment, then ringing.

'Vivienne?' asked her mother, immediately.

'Elora,' she replied.

Her mother exhaled. Two long and practiced breaths. 'Where are you? Are you okay?'

'We're fine, Mum. We're on a farm near the mountains. There was a strike on the highway into the city.'

'You got the windscreen fixed?'

'No. Vivienne just dumped her car and hired another one,' said Elora. 'How did you know about the windscreen?'

'I spoke to Frances. She said you called.'

'Sorry, Mum. I was going to call you too, but Vivienne came back with dinner and I was worried I would cry when you answered.' Her voice cracked. She swore silently and wiped her nose and eyes on her sleeve.

'It's alright, sweetheart.'

'We've been trying to call you ever since.'

'The lines were down in town. Only a few of them have come back.'

'Have you had showers there?'

'I think everywhere has.'

'Are they blue? It's crazy blue out here, Mum. Like the ocean.'

'Yes.'

Elora caught something in her voice. 'Are you and Dad okay?'

'We're fine,' she replied, then paused. 'We've had some strikes down here.'

'Oh my god. Whereabouts?'

'In the archipelago, mostly. But also just outside of town.'

'With shockwaves?'

'A few.'

'Oh, Mum, I'm so sorry. Do you have the shutters up? And fuel for the generator?'

'Of course.'

'Are the roads still open?'

'One of them is open, but your father says the other one is a mess.'

'How is Dad?'

'He's good. Out at the shops on his way home from golf.'

'They're still playing golf?'

Her mother laughed. 'They'll putt into craters out there if they have to.'

Elora smiled and tried to settle her breathing.

'Is Vivienne there with you?' asked her mother.

'No, she's next door. We had a fight. She wants to drive us through the mountains.'

Elora prepared to spill all of the details of their journey. To build a case with her mother that Vivienne could never defend.

'I don't want you to come back here, Elora,' said her mother.

Elora was silent. Shocked. The satellite signal flickered, then returned. 'What?'

'It's not safe.'

'It's not safe anywhere, Mum.'

'I know that. But if the other highway is hit then people won't be able to leave this place. We don't want you to miss university.'

'But I don't even think I want to go anymore,' said Elora, tearing over again.

'It's better to go and find out. Kids down here aren't coping well.'

'What do you mean? What did Frances say?'

'Frances is fine. I saw her at the supermarket yesterday.'

'What about Donnie and Jenna?'

Her mother hesitated. 'Your father says they left town when the first highway was hit.'

'Donnie? To go where?'

'I don't know, Elora. We haven't had the phone, and most people have been behind their shutters or heading out of town.'

The deserts, thought Elora immediately. Her head was throbbing. How was it that her home had been flipped upside down so violently?

'What is Vivienne planning to do?' asked her mother.

'Keep driving to the city, of course.'

'Good. I think that's the best idea. Just be careful on the roads. Only drive when the road crews say it's safe. Pull over if the showering gets too heavy.'

'Vivienne is crazy, Mum. I want to come home.' Elora cried properly now. Her face slick with snot and tears.

Her mother took a steadying breath. 'We thought we might come up to the city at semester break,' said Janine, soothing and calm. 'Once all of the showering has settled and the roads are clear. We could stay in a flash hotel for once and see where you're studying.'

Elora sniffed and wiped her nose. 'Okay,' she replied, eventually.

'Do something nice when you get to the city. Go and see a play, maybe. I'm sure there'll be one on somewhere.'

Elora took a breath and nodded. The icon on the phone started flickering once again. 'Can you hug Frances for me?'

'I did already,' said her mother. 'But I will again if she lets me.'

Elora smiled at the thought of this.

'She was going on and on about a salt lake somewhere. You know what she's like when she gets stuck on something.'

'What salt lake?' asked Elora, her voice distorting with static.

'Can you call Vivienne over?' asked her mother, not hearing her.

'She's down the hall, but if you hold on a sec, I can–'

The line dropped.

'Mum?' Elora kept the phone at her ear, waiting for the connection and her mother to return. The icon remained cold and vacant.

A heavy silence resonated throughout the room.

Elora placed the phone back on charge. She found a crumpled tissue in her pocket and cleaned herself up the best that she could. A numbness swept over her. Too many things had just come to pass, and her emotions couldn't settle in any one place. She sat there, staring blankly at the view as it etched into a corner of her memory where it would remain forever.

Eventually Elora left the room and retraced her steps down the hall. Halfway along she paused and found Hayden cross-legged on his bedroom floor. He was seated on a rug playing a video game. A figure was running through a streetscape on the screen in front of him, leaping from building to building, a cape dancing in the wind behind him as enemies darted in the periphery. Hayden paused the game and looked up at her, his eyes young and bright, his arms long, the t-shirt grown too small like the many before it.

'Can I play?' asked Elora.

Hayden shifted over and untangled another controller. Elora sat on the rug and familiarised herself with the controls. Hayden didn't ask about the phone call, just leant back against his bed and led her off into the dystopia. Elora's breath returned and she gratefully disappeared into the oblivion of the game. They stayed there, beside each other, as the daylight faded and Draconis arrived again, sparkling like an upturned aquarium in the windows of the homestead.

Avatars racing onwards, side by side in an unspoken quest.

* * *

Late that evening Elora was pulled from the edge of sleep by a voice in the dorm: 'Are they okay?'

It came without warning, and Elora was caught out by Vivienne's question.

She and Hayden had missed the regular dinner service, instead eating leftovers while the kitchen was cleaned and workers resumed their harvest.

Vivienne was in the bathroom when Elora finally returned to their room. They spoke once in passing about the dampness of their towels, then nothing further as Vivienne curled into bed and Elora took out her torch and novel. That was more than an hour ago and she had assumed that Vivienne was deep into sleep.

'Draconis is striking down there,' Elora replied, her voice quiet in the darkness.

'So are they okay?'

Elora hesitated, swallowing down her tears once more. 'Yeah. They have power, and one of the roads is still open. So far the strikes have been out of town.' Elora tried to think of something else she could share. She felt selfish for consuming so much of this precious conversation. 'Dad's still playing golf.'

Vivienne didn't say anything but Elora could hear the soft rhythm of her breathing. Laying above her in this moment she was reminded of when they first arrived in their town from the city, sharing a bunk in the house their mother had found. Elora tingling with excitement at this new proximity to her sister and trying her hardest not to do anything annoying or immature. Hoping naively that somehow they might continue to share both a bedroom and a life.

'And Mum says we should keep going,' she said, after a while.

Vivienne sniffed once in the silence, then rolled over and was still.

Chapter Fourteen

The three of them left before dawn, Draconis twisting and heaving above like the intestines of a great blue monster. Elora had been nudged from sleep by her sister, and now sat upright but dozy in the car as they rounded paddocks and traversed the charcoal slopes to the south. Occasionally there were lights in the distance. Workers heading out for another shift, or the lonely glow of a neighbouring homestead. Beyond these lay the ranges, etched black against the electric glow of the sky. Suddenly they appeared foreboding and imminent. Elora tried to remind herself why she had been so taken by these peaks.

It was winter when she passed through them with her family in their car. The route wasn't a complete detour, but her father had made a point that they 'could still see a few things' as they fled the city for their coastal haven. Elora had switched sides with her brooding sister and glued herself to the view that came pouring through her window on the second morning of their journey. The ranges were a rich and constant green. In school she had only heard of one mountain, but beside her there seemed to be a dozen or more, cutting across the skyline as a gateway to the mysterious lands beyond, like the maps in her father's fantasy novels. Elora would often finger through the thick and colourful books she found on his bedside table or those he left beside empty teacups in their garden. She was taken by the idea that the worlds within these books had their own maps. Surely if a place had a map, then somewhere, at some time, it must be real. Her father answered pragmatically when she raised this with him, saying that even now there were places on Earth where nobody had been, and many, many more throughout the universe.

As the mountains grew nearer, she caught her father's gaze in the mirror and the two of them had shared a smile.

'Look at the tops,' he said.

Elora refocused on the peaks, tracing the mat of green foliage from the lower slopes, unbroken but for the occasional rocky outcrop, on and on away from them for what seemed like forever. Then she saw it. A shift in colour, sudden and deceiving against the clouded sky. The peaks were dusted in snow.

She had inhaled audibly. Her mother glancing back, concerned, and her father laughing. Elora looked at him in the mirror and he nodded. On this morning she had seen both mountains and snow.

They looked different now. Dark and burned dry from the summer. A graveyard of craters, cars and hobos, if the stories were true. At least Elora now knew some of what lay beyond this mountain wall. Her parents, friends, home – but also Draconis, fickle and relentless in her destruction.

She shifted in the middle seat, already cramping and with no real room to move. Vivienne sat beside her in the passenger seat, knees hugged up to her chest, eyes scanning the roads ahead of them. A wariness had crept into her sister's eyes. Too many obstacles had been thrust up in front of her on this trip, shouting something about the world that Vivienne didn't want to hear. The very same thing she had refused to acknowledge since adolescence. Vivienne had no agency over the universe. None of them did.

They slowed on an incline and Hayden shifted down a gear. The ute revved angrily then smoothed out and crested another small escarpment. Hayden struck a mixture of comfort and apprehension. Elora had the feeling he had driven these roads a thousand times over, but never under the close eye of such strangers.

His presence was still a mystery to her. He had offered a few clipped sentences as they loaded luggage into the dusty tray of the ute: 'The roads are four-wheel drive only.' 'We can't spare the car to give you, but Vivienne has paid double for the fuel.' 'Someone will cover my shifts while I drive you to the highway.' Elora had nodded along, foggy with sleep and becoming immune to the constant shifts in their plans. Before she knew it they were bunched into the cabin together, any thought of conversation stolen by Draconis and the complicated pathway through the back of the holding. Elora was aching to know how far Hayden was coming and why he had agreed to do so. Was it Vivienne's manipulation, or did he, like her, feel some sense of the magnetism that had kept her awake each night since their arrival?

The sun rose beside them, burning Draconis from view and drawing shadows across the farmland that trickled up to the base of the ranges. They left the holding through a nondescript gate and travelled on a sealed road for a few kilometres before Hayden picked out another gate on the southern side.

'Is this your farm, too?' asked Elora as they idled and Vivienne opened the gate.

'The neighbours,' said Hayden. 'They run cattle on the west side of the ranges. It rains more there.'

Elora looked around. 'Are we driving through their property?'

'Just for a minute. Then we'll hit the old tourist road.' He edged them forward and they waited for Vivienne to close the gate and rejoin them.

'Do you come up here much?'

'To the mountains? Not since I was a kid.'

'Before Draconis?'

Hayden glanced at her and nodded. Vivienne climbed back in and they set off along the rocky, shifting road.

The tourist road was sealed, and in good condition but for the leaves and small branches that dusted the surface like a browning carpet. Elora made out the occasional tyre mark, but none that looked recent, and nothing else that spoke of regular traffic. The smoother road brought a silence to the cabin, and Vivienne quickly filled it with music she plugged into Hayden's stereo. He seemed to appreciate this, and the three of them kept to their thoughts as the first mountain crept in from the horizon to take on shape and depth beside them. Elora immersed herself in its lines and shadows until they passed it by and another emerged like the graphic tick of a heart on a screen.

Occasionally Hayden slowed them down to bypass a larger branch or some rubble on the road. They weren't speeding through the country, but Elora had expected a fiercer battle.

Mid-morning, they stopped for the toilet in a rest bay. Hayden waited awkwardly by a faded old tourist map, feigning interest in the attractions while Elora and Vivienne squatted beneath neighbouring trees. As she emerged from the bush, Elora caught a glimpse of two craters in the side of the upcoming range. The bush on this slope had been transformed into a moonscape, barren and grey, with lines of radiating white where the earth had been burned by a heat beyond description. Vivienne stopped and followed her gaze.

'Why does Draconis strike more out here than other places?' asked Elora.

'It doesn't,' said Vivienne.

Elora looked at her, confused. They had spoken little since the argument in the dining hall, sharing only measured sentences that covered practical matters and nothing further. *Back to normal* thought Elora.

'You just see more craters because the land is raised.'

'So why don't people drive through here anymore?' she asked.

'Landslides,' said Vivienne. 'Meteorites trigger landslides when they strike in mountains. You've seen the videos.' She continued back to the car, leaving Elora alone by the edge of the bush.

There were whole channels online dedicated to meteorite videos – a novelty at the start of Draconis, now morphed into a collection of weird and disturbing footage. Things like rocks landing amid traffic, or cows sent airborne by shockwaves. They didn't spark much interest in Elora, and the internet at their house would often struggle with videos anyway. But Vivienne was right – Elora had seen footage of landslides and avalanches caused by Draconis. The slow and terrifying roll of terrain caught by a faraway camera, or the frantic engulf of dust or snow on a hiking trail. In a flat and barren state these things felt a long way removed from the Draconis that Elora had come to know.

As the craters grew on the slopes above them, so did the debris on the road. On some stretches they found trees and foliage pushed over the road by a shockwave. Other areas were strewn with rubble and boulders that had, alarmingly, erupted from above and cut a path through the slopes below. At times these trees or rocks were heavy enough to sever the road entirely. Hayden slowed to a stop at the first of these stretches, locking the wheels and activating the ute's four-wheel-drive. He edged them down onto the shoulder of the road where, luckily, the foliage was thin enough to roll over until the road became clear once more. As this happened more and more, they realised that these areas had been cleared by others to allow them to pass. Larger trees were stumped or stripped of their branches, boulders pushed aside as much as was possible. At one stretch where a shockwave had brought trees down over rubble and sand, an entire bypass had been cut into the bush to one side.

'Is this road crews?' asked Vivienne as Hayden bumped them along through the remaining trees.

Hayden shook his head. 'They don't work like this.'

'Who is it then?' asked Elora.

'Dad says people still camp and hunt out here. Sometimes we see their smoke from the homestead.'

Elora thought of the campers they had seen at home. People hunkered down in the wilderness with their vans and generators in places where Draconis hadn't ventured. Yet these ranges were littered with craters. Living out here seemed, to Elora, like taking shelter in a hailstorm.

The road ended at an intersection with a highway running east to west through a channel in the ranges. It came into view abruptly, without signs or warning. As Hayden geared down and prepared to turn them west, a campervan passed by on the road ahead, bulky and white against the grey of the mountains. There was nothing remarkable about the vehicle, but its presence sent a charge through the cabin. Elora sat upright, suddenly alert.

As they idled at the intersection, two more campervans passed by in front of them, gas tanks and tyres strapped to the back, shutters covering the glass but for the windscreen. Both of them headed east.

'Great,' sighed Vivienne.

Hayden and Elora glanced at her, but neither said anything.

They set off in the other direction. The sun was high and bright, and Draconis seemingly quiet beyond this. A procession of campervans, minivans and cars towing caravans passed them by. One after the other, the bright dots appeared on the road, grew larger, then shuddered eastward. Elora began to catch glimpses of the people inside. Many were old and greying like the tourists who filled the holiday parks at home each summer, but she also saw families through the windscreens, and occasionally younger people. Most wore sunglasses against the glare of the day, and it was difficult to garner any kind of emotion from their faces. For a second Elora did catch the eye of a young boy, maybe five, in the seat between his parents. There was wonder in his gaze: a child seeing something of the world for the very first time. But it wasn't a new bike or a dolphin or the moon, just three young souls driving west to the city.

Hayden reached past her and switched on the two-way that was wired to the dash. Vivienne glanced at him as it scanned for chatter, picking up garbled snatches and the looping government weather reports. He was about to switch it off when a voice cut through in a clear and solid tone. Their eyes drew to the small speaker.

'There are nine kilo refills at the station out by Menzies,' the voice said. 'More at Laverton if you can wait that long.'

The reply was less clear, something like 'thanks' or 'cheers'.

Then another voice chimed in. 'Laverton was run dry yesterday. No diesel either.'

A few voices all at once. Nothing decipherable amid the static.

'Where is Laverton?' asked Vivienne.

'Inland,' said Hayden. 'Middle of nowhere.'

'They're going to the desert,' said Elora.

Vivienne grabbed the two-way and held it up to her lips. 'Anyone out here coming from the city?'

The frequency went quiet for a moment, people taking stock of this strange new voice.

'We're from Bullsbrook,' came a reply, eventually.

'Coogee,' said another.

One more: 'Armadale.'

Vivienne spoke again. 'What's happening with Draconis back there?'

More silence. Elora felt a thin layer of sweat building upon her forehead.

'Big showers in the hills,' came a reply.

'Big showers everywhere,' came another.

'Striking?' asked Vivienne.

'Just a matter of time on the coast. On-shore breezes sweeping it all across from the ocean.'

'We've been tracking these blue showers for months up in the hills. Got a twelve-inch scope pointing straight at Draconis. All manner of rocks ...'

Vivienne switched off the radio.

'What?' asked Elora.

'They're preppers,' said Vivienne.

'All of them?'

'Well, they're driving caravans out into the desert.'

Elora was silent, feeling awkward for Hayden in the car beside them.

More and more vans passed them by. They crested a ridgeline and caught a sweep of the land ahead: a slow snake of white vans continuing on as far as they could see. They were in the heart of the ranges now. Sharp and ragged mountains bordered them to the north, their reaches sheer and angular in the afternoon light. The mountains were larger again to the south, matted with heavy foliage and the faded remnants of hiking trails. Together they funnelled the traffic toward a narrowing eastern gateway.

'Why are they coming through the ranges to get to the desert?' asked Vivienne.

'The northern highways must be out,' said Hayden.

Elora watched as the vans hummed along neatly. Uniform, like a cult or convoy. She had to remind herself that the people inside didn't know one another. They were from all over the state and city. Each with their own life and story.

'What will they do when they get to the desert?' she asked.

Vivienne glanced at her but didn't say anything. Hayden focused forward, unsettled by more questions without clear answers. For a moment it looked as though he may say something in response, then three meteors exploded in the sky ahead of them.

The flashes were condensed and rapid. Blinding bright and flaring outwards like the floral bloom of fireworks.

Hayden braked hard and swore. The shockwave arrived almost immediately, a buffeting of acrid air against the car. Dirt, leaves and foliage hurtling from one side of the road to the other. The crack of a tree trunk snapping. Sand spitting against the windscreen like hailstones.

A moment later they were stationary on the road, hands braced against the dash, eyes wide and searching the ranges for signs of movement on the slopes above.

'Keep driving,' said Vivienne.

'Jesus Christ, Vivienne.'

'She's right,' said Hayden, taking off again. 'We need to clear the mountains.'

He hammered through the gears, the ute straining for breath. There was another flash in the sky, this time distant and southwards.

Elora began to count.

Ahead of them the road appeared to narrow. An approaching campervan looked as though it was taking up both lanes. Hayden leant forward and squinted through the glare. Elora caught herself looking at him rather than the road or sky. He seemed suddenly older now they had left the holding. A shadow across his jawline, arms taut and strong on the wheel.

'Oh, those fuckheads,' said Vivienne.

Hayden hit the brakes again and Elora's eyes darted back to the road. There were vans driving towards them on both lanes.

'What are they doing?' she said.

The vehicles grew large and close ahead of them. They were hammering forward, headlights flashing manically. Elora caught sight of more beyond them. The convoy had panicked and claimed the road like a herd of spooked cattle.

'We need a turnoff,' said Hayden.

'There isn't one,' said Vivienne.

Hayden pulled up and began reversing. Frantically they scanned the roadside. The shoulders of the highway dropped away steeply into bush on either side of them. Beyond this they were hemmed in by the rocky foot of the mountains. Elora watched the vans draw closer and closer. She realised then that the people driving these vehicles weren't going to move for them.

'The rest stop,' she barked. 'We passed one earlier.'

'How far back was it?' asked Vivienne.

Hayden swung them around, not waiting for an answer. He pushed the ute hard, but they had none of the momentum of the thundering convoy. Horns joined the headlights behind them. Vivienne put her hand out the window and signalled for them to slow down. Elora grabbed the radio and screamed at the drivers to stop. Another meteor cracked and burned in the sky somewhere above.

'Left or right?' asked Hayden.

'What?' asked Elora.

'The rest stop.'

'Right.'

He scanned the bushland flashing by beside them.

'No – left! Sorry. Shit.'

The campervans were all but on top of them.

'There,' said Vivienne.

Hayden started braking and any space behind them and the convoy evaporated. The rest stop emerged from the bush, tiny and imminent. *Too fast*, thought Elora. Hayden braked again and a campervan roared past in the opposite lane. Elora caught a frame of the people in the van behind them – above them – in the mirror. A man and woman her parents' age, eyes cold and steady, prepared to do anything but be caught by Draconis.

They veered onto gravel and the back of the ute kicked out violently behind them. Vivienne fell sideways into her. The windows were suddenly a carousel blur of bush, vans and dust. She looked up for something stationary but could no longer find the sky above them. Instead there were rocks and dirt, and Elora thought that Draconis had finally come for them all.

Chapter Fifteen

Elora sat with Hayden on a fallen tree as two children drew bubbles from a neon tube and chased them around the gravel. Occasionally one would escape their grasp, drifting high enough to catch a breeze that sent it southward above the mallees and onward to the mountains. The children screamed in anguish, but were also taken by the wonder of such a thing. Something from their own hand setting out into the wild.

Their father watched them while he made a kettle of tea on a gas stove by the caravan. He seemed young for a parent, a blush of acne still present beneath his beard, his hair cut short in the faded style Elora had seen in others from the city. The sky had calmed and the convoy gone, but Elora saw an apprehension in his shoulders. He wanted to be back on the road with his wife and children, not making tea for three strange people that were headed to the city.

She smiled gratefully as the father approached with two mugs. The children circled in front of him, laughing like maniacs until he ordered them away from the steaming liquid. They took a seat at the other end of the log, mirroring Elora and Hayden and laughing some more.

'Sorry,' said the father, wearily. 'They haven't had a run around since we left.'

He passed them the mugs and they thanked him in unison. A van approached from the west, quietening the bush with its rumble, before shuddering past. The three of them watched it as the children resumed with the bubbles. The father stood awkwardly, not knowing what to do now he had completed this task of making tea. Behind him his wife was tending to the cut on Vivienne's elbow. She looked slightly older than her husband, hair bobbed but pulled away from her face in a ponytail, dressed in sneakers and tights as if she were about to go running. She seemed calm and relaxed, smiling at the children as they drew in to watch their mother's careful movements with the gauze and bandage.

Elora caught her sister's eye, and the two of them looked at each other for the first time in a while. *So fierce*, thought Elora. *Even here with her arm in bandages, stuck in the mountains with their ute flipped upside down.*

'You're all heading to the city for uni?' asked the father.

Elora glanced at Hayden then nodded for the both of them. 'Is that where you're from?' she asked.

'Eglinton,' said the father, tracing his eyes across his children's movements by the van.

'Sorry,' said Elora. 'I don't know the city that well.'

'It's north of the city. A new estate. We just built a house there.'

Elora smiled a little awkwardly and glanced back at the caravan. It looked to be loaded with luggage and boxes, as was the car in front. She shook off a vision of the house in this foreign suburb, freshly built and abandoned, bunk beds stripped of sheets and the lawns slowly dying.

'We can use the winch on your ute,' said the father to Hayden. 'Once you finish your tea.'

Hayden nodded and sipped carefully from his mug. The father wandered away to check the tyres on the van. The children shadowed him, tapping the wheels with their bubble tube.

'You okay?' asked Elora once they were alone.

'Yep,' said Hayden.

'I just said that about uni so we didn't have to explain everything.'

Hayden nodded.

They watched the father tinkering with the van against the patchy afternoon sky.

'I don't think he was that interested, anyway,' said Elora.

'He wants to get going. Clear the ranges before dark,' said Hayden.

'That's fair enough. They didn't have to stop for us. Nobody else did.'

They drank from their cups. It was just regular tea, but watching the steps involved in preparing it – table, gas, kettle, cups – against the backdrop of such wilderness made the liquid feel sacred. Elora cradled it close and focused on the smoky, floral aroma.

'Is Vivienne okay?' asked Hayden.

'Yeah,' said Elora. 'It's not deep. Plus the mum is a nurse.'

Hayden nodded and shifted some rocks with his feet.

Elora watched him for a moment. 'It wasn't your fault.'

Hayden was silent.

'Seriously, Hayden. We dragged you out here in the middle of a meteor shower. And those caravans were insane driving like that.'

'Arseholes,' muttered Hayden as another van rumbled by.

'An arsehole of caravans,' said Elora, smirking.

'Collective nouns,' he said. 'Very funny.'

They shared a smile, and watched as the father unclipped his winch and walked it over to the upturned ute. It looked oddly fragile with the tyres and undercarriage exposed to the sky.

Like an insect flipped by the wind and waiting to see what fate would decide.

'God. I'm so sorry about the car. We'll pay for it. Or Vivienne will.'

'It was banged-up anyway.'

'You can head back to the homestead. You should. Being out here is stupid.'

'I thought you were going home?' asked Hayden, looking at her.

'Mum told me not to.'

'Were there strikes in Esperance?'

Elora sniffed and felt the flood of everything tipping over once more.

'Sorry,' said Hayden.

'It's fine. I think they're fine. My mum was in the showers that hit the city at the start of Draconis.'

'Was she okay?'

'Yes and no.'

Vivienne stood up from the chair across from them and tested out her bandaged arm. They watched as the mother offered some final advice.

'Anyway,' Elora said. 'You should totally head back home. We'll figure something out. Maybe bunk in with these kids.'

Hayden smiled. Somehow the children had found mud in a place without rain, and were holding up their hands for the father to wipe clean.

'I was going to head away somewhere with some friends after school finished,' he said. 'Maybe the city or the coast. But the harvest came early.'

'Leavers,' said Elora.

'What?'

'It's what they used to call the parties between school and uni.'

'Leavers,' repeated Hayden.

'What did you want to do when you arrived?'

Hayden thought about this for a moment – for the first time. 'I don't know,' he said. 'Does that matter?'

Elora looked at him and smiled. 'I don't think so.'

There was a clink across from them and the winch grew taut. They rose from the log and joined the others by the side of the ute.

* * *

They resumed their journey westward in silence, Vivienne now driving and Hayden staring at the sprawling ranges through the fractured glass of the passenger window. He had listened to Vivienne say the same thing as Elora about him leaving them and heading back to the homestead. Offered the same casual decline as he reloaded their bags into the tray and checked the tyres.

Elora remained seated like a child between them. She couldn't shift her thoughts from the family fleeing into the desert behind them. Before they left, the mother had hugged each of them as if she were a favourite aunty. The children clinging to the legs of their father, and cackled as he humoured them and continued to pack up regardless. Elora caught a glimpse inside their car of boxes, overflowing and still open at the top. A totem tennis pole and inflatable pool. A filing cabinet wedged between the front seat and back. The dinner bowl for a dog or cat hiding somewhere inside. Meeting the people within one of these caravans – people so ordinary – had destroyed any notion that things were in any way normal. If these people were willing to abandon their hard-fought homes, to bundle their children into a caravan and head for the desert, what kind of life could possibly be awaiting her in the city?

They all left at the same time, beeping their horns and pulling back out onto the highway. Elora looked at her sister to see if she were feeling something similar, but she was already looking west, eyes shielded by glasses against the lowering sun.

Draconis grumbled and cracked like fireworks all over the ranges. Many of the lights were hidden by peaks or lost in the sun, but occasionally the cab blinked with a pale flash of blue. The road was intact, and more campervans passed them in the opposite direction. It would be nightfall before any of these people reached open terrain. Elora found herself silently urging them on, wishing them safety and solace in the east as the three of them continued blindly into battle.

The meteors had thrown a dust into the air that coated the windscreen and kept them from seeing anything beyond a few kilometres. Vivienne slowed warily whenever the road became unstable beneath them. Rocks and debris had been spread like seeds across the highway and surrounds. Eventually these sections became so frequent that she abandoned any hope of moving beyond fourth gear.

They ground on and on in the lingering afternoon. Elora was still taken by the drama of the ranges beside them, but yearned for a sense of their boundary. For the farmland, or whatever came next, to manifest. Instead the dust appeared to thicken around them.

Hayden drew down his window to catch a whiff of the air. 'Smoke,' he murmured.

Vivienne glanced at him and leant forward to survey the road ahead. The air was swirling and murky. The campervans that passed seemed to manifest out of oblivion before fading like ghosts behind them. One of these vans flashed them with their headlights.

'What's that supposed to mean?' asked Vivienne, slowing down further.

They sat upright, straining to see what might lay ahead.

Elora caught a glow of red on a ridge to their right. Looking closer, she could make out a messy line of flames fanning downward. 'There's a fire up there,' she said, pointing ahead of them.

'Of course there is,' said Vivienne. She closed their vents and checked that her window was sealed. 'Hayden, what do you think?'

He hesitated for a moment. 'The road must be clear if the vans are still coming through.'

'What if it's behind them?' asked Elora.

'I guess we'll find out soon,' said Vivienne.

She stared hard at the way forward. Smoke and dust in a thick, soupy haze. Another caravan emerged from the darkness ahead of them. Vivienne swerved them out of the way as it hurtled past, hogging the road.

'Shit,' gasped Elora, hands braced on the dash.

'I can't see the fire anymore,' said Hayden.

The ridge to the right of them had been lost to the smoke. Elora turned in the other direction and realised that everything was now hidden but the road in front of them. It felt as though the sun had gone and night was suddenly upon them. Vivienne slowed even further, and Elora could feel her frustration radiating through the cabin.

'Try the spotlights, maybe,' said Hayden.

'What?' asked Vivienne, looking around the dash.

'By the ignition.'

She flicked a switch and an extra glow of light spread out across the highway. 'Jesus Hayden. What else do you have hidden down here?'

Elora smiled. She felt like laughing, but was worried this would quickly spill into tears. Hayden watched them both, still at sea within their strange and shifting relationship. He smiled too, but the moment had passed.

Vivienne increased their speed just slightly amid this new light. Objects emerged out of the fog like fossils left behind in the bed of a great river. Stones scattered upon the road, the heavy barrel of a rubbish bin, charred branches from incinerated trees. She rounded these carefully, terrified of blowing out a tyre and leaving them stuck by the roadside.

The smoke deepened further. Elora watched as it shifted past their windscreen, now not a hovering blanket but ragged and puffy plumes. Vivienne slowed them to a stop and sat, staring at the smoke ahead of them.

'What is it?' asked Elora.

'No more caravans,' said Vivienne.

'You think the fire's on the road?' asked Elora.

She didn't answer, instead rolling them slowly forward. The smoke thickened again until there was nothing more to see, just greyness and the feel of the road beneath them. Elora felt herself sweating and realised that the dash had grown warm beneath her hands.

'We need to turn around now,' said Hayden.

They continued to roll forward. A bead of red light danced and twirled past the windscreen. Then another.

Embers.

'Vivienne!' screamed Elora.

Her sister crunched the car into reverse and turned to see what lay behind them. Hayden followed. Grey nothingness, then a flash of brilliant blue.

One one hundred. Two one hundred.

They braced for a shockwave. There was a deep and mournful groan. Smoke shuddered in the glass surrounding them, then resumed its thick and endless roll.

'Go forward,' said Elora, still facing the windscreen.

Vivienne and Hayden turned and looked at her.

'I saw the road in front of us. We're in the fire right now, but it ends soon and there's a highway ahead.' Her voice sounded strange in her ears. Resonant and certain in a way she wasn't used to.

Vivienne hesitated. Found her hand trembling against the wheel.

'Go,' repeated Elora, crunching the gearstick into first.

They leapt forward, blinded again by the smoke.

'The road is straight. Just keep going straight.'

Vivienne followed her orders as more embers circled above. Elora found herself gripping hold of Hayden's hand. She didn't remember when this had happened but was sure that it was he who had reached for her. They moved ahead blindly into the abyss.

It felt as though the ranges had warped them to another realm, one where Draconis had already taken humans from Earth and was toying with ideas about what might come next. Elora felt a deep emptiness to be suspended in a place so liminal. She could navigate the before or the after, but no longer this broken-down realm in between. Hayden's hand contracted in hers and she burrowed low into the seat.

Light reached them again. It was orange this time. The last hue of the sun before nightfall.

Vivienne exhaled. In an instant they had cleared the smoke and now travelled alone on a wide and empty road. She lowered her window and switched off the spotlights.

Elora turned and caught a sweep of the chaos behind them. Ranges climbing madly away from smoke, fire and the crater-filled earth. As Vivienne sped them away towards the southern highway, Elora saw a glimmer of white on the very tips of the ranges. This time it was ash, not snow.

They arrived at an intersection running wide and clear to the north and south. Vivienne idled there a moment and none of them could find anything to say. The sun had gone and a calm and violet dusk settled in over the rolling farmland to the west. A sign pointed to a town not far from where they waited. It was a name Elora didn't recognise from her maps, dreams or nightmares.

CHAPTER SIXTEEN

They checked into a hostel built for hikers planning expeditions through the nearby ranges. The building was sprawling, yet homely, with timber cladding on the walls and gentle sloping roofs made of corrugated iron in the colour of the grassland. The common area housed a singular long table etched from the colossal trees of the southern forests, its grain gnarled and mysterious beneath the plastic dinnerware and coffee mugs. Beyond this was a broad kitchen with two fridges and an eclectic array of cookware hanging from hooks drilled into the low ceiling. There were windows framing the landscape to the east as it rippled and grew into what would eventually become the ranges. One of the walls had a pinboard with postcards, notices and photos of guests drinking beer or standing ready with their backpacks. Another had a framed poster of a hiker made famous by a book, then a film. Running off this common room was a lounge area with several old couches and a coffee table littered with paperbacks and magazines.

A scattering of guests inhabited these spaces. Elora and Hayden watched them curiously, taken by the gentle and everyday atmosphere of this place. People were chopping vegetables and waiting on water to boil in the kitchen. Relaxing at the long table with wine from glass tumblers. A girl their age was sprawled on the couch with a paperback as if she were at home in her lounge room. Another was seated at a communal computer waiting on the internet. There was music coming from somewhere too, folky and sombre, with lyrics about the kitchen garden of a cheating lover.

As evening descended calmly over the town, a woman led them outside and across a walkway to their rooms. The stars were heavy above them, and Draconis gathered ominously in the spaces between. Elora couldn't find the moon, but she saw Mars, red and angry, in the northern sky, consumed with her own war against the rocks of Draconis. The woman seemed oblivious to the sky, instead talking of the vegetables they were growing and the water being recycled from the laundry. Solar globes lit the decks connecting each room, and they gratefully accepted a line of three by a sunken fishpond. Dropping their bags on the floor, they returned wordlessly to the kitchen for something to fill their strained and anxious stomachs.

Hayden's mother had packed them a cooler with a cut of beef and some vegetables pulled from the ground that morning. They found a free corner in the kitchen and Elora set about dicing the potatoes and carrots while Hayden found a pan for the steak. Vivienne moved over to some people still seated at the table and asked if she could buy some of their wine. They refused the money and happily filled up three tumblers with something dark and red. She brought them back to the kitchen and stood at the bench sipping her glass and staring blankly out of the window. Elora glanced at her and wondered what was swirling around in her sister's head. They had a clear run to the city now – could be there by midday tomorrow, back to the life that had been hovering out of her reach for all of these days. Elora pictured Vivienne there now, craters erupting all around while she went about her business.

They sat and ate in silence as other guests drifted about the space making tea and talking about their plans. Elora caught snippets of their conversations – people spoke of showering in the ranges, the state of certain roads and trails, rumours of weather occurring to the west of them. Most of the guests seemed to be just waiting things out. Some of them would stand at the windows, staring out at the flashing ranges as if they were beset by a passing winter storm. It was a long way removed from the image she had built of frenzied mountain people, hunting and trekking amid landslides and bushfires.

Elora also noticed that the hostel had a lot of glass. She couldn't remember seeing shutters on the common area, nor on any of the dorm rooms. Something about this, and the idea of these hikers still hoping to venture out into the ranges, felt reassuring to her. Something about the town even, although she had yet to see more than a street or two.

After eating they slumped back in their chairs and finished the wine while a couple played records from a pile by the lounge. Eventually Vivienne rose from the table, stacking up their empty plates and glasses. Elora and Hayden trailed her over to the sink and they shared the washing up like siblings away on a summer holiday. Elora watched their reflections in the windows. The journey through the mountains had stolen the life from their eyes and the sharpness from their movements. She doubted whether sleep would be able to bring these things back. Questioned whether they could exist at all in a world such as this.

The air outside had cooled, holding a bite that spoke of altitude and something beyond the summer. They followed the lights back to their rooms and hovered for a moment outside.

'When do you want to leave tomorrow?' asked Elora.

'I don't know. I'm tired,' said Vivienne. 'Just whenever we wake.'

Elora nodded, relieved.

Vivienne turned for her room and the shower, but stopped. 'Thanks for driving us here, Hayden.'

'No worries,' he replied.

'I'll get some cash when we hire a car tomorrow. Pay you for the ute.'

He nodded, scuffing his shoe on the deck.

Elora stood by awkwardly, wishing there was something she could add.

'You guys should head into town,' said Vivienne. 'There's probably a bar or something open somewhere.'

She disappeared inside her room, then returned carrying a towel and wandered away to the showers.

Elora and Hayden lingered in her wake.

'I'm wrecked, but it would be good to see the town,' said Elora.

'Let's do it,' said Hayden.

Elora looked at him, surprised by the definite response.

'Leavers,' said Hayden.

'Leavers,' repeated Elora, smiling.

They showered and changed. Elora spent a few minutes putting on makeup and pinning up her hair. When she emerged from her room she found Hayden seated on a bench wearing jeans and a fresh black t-shirt. His arms were tanned and muscular beneath and she pulled her eyes away from them. They left the ute, dented and snowy with ash, and set off into town on foot.

The hostel was at the end of a wide street where rambling houses stretched away comfortably on either side. Most of these were clad in timber with pitched iron roofs and chimneys reaching upward from the kitchens and lounge rooms inside. In place of fences there were sprawling trees and thick, motley gardens. Elora saw shutters on some of the windows, but also others that lay bare and now glowed warm and yellow with light. The street had no footpath, so they wandered down the middle, peering into the houses and occasionally catching a glimpse of the people inside. This street made its way into another which looked much the same but for a glow of lights at the end that signified their destination.

The town centre spoke of many of the others they had passed through on their journey, set high with a view of the surrounding farmland and ranges. Dual hotels perched central in the street with hovering balconies and rows of stained-glass windows. Beside these were smaller stores, a park with a memorial, and shelters for people awaiting buses. Yet rather than hiding behind timber and iron, this town threw a stoic yellow glow out into the darkness. Shutters were open on shopfronts, items displayed proudly inside. They passed a craft store, chemist and supermarket. Many of the windows had signs advertising local events such as a school fete or the monthly farmers' market. A bottle shop was open, with people drifting in and out from cars parked at neat angles along the street. Beyond this were neon signs for takeaway restaurants selling fish-and-chips and kebabs. The smell of fat and salt spilled out as a family carried paper parcels back to their Landcruiser.

Elora and Hayden lingered for a moment before moving on to reach another intersection where the town centre continued partway down a quieter street running to the south. More shops and a service station glowing green in the distance. Something caught Elora's gaze in the foreground. A few doors down was a restaurant with soft lighting and people drinking and eating dinner at neat circular tables. There was a menu on the footpath, and music drifted out that sounded like jazz. They stopped and stared as if the scene had been transported from another time and universe.

'Are you still hungry?' asked Elora.

'Not really,' said Hayden.

They hesitated.

'Should we go in anyway?' he asked.

'Yes,' said Elora, smiling.

The door opened to a wash of cooler air and the smell of garlic and wine. They stood in the entry for a moment, neither totally sure how to proceed. A moment later a woman their mothers' age emerged and ushered them to a table by the bar and service area. Elora noticed that all the tables near the windows were already taken. People laughed and ate by the tall glass panes without distraction.

Before they could talk, the woman re-emerged beside them with some menus. She paused and eyed them curiously.

'Will you kids be needing a wine list tonight?'

They dug around in their pockets for their ID until the woman put a hand on Hayden's shoulder.

'It's fine, love. We're not the police.'

She placed menus in front of them and they shuffled through the pages, trying to work out where they should be looking. Elora found the wine list but was lost amid the names and varieties.

'The cabernet at the top is local and lovely,' the woman said. 'And cheap.'

'Thank you,' said Elora.

'Anyway, I'll come back in a few minutes and we'll work it all out.'

Hayden nodded, upright and proper in his chair. Elora looked at him and laughed.

'What?' he said.

'Nothing.'

'What?!'

'Just this day.' Hayden smiled and relaxed a little. 'For a while there I thought we would be sleeping out in the ranges.'

'I keep thinking about that family,' said Elora. 'I hope they're okay.'

'They should be in the Goldfields by now.'

'Kalgoorlie?'

Hayden nodded.

'Have you been there?' asked Elora.

'Dad took us once. It's hot out there. Not as bad as the Kimberley, but still pretty baking. We spent most of the time in the pool.'

'It seems like you've been to a lot of places.'

'I guess so. We go away somewhere every year for Christmas.'

'Where did you go this year?'

'We didn't go this year.'

'How come?'

'I guess I was meant to be going away after school. Then the harvest came early. Then Draconis.'

Elora nodded. A waiter drifted by and placed some water on their table.

He continued. 'Mum and Mia were talking about going back to Ningaloo before the road was cut.'

'How old is your sister?'

'I have two. Mia's fourteen and Macy is twenty. She lives in town now. Works at the hotel.'

Elora thought about Hayden's mother. How young she must have been when she had Macy, then Hayden just two years later. What it would feel like to stand with a baby on the hip, gazing over paddocks of wavering grain. Nobody for miles and a sky so clear that it burned the eyes.

'Is Vivienne much older than you?' asked Hayden.

'Four years.'

'It seems like more.'

Elora smiled and looked down at her water.

The woman arrived back with two glasses of the wine she'd recommended, and they ordered a few smaller dishes to share. Hayden said yes to all of the woman's suggestions. It would be too much food, but it also felt exciting and mature. They were given bread and olive oil then left alone as other diners filtered in and out of the building. The food was being prepared just across from them, two chefs bustling about in a galley beneath the hum of a hovering rangehood.

'It was different before Draconis,' said Elora. 'We used to mess around. Put on shows for Mum and Dad. Vivienne was always the one who would make everyone laugh. She does great impersonations.'

Hayden drank some of his wine. It was hard to tell if he was enjoying it but he continued regardless.

'Do you remember much from before the showers?' asked Elora.

'Just farm and school stuff,' said Hayden.

Elora nodded and chewed on a slice of bread. Her life had shifted irrevocably when Draconis arrived, and she had to remind herself that this wasn't always the case for others.

'I remember going to Bali one Christmas when I was six,' said Hayden. 'We flew over at night but I couldn't sleep. Out the window you could see these pockets of light all the way up the coast. Lancelin. Geraldton. Exmouth. Then just blackness and tiny lights in the ocean that Dad said were oil rigs.'

'What was it like when you got there?'

'The hotel was on a beach with shops all along the sand. You could buy t-shirts and drinks and ice-creams. I remember Mum getting massages while we swam in the pool with Dad. Then Macy cut her foot on something and couldn't go in the water again for the rest of the holiday.'

Elora grimaced.

'We went up into the forest to see some monkeys instead. The traffic was crazy. Dad was beeping and swearing at everyone.'

Elora laughed, and they took turns dipping the bread in oil. Hayden thought of something else, and his brow turned focused and taut. Elora had seen this in him a few times now, as if a question kept resurfacing that he had been unable to answer.

'I remember local kids eating dinner with their hands in the back of a shop. They were just scraping up rice with their fingers, one plate for all four of them. Macy got upset, started crying in the shop, and Mum had to take us outside. She told us that this was how they ate. That they were happy because their parents had work when people like us took holidays.'

They were silent a moment, and glad when some food arrived to take their attention. The woman asked if they would like more wine. Hayden nodded immediately and Elora laughed.

'Did you go on many holidays before Draconis?' he asked.

'Not really. Dad used to travel for work so we would usually stay home when he wasn't working. It's kind of a holiday town where we live now though, I guess.'

Elora dipped her arancini in a swirl of bright-orange sauce. The food was delicious and she wished she had more of an appetite. 'Where would you go if Draconis stopped?' she asked, eyes dancing with excitement.

'I don't know,' said Hayden, honestly. 'Where would you go?'

'New York and London.'

'Because of the theatre?'

Elora nodded, impressed. 'Then Hawaii to surf,' she added, smiling.

'Hawaii would be cool. Jurassic Park was filmed there.'

'That old dinosaur movie?'

'Classic dinosaur movie,' corrected Hayden.

Elora smiled and drank some more of the wine. As they continued to eat and talk she felt a deep calm radiating throughout her body, as if she were floating on her board at the end of a long session, the breeze spraying her with mist as she waited for a final wave to usher her to the shore.

Eventually the woman arrived at their table to clear some of the dishes. 'Will you be having dessert?' she asked.

Hayden and Elora looked at each other.

'Are any of the bars in town still open?' asked Elora.

The woman smiled. 'If you're quick you can catch the karaoke at the inn.'

They paid for dinner then retraced their steps back to the second of two hotels on the main street. There were still cars parked in the bays outside, and light spilled out from the decorative windows of the frontage. Elora led them across the road and inside through the heavy wooden door. Guitar greeted them, along with the low rumble of a man singing Johnny Cash. He was bearded and largely bald, jeans and a flannel shirt dressed up by decorative boots and a bow tie resting just beneath his beard.

The man offered a theatrical nod as they traversed some dining tables between the entrance and the bar. The stage was comprised of several square platforms dragged together beneath a rusty old mirror ball. A cluster of people were listening from a space below the stage. They were rugged and greying, with a hint of the alternative like the singer above. There were also the remnants of what looked to be a mothers group out for a night without the children. Beyond them a gathering of younger people were dressed in clothes that Elora had seen her sister wearing.

The man finished the song to healthy applause, and they made their way to the bar. Hayden ordered them shots of vodka, then a combination of something sweet and creamy that neither had tried before.

A woman began to sing – an old pop song with a chorus that some of the crowd seemed to know. Elora took a song list from one of the tables and started browsing. Hayden wasn't interested and instead looked around at the sprawling space. There were pool tables, dart boards and a numbered wheel to spin for raffles. The bar stretched away into a dining area where they had entered. Beyond this were stairs going up to the accommodation on the floor above, and others that were roped off and headed down to what he assumed must be a basement. There was a sign at the entrance to this space. Elora followed his gaze and they squinted to make it out: a capacity limit and a graphic of a person wearing an oxygen mask. Designated shelter sites like this were scattered all over in town halls, churches and school gymnasiums, though neither of them had seen one that was roped off in this way.

Hayden looked for a while longer, and when he turned back he found Elora had disappeared from his side and was now standing central on the stage.

She cleared her throat theatrically, and Hayden waved from the bar. There was a whisper of silence before guitar licked out into the room, warm and familiar. A few people whooped and clapped in recognition. Elora let her hair out and lowered her head so it fell like a curtain about her face. She felt a swell in her stomach that had been missing forever. The potent swirl of stardust.

A drumbeat sounded and she lifted her head.

More whooping, and this time Hayden joined them. Elora took the mic from the stand and drifted around the stage, mesmeric and transported beneath the glimmer of the mirror ball, a song about searching beneath the Milky Way. She sang to the faces of this strange haven they had stumbled upon, then to Hayden standing proudly beyond them, then to the sky raging above them all. Time disappeared, and Elora found herself in a place where the world could no longer reach her. No Vivienne. No Draconis. No roads without an end.

Eventually the music faded and her head dropped once more. People clapped and cheered. Elora was smiling and crying. A lady squeezed her on the shoulder as she returned to Hayden at the bar. He stood there, rigid and confused as she buried her head into his chest. After a while she sniffed, then reached up to kiss him, then moved to the bar for more drinks. Hayden put his hand on the small of her back and Elora felt like crying all over again.

They chatted to the barman for a while and ordered local beers served in long white cans. Someone else started singing and the bearded man approached them from along the bar.

'Pretty good singing there,' he boomed.

'Thanks,' said Elora, smiling.

'People here get a little tired of my Johnny Cash.'

'It sounded cool,' said Hayden.

'Thank you, young man. I'm Johnny,' he said, extending a hand.

'For real?' said Hayden.

Elora laughed into her drink.

Johnny looked at them both, then erupted into laughter himself. 'For real,' he replied.

They took turns shaking hands. The barman arrived with a wine for Johnny.

'You're on your way to the east?' he said.

'Nope. The city,' said Elora.

'Good to hear,' said Johnny. 'No place for a voice like that out in the desert.'

Elora smiled.

'Do you live here?' asked Hayden.

'Born and bred. Of course, I left for a sabbatical in my twenties, then again thirty years later when the kids had moved on. This was when you could fly into Amsterdam and smoke by the river in the morning, then over to Manchester for football and black pudding at night.' He paused. 'Of course, she doesn't allow for that any longer, except by boat if you can stomach it. So, what do we do?'

He paused again, and Elora wondered whether she should attempt to answer.

'We keep our feet on the ground and live our best lives,' said Johnny. 'Just this morning I took a kilo of heirloom tomatoes from a seedling that had grown in the twist of a garden path. No regard for her rocks or dust or any other business.'

'You mean Draconis?' asked Hayden.

'I do,' replied Johnny. 'But I prefer to call her a wolf than a star.'

'How come nobody here is worried about the showers?' asked Elora.

'Well, it's the weekend,' replied Johnny, smiling and downing his wine.

'Have you had any strikes here?' asked Hayden.

'Two last week,' said Johnny. 'And all that silliness up in the mountains.'

'But no one uses their shutters,' said Elora.

'Not true, young lady,' said Johnny. 'I rolled down a couple just this evening to keep the dogs inside.'

'Okay, but I've seen a dozen small towns over the past week, and this is the only one with shops sitting open to the sky.'

Johnny applauded another singer as they took to the stage.

'You figure what's the point?' said Hayden.

Elora and Johnny turned to him.

'That's why the shelter site is roped off. You figure if Draconis is coming for us then what's the point.'

Johnny nodded solemnly and patted Hayden on the shoulder. 'It is how we started and how we will end,' said Johnny, watching the singer.

The two of them looked at him. Children at the feet of a strange new teacher.

'This, now, is our remit,' said Johnny, spreading his arms in a wide arc. 'What we choose to do while she makes her way toward us.'

They stood and drank as a woman stumbled and laughed her way through a country song. Elora leaned into Hayden and wondered about the things that were shifting inside of him.

Johnny left them to sing some more, and eventually he coaxed Elora onto the stage with him. Their duet drew the biggest cheer of the night, and some people even danced on the floor below as they sang. Hayden drifted about the bar, speaking with farmers and locals with an ease that struck Elora as almost diplomatic. She caught an image of him from deep into the future, talking at the front of a packed town hall, upright and calm despite the stirring in the crowd and the heaving sky in the windows.

People booed when the lights eventually came on, so the publican simply turned them off again. When they came on a second time, Elora and Hayden funnelled out onto the street with the others. People drifted away on foot, abandoning their cars to walk home beneath the meteors in a way that felt routine. Elora looked around for Johnny to say goodbye, but they hadn't seen him since his voice gave out during his final, rambling song. He'd stayed on stage, instead attempting an Irish dance to the clap of those who remained below.

Lights had timed out in the shops and Elora pulled Hayden beneath the porch of a gift store where they made out properly against the cool limestone walls. After a while she paused and looked at his face, so close now. The straight bridge of his nose. Lips with a softening overbite.

'Let's go back to the hostel,' she whispered.

Hayden nodded seriously and Elora laughed.

'We'll have to be quiet,' she said.

They kissed again until a humming noise stole their attention.

'What is that?' asked Elora, looking upward with a degree of apprehension.

Hayden followed her gaze and they found a light flashing rhythmically in the sky to the south.

'A plane going east,' said Hayden.

Elora looked at the flashes, wings then tail, wings then tail, diminutive and fragile against the heave and thrust of meteors all around. It was like a space explorer. The sky had been claimed back by the universe and was no longer the realm of humans or their machines.

'I can't believe some people still do that,' said Elora.

Hayden looked at her. 'Are you worried about Vivienne?'

'Why?'

'Flying to Sydney.'

Elora's breath caught in her throat. She felt weak and dizzy, as if a secret she'd ignored since childhood had finally caught up with her.

'When?'

Hayden studied her. 'You didn't know?'

Elora shook her head.

'She asked to use the phone at our place to check some flight information. Before you called your parents. A lot of flights were cancelled with the new showering. People were saying that they might stop them altogether. Vivienne found one of the last seats to Sydney this week.'

A moment passed when Elora couldn't speak. Vivienne had chosen this above calling their parents. Above everything they had been through since leaving.

'Did she say why she was going?'

Hayden shook his head. 'They have a new satellite program over there. I figured she was going for work.'

Elora was silent, tracing the plane as it faded into the lights above the ranges.

'Sorry, Elora.'

'I don't want to go back to the hostel right now,' she said, eventually.

Hayden lingered, uncertain of what to suggest. 'What should we do?' he asked.

Elora looked around, then took his hand and led them down the side of the building. It was dark and the gravel crunched loudly beneath their shoes. Elora ignored this and found a small porch at the back of the building. On the timber slats there was a bench with faded floral cushions and a teapot left behind from a lunchbreak. Hayden stepped up and sat down on the bench. Elora followed, but instead of sitting beside him, she climbed onto his lap and kissed him seriously. Hayden put his hands on her back and Elora moved them to her legs. A moment later she slid off and unzipped her jeans. Hayden watched as she took his hand and put his fingers inside her. Elora carefully climbed back onto his lap and they continued to kiss. Draconis flickered a wicked blue in the window behind them, and a rumble sounded somewhere distant. Elora closed her eyes and tried to stall the soberness that had swept through her so abruptly and completely. It was no use. She still felt the world all around her, mocking and relentless in its pursuit.

CHAPTER SEVENTEEN

The ranges evaporated into a rolling beige horizon of farmland as they took the highway north into the city. Trees grew in haughty clusters by the roadside and in the hollows of dried creek beds. Engulfing them were healthy paddocks of grain and the occasional burst of green signalling a crop of vegetables. Fences were neat on these properties, and roads well-worn. Hayden had explained how the drought was less severe to the west of the ranges where cold fronts would still scatter their rain in the shortened winters.

They passed quaint country towns with artwork on silos and tiny banks with decorative facades. The nearest coastline was west of them now, and signs pointed to places Elora had seen on the internet. The city with the endless jetty and abandoned aquarium. The river that snaked through vineyards and out to an ocean she hadn't visited since she was a child, pounding swells and point breaks that still drew surfers in convoys from the east. The sprawling southern arm of the city where people with boats would go to retire on perfect canals. The ocean seemed close, just beyond a rise or tree line. Elora felt an urge to swerve them away from the city and plunge herself deep into the nearest water. She reeled with a thirst that she felt both inside and out, as if her skin needed liquid as much as her throat and stomach did and until she had both the parching would continue.

Traffic was constant in the lane opposite them, an endless procession of campervans heading south to a point where the roads would funnel them east into the desert. There were regular cars now, too, often without luggage strapped to the roof or a caravan trailing behind. Just cars and the people inside them. Some flashed their headlights in a hollow and indiscriminate warning, others stared at them with a harried gaze that reminded Elora of families she had seen on television, awoken by bushfire or flood in the dead of the night. But most passed by blankly, shapes and colours rather than people. As if the highway was a liminal space where souls lay suspended until their bodies could arrive at someplace new.

They had only seen a handful of other vehicles heading north. Some exited down backroads and driveways, others disappeared into the landscape ahead of them. The hire car had a two-way, but Vivienne kept it dormant by the dash. It was clear what was happening, and they didn't need a barrage of panic and rumour to fuel their anxiety. Draconis was now dripping and surging in the daytime sky as well as the night. A canvas of light and explosion, drooping beneath the sheer weight of activity, as if the atmosphere would soon be overrun and seek a desperate refuge on the land below. Already there had been crackles and the brief shudder of a distant shockwave. Vivienne ignored these, as always. Her hands were steady and eyes were lowered, as they had been when they left home all those days ago.

Elora looked around the cabin of yet another car. Soulless and clean. Just a sticker with the designated glass repair company and a selection of complimentary mints in the console. She took one and bit down into the sharp and acid flavour. It cleared some of the alcohol from her breath, so she took a fistful and ate them one by one. Vivienne glanced at her momentarily but said nothing.

They hadn't spoken more than a sentence since leaving the town. By the time Elora was awake, Vivienne had eaten breakfast, organised a hire car and loaded it with her things. She sat at a computer in the common room while Elora and Hayden shuffled about making coffee and toast. Elora took her time, making a second pot of coffee and drinking it with a magazine on the couch. Hayden watched the two of them with a quiet anticipation, suns in pensive orbit of each other. She doubted whether anything Hayden had encountered in his life so far was as complicated and impenetrable as the relationship between sisters.

He was still eating cereal in the kitchen when they drove away, his face full of sleep and gaze fixed blankly on the bench across from him. Before they left, Vivienne gave him an envelope of cash for the ute and told him to drive carefully back through the ranges. Then she said something else that Elora didn't hear from the doorway. Hayden smiled and looked Elora's way, and Elora felt bitter and jealous in spite of herself. She hovered there, not wanting to trigger any more of her emotions.

She and Hayden had said their goodbyes before bed on the previous evening, standing outside while the hostel slept around them. Elora had asked him then what he would be doing in the morning.

'Get the ute fixed. See what happens with all of this,' he said, gesturing up to the sky.

It made sense to Elora, and she wasn't surprised. Heading to the city no longer seemed logical to anyone but Vivienne, so why would Hayden choose to continue on? His life and family were back beyond the ranges. Still, she felt a sting of salt in her eyes.

'Can you call me once you're back at home?' she said. 'If you reach the student village at the university, there will be a number for my room, I think.'

Hayden nodded. 'I might not go home straight away.'

'Will you stay here in town?' asked Elora, confused. She shook off a sanguine vision of her and Hayden in the town forever. A house with a vegetable garden. A dog wandering around while she tended the plants. Laughter from inside as Hayden prepared a dinner and played with their child. Karaoke at the inn, and weekends hiking out in the ranges.

'I might head south,' said Hayden. 'Look around for a while before I'm back on shift.'

'Leavers,' said Elora.

'Leavers,' replied Hayden.

They shared a smile.

'Well, just call me whenever you get there,' said Elora.

He nodded again and they stood for a moment in the calm of the night, eyes down and away from the lights above.

'Most of our grain ships out of Albany,' said Hayden, abruptly.

Elora looked at him.

'But sometimes the port gets backed up. If there's heavy showering coming in from the west, or something going on in the city. Sometimes we send the trucks further east.'

'To Esperance?' asked Elora.

'I could try to get a message to your parents. In case the phones are down in the city, too.'

Elora felt herself wavering. She hadn't considered this. 'Only if you want.'

Hayden waited, unsure if he'd done the right thing.

'Just tell them we're almost at the city,' said Elora. 'And that we're still together.'

He nodded and they stood in silence.

'Do you think Johnny Cash is right about how we all got here?' asked Elora, after a while.

'From a meteorite?' asked Hayden.

'Yeah.'

Hayden nodded. 'But I'm not religious.'

'Neither am I,' said Elora.

'But you're not sure about the meteorite?'

Elora stared past him to the black and reaching landscape. 'I don't know. Everything just feels so random, doesn't it?'

Hayden didn't have an answer. 'You kept your eyes open when that meteor flashed during the fire,' he said.

Elora turned back to him, trying to determine his expression in the darkness. 'I didn't mean to. It just happened before I had time to close them.'

'What did you see?'

'What do you mean?'

'When the meteor exploded, what did you see?'

Elora thought about it for a moment, for the first time since they escaped from the fire. 'The Earth with no shadows.'

Hayden smiled, a hint of wonder in his eyes. 'Like the dinosaurs,' he murmured.

He sniffed a little in the cool of the night and Elora reached up and kissed him on the forehead. 'Night, Hayden.'

★ ★ ★

Elora buried herself back into the fantasy novel. The story had splintered into three threads, each one now as desperate as the other. She found herself racing through chapters on the elven war and the crumbling monarchy to focus on the journey of the two young elves tasked with unlocking a magic that some believed could halt the demons. Both of them were fighting an inner battle to accept a fate that they could not yet reveal to the other. Elora spilled tears behind sunglasses as she re-read their story, shocked at her fragility that grew with every day that passed on their journey to the city. She was continuing now only because of her mother.

The land began a steady incline in preparation for the hills and forests to come. Livestock appeared on the properties beside them, clusters of sheep and rangy cows with their heads turned to the highway as if stunned by this sudden noise and movement. A larger town emerged from the roll of the hills, streets and houses spreading back from the highway and a statue of a giant ram. They took their turn queuing for petrol.

Up close to the other cars and vans, Elora noticed how many of them had fractures on their windscreens. The repair outlet beside the service station was overrun; most people just continued onward regardless. A television played inside the building, and Elora could see news footage of a beach struck by a tsunami. Boats invading houses. Trees cut down like sugarcane.

Vivienne drained the last of their fuel cards and stocked the back seat with water and snacks. Before she returned to the car, she took a window cleaner from a bucket by the bowser and tried to remove some of the dust that now hung in the air like smoke from their windscreen. As she took her final stroke across the glass the entire street pulsed with the light of a careening meteor. People ducked and screamed, but somehow they were spared a shockwave. There was a moment of silence, then the station erupted with noise and movement. People ran from the store carrying children and supplies, abandoning their place in the queue and taking to the highway. Vivienne and Elora locked eyes through the glass. A thousand things to say but no time or words for any of them.

They hurried out of the town and turned onto a highway with another name. It was wide and smooth, two lanes in either direction. Vivienne kept them hugging the left shoulder, away from the hurtling convoy across from them. She tried a few times to initiate a conversation, asking Elora about university and her night out with Hayden. Elora was blunt in her replies, and eventually Vivienne gave up and switched on some music. She seemed edgy in a way that Elora hadn't noticed before, worried the city might be prised away from her at the final stretch.

The roll of the hills intensified, and pockets of forest appeared beside them. Trees with arrow-like trunks that thrust skyward before spreading into thick green clusters. Elora saw dirty plumes of smoke among them from strikes that had cut holes in the canopy like a message in Morse code. As they continued the pockets of forest grew larger, then combined. Within an instant their view of the surrounding land disappeared – they were walled in by a fortress of shade and green, with just a ribbon of Draconis now visible above. It would continue on in this way until they reached the city. Elora remembered this from their journey all those years ago, how her ears had popped as the city evaporated into forest and they left their home behind.

Vivienne slowed at the sight of some activity on the road ahead of them. Cars were banked up and passing into their lane from the other direction. The forest had been cut back by a crater on the side of the highway. It was black and smouldering.

Recent, thought Elora.

Three of the four lanes were covered with debris. Theirs remained clear, but was now being commandeered by the convoy heading south.

'Awesome,' said Vivienne, pulling them up to an idle just prior to the start of the debris.

Vehicles funnelled through in an endless line, manoeuvring around the branches and shrubs before accelerating away with fervour. They waited for a gap in the traffic but it didn't come. Eventually Vivienne edged them forward a touch and a Jeep flashed them through. Both of them waved in thanks at the family inside. There was beeping and flashing along the queue; the driver hurried along without a reply.

They continued on and the traffic thinned back to a rushing, constant river. A road crew overtook them, lights angry and orange against the green. It was the first vehicle they had seen travelling north on this highway, and Elora felt a degree of relief, despite what this said about the roads ahead. The driver peered sideways at them as he passed, eyes hidden behind sunglasses but still cutting in their judgement. Elora waved, awkwardly, then watched the ute disappear beyond the next hill. An ache was growing in her temples, and she fished around for a water. As she took her first sip Elora saw the bottle fill with white light before her eyes.

The accompanying sound was monumental. An explosion of bass so low she felt her teeth contract. People swerved, heads down and eyes closed in their fragile steel cabins. Somewhere in the forest beside them a meteorite had struck earth.

'Shit!' screamed Vivienne as a car flung out into their lane.

She braked and the other car corrected, swerving violently back to the right. They had barely gathered themselves when another flash lit up the highway.

One one hundred. Two one hundred. Three one hundred.

A line of windscreens blew out ahead of them. Glass glittered over the road like water.

The highway turned to chaos. People pulled over or overtook one another. A Landcruiser ploughed on without a windscreen or mirrors.

'This is fucking insane,' said Elora.

Vivienne gripped the wheel like a vice and crested a hill. They saw another blot of fire knife through the sky and bury with a tremor into the forest to their left. It was several kilometres away on a ridge by the highway, but something about seeing the whole thing – a rock from space smashing into their own planet – brought a shudder to Elora that she couldn't shake. 'Stop!' she shouted.

'Where?'

'Anywhere.'

Vivienne slowed without conviction. The forest was thick and impenetrable. Some people had pulled up at its edge and run into the trees to escape the glass in their cars. They looked shaken and vulnerable, and neither Elora nor Vivienne wanted to follow.

More booming from somewhere they couldn't see.

Vivienne picked out a rest stop on the highway ahead. It was on their side of the road and didn't yet look to be overrun by cars. She slowed as they approached and pulled them onto the red gravel entrance. The road swung into the forest before opening up into a wide bay with picnic tables, bins and an emergency landline.

The EL was empty, as were a messy gathering of cars and vans parked throughout the bay. Vivienne slowed them to an idle.

'Where is everyone?' asked Elora.

Vivienne stared hard at the scene, her brain ticking over. The sky was lost to them beneath the canopy, but it groaned and creaked like a beleaguered machine.

'Under the cars,' said Vivienne.

'What?'

'Come on.'

Vivienne shut off the engine and stepped out of the car. Elora followed, still confused, but not wanting to be left behind. They clambered down to the rough gravel floor and shuffled in under the car as much as they were able. Elora felt breathless and claustrophobic. She took a few shaky breaths and looked out across the ground. It was then that she noticed all the other people beneath their cars. Bodies, clustered and still, some lined up like sardines beneath the high arch of a four-wheel-drive, others barely wedged under the bumpers of sedans. A child cried out and was hushed by a father, as if Draconis might be listening above.

'This is stupid,' said Elora. 'Cars aren't going to protect us from a strike.'

'Trees,' said Vivienne, lying across from her.

'What?'

'The strikes bring down trees.'

She nodded to an area at the edge of the rest stop. A mass of tangled branches and foliage had been thrust out of the forest like a splash of paint on canvas. Trees were severed in the canopy above. A century of growth stolen in an instant. Elora looked again at the clumped foliage and this time made out the cars stuck beneath. They were buried and crumpled. Someone had thrown blankets and tarpaulins over them the best that they were able. Elora's mouth filled with a wash of vomit, the headache and hangover overcoming her now. She gagged and coughed a string of bile onto the ground in front of her face. Vivienne watched on and the child cried again.

'I'm going home,' said Elora, wiping her mouth.

Vivienne looked at her. 'This isn't normal, Elora. It will probably all be over in a day or two.'

'I don't care.'

'You're going to change all of your plans for the future?'

'Yes, Vivienne. In light of the meteorites killing people all around me, I'm going to change my plans.'

Vivienne sighed.

'You might want to think about it too,' Elora said, 'rather than flying up into this.'

Vivienne looked at her, then back out at the forest. A thump resonated through the earth from somewhere distant, like an Airbus touching down on a runway.

'What are you going to do over there?' asked Elora.

'Study. Work.'

'Do Mum and Dad know?'

'They know I applied.'

'So why didn't you tell them you got in?'

'You know why, Elora.'

'No, I don't.'

'Because Mum is enough of a wreck already,' barked Vivienne, harshly.

A couple of heads turned their way from the car adjacent.

'Having you disappear to Sydney will really help.'

Vivienne sighed. 'Obviously I will tell them. When I get there and all this has stopped, I will tell them.'

'Mum will still freak out.'

'I can't control that, Elora. And she wants us to live our lives. Didn't she say that to you on the phone?'

'In Sydney? Where half the city has been flooded out? Even before all of this.'

Vivienne shook her head.

'And you couldn't just drive?' asked Elora.

'The roads are a mess,' said Vivienne. 'It would take forever.'

'The sky looks pretty messy right now, too.'

'You still don't get it,' said Vivienne, staring out at the trees.

'Get what?'

'You can't hide from Draconis. All of those people running away to the desert. They could be driving out to a great big coffin.'

Elora shushed her, worried about the others listening around them.

'Draconis strikes on a whim,' whispered Vivienne, continuing. 'City, country, desert – wherever. Dad didn't move us south because it was safer. He got a job there when people were getting laid-off all over the place.'

'Then how come there hasn't been any strikes down there?'

'Luck.'

Elora sighed.

'Plus, there has now, hasn't there?'

Elora didn't answer. It was quiet in the car park. Insects resumed a choral drone in the canopy above.

'I just don't understand what's back there for you,' said Vivienne.

'My parents. My house. Friends.'

'And what will you all do together? Sit out on your balconies and cross your fingers that Draconis stays away?'

'Sounds fine to me.'

Vivienne sighed and appeared to give up. There was some shuffling nearby. Car doors opening and closing and an engine turning over. Others followed shortly after. People had taken the quiet as a sign that Draconis had moved elsewhere. Vivienne and Elora lay watching from beneath the car.

'You know there are cities in Europe right now where people get weather reports from satellites straight to their phones,' said Vivienne. 'Where you can take a flight to another city, or even another country, for the weekend. Places where people don't have to hide behind shutters because the glass in their houses doesn't shatter.'

'Well, maybe you can go there once you're done with Sydney,' said Elora, looking the other direction.

Vivienne mumbled something and shuffled out from beneath the car.

'Where are you going?'

'To see if any of these people have room to take you with them.'

Elora watched her sister walk away across the gravel. She felt numb, and no longer worried about being left on her own. A great tiredness had descended upon her and she yearned for the soft morning light of her bedroom. The sounds of her parents about the house as she lay in until midday, their eyes on the world so that hers could remain closed and still.

More people returned to their cars and Elora crawled out to stretch warily beneath the trees. She watched as people checked their tyres and the luggage strapped tightly to the roof. Fathers took children to the toilet in the trees then settled them back inside cars with books and snacks. Mothers checked maps and held up phones in the hope of a signal. A girl that looked to be Elora's age slumped sullenly back into a seat beside her hyperactive younger brother.

Elora lost sight of Vivienne. She lingered by the car and drank some water, then wandered over to the edge of the bay where the first severed tree rose up to a charred and blackened stump. More of these followed, trailing away like a row of used candles. She needed the toilet but couldn't really see anywhere that was hidden from the car parks without heading past the wrecked cars and moving deeper into the forest.

She looked again. Something caught her eye amid the foliage: a red car, small and with a sticker on the back that she'd seen once before.

Elora picked her way through the web of branches. There was glass all over the ground and it popped and crunched beneath her shoes. An old Landcruiser emerged, looking relatively intact but for the missing windows and a branch that had neatly disembowelled its engine. A P-plate had blown into this void and become stuck, like a Christmas decoration, amid some foliage.

The debris became thick past this car; Elora had to crawl through tunnels of sticky, weeping leaves to continue forward. She emerged into a patch of grass sheltered by the height of the cars beyond. The first of these was a blue sedan covered loosely by a tarpaulin that was flickering inwards in the breeze. Next along was the red hatchback. There were P-plates on both of these cars. And all of the others she could see.

Elora's heart was pounding. She reached the hatchback and stopped. A tarpaulin was covering the windows and roof to a point where it had buckled beneath the weight of three thick branches, fallen like spears from above. The forest felt gentle and quiet around her, as if she had travelled deep into the canopy. She lifted the tarpaulin, but for a long moment she was unable to look inside. When she finally turned it was only for a second, then she returned the covering and retraced her steps back out into the bay.

Vivienne strode across impatiently when Elora emerged from the forest. 'These people will take you, but they're leaving in a few minutes.'

Elora walked past her and continued to the car without responding.

'Elora!' said Vivienne, annoyed.

Elora reached the door but couldn't find the strength to open it. Instead she stood there, frozen like a mannequin, while more cars edged past them and back out onto the highway.

'Elora. What is it?' asked Vivienne, beside her now. She looked over her shoulder to the place where Elora had emerged. 'Why did you go over there?'

Elora stared at the gravel, watching ants pass news down a line beside her. 'Annabel's car is there.'

Vivienne froze.

'And a bunch of others from the party.'

'We don't know if they were inside,' said Vivienne, rapidly. 'They might have been sheltering somewhere else. Maybe they just dumped their cars here and got a ride with a road crew. You'll probably see them tonight when we get to the city.' She was shuffling about, agitated, as the last of the cars prepared to leave the bay.

'They were inside,' said Elora.

Vivienne stopped and looked at her.

'Some of them are still there.'

Elora heard a sniff and turned to find the foreign sight of her sister crying beside her.

'Sorry,' said Vivienne.

Tears also dripped from Elora's eyes, yet she was unable to feel them upon her face.

'Sorry,' repeated Vivienne. 'It's not normally like this.'

Elora caught a glimpse of the two of them in the window of their car, haggard and small against the ominous loom of the forest. She leant into the glass and wept while Vivienne sniffed, trying to swallow down whatever it was that was rising within.

She put a stiff hand on Elora's shoulder.

'I'll take you home,' she said. 'We'll call the police and get them out of there, then I'll take you home.'

Elora took a long moment to find her breath and pull away from the window. She stood upright for a while and let the breeze drift across her raging skin. All of the cars had gone now, and the forest ticked and hummed like the reefs emerging from the tides of her beautiful home.

'No,' said Elora.

Vivienne watched her silently.

'No,' she repeated. 'I'm going to university.'

Chapter Eighteen

It had taken hours for the police and ambulance to arrive, then
longer again for them to ferry the crumpled bodies from the cars.
Annabel and her friends weren't alone. Others had abandoned
the highway for the trees and suffered the same fate. Elora didn't
know how many were students from the party and how many
were other people travelling to work or home. Maybe even some
on their way to holiday in towns like her own. She couldn't watch.
Couldn't move, even, except to turn the pages of the fantasy novel
from the back of their car in a stupor that felt to her like heavy
drunkenness.

Vivienne hovered anxiously, then used the EL to try to find
contacts for some of the students. She passed these on to a young
officer who appeared grateful yet harried. Vivienne wanted to
know that these people hadn't been abandoned beneath the trees

and deluge. That the phone was down, and that someone had covered them only so they could return with help. The world was shifting too swiftly both beneath them, and above. Vivienne needed to deliver her sister to university as promised. To call their mother with this news and board her flight without the guilt that now followed her everywhere.

There were photographs taken of the scene. Radios that chattered without pause. A kind paramedic who walked over to check that they had water and petrol to continue their journey. They took some water and avoided any mention of their destination.

Elora remained in the car as the convoy finally rolled back out onto the highway. It was hot and now well past midday. A haze of dust hovered in the stillness of the abandoned car park. Vivienne slid back into the driver's seat and sat with a silence that drew Elora's attention. A moment later she left the car again and walked back over to the forest. Elora put her book aside and gingerly stepped out herself. Her legs were cramped and she hadn't eaten since the morning. She steadied herself and watched as Vivienne selected an array of branches from the edge of the forest and carried them back to the centre of the car park. She dumped them there, then returned for more. Elora couldn't fathom that her sister would be preparing a fire in the heat that surrounded them. Neither could she reconcile the idea of spending the night in this place with Draconis haunting them from above.

'What are you doing?' she asked, moving over to the pile of sticks and branches.

'We need to make a temple,' said Vivienne.

'What?'

'A temple,' said Vivienne. 'To burn.'

Elora nodded, remembering their conversation about the festival in the desert.

Vivienne returned from the forest with a final pile of sticks, then knelt down and assessed the ground.

Elora joined her. 'A whale, maybe?' she said, after a while.

Vivienne nodded, and the two of them set about putting it together. One of the branches was longer than the others and somewhat curved when stood upright on the ground, so they used this for the spine of the whale, Vivienne holding it up while Elora built a support frame of smaller branches that resembled a rib cage. It slumped to one side when Vivienne released her hand, but they were able to reinforce the spine with additional branches until it was roughly symmetrical. Elora worked away at the tail while Vivienne gathered kindling to start the fire. The process felt slow and meditative. Elora put her thoughts on hold and tried to absorb herself into the task. Cars streamed by on the highway and there were meteors in the sky to their north. When they grew louder, Vivienne paused her work to put some music on in the car across from them – soft, golden songs from an American folk singer.

The tail was made from an outward fan of sticks pinned to the ground by a pile of rocks and gravel. The fan reached upward with a long and skeletal tick, as if the whale was preparing to plunge back downward into the ocean. Elora covered this with flowers and foliage, choosing carefully from the surrounding forest as the shadows lengthened across the car bay. Eventually she stood back from the sculpture and noticed that Vivienne was leaning by the car, finished with her work and waiting calmly for her sister to be satisfied.

Elora gave a small nod and they gathered by the edge of the whale. It was just over waist high and thick with timber. Vivienne took out a lighter and wove her arm through the rib cage to a line of twigs and bark inside. She lit the first cluster, then quickly worked her way along to the others. As the flames took hold, Elora realised that each pile was a letter and together these piles of kindling spelt Annabel.

'I didn't know the others' names,' she said, standing back beside Elora.

'That's okay.'   •

'At Burning Man they say that the names are personal, but the temple is for everyone.'

Elora nodded. 'Thanks, Viv.'

Vivienne offered a brief and tired smile as the spot fires grew larger. Suddenly the letters swamped together and the flames licked up hungrily for the rest of the whale. Some of the timber was young and green, but the flames were tall now and took hold on the rib cage, rapidly making their way toward the spine. Vivienne and Elora stepped back, a swirl of heat and smoke engulfing them and spreading throughout the clearing.

'Shall I take a photo?' asked Vivienne.

'Is that what they do at the festival?'

'You do whatever the hell you want at the festival.'

Elora sniffed and smiled. 'I think take one. We can give it to her parents.'

The whale erupted into flame before them, and Vivienne took a photo just moments before it crumbled inward. The fire grew momentarily, heat and light flickering in the trees as the flames searched for something further, then gradually diminished until only the tail remained, a fan of orange against the dense green of the forest. Elora stared at it through stinging, glassy eyes. She had never felt so close to her sister, yet so removed from the world.

* * *

Draconis eased and then came again, angry and loud, as they made their way north through the dark roll of the forest. The trees seemed clustered closer than they had been earlier, brooding and guarded beneath a sky that hurtled down to pluck away their kin. Days were long in February, and the sunlight endless, yet in the forest it still evaporated by mid-afternoon. Then followed an hour or two of dappled, dream-like hue, where each trunk was caught in a heavenly silhouette. Then shadow. Then night.

They hadn't spoken about whether they would continue when night arrived or find shelter somewhere amid the trees. It wasn't yet dark, and cars still streamed south with their headlights beaming, a shifting river of yellow that forced their eyes down against the glare. Elora glanced up at Draconis whenever the forest fell back and offered a vista. The blue fire that had descended during their stay at the salt lakes had morphed into a deep and bruise-like purple. Rocks were burning up in the atmosphere like giant, wilting flowers. Elora was sure she could feel their warmth. Different to the sun. A sharp and knifing heat. Invisible needles burning the epidermis of her skin.

Vivienne kept the music playing on the stereo, and they ate their way through anything that was remaining in the car. The green road signs now spoke of the city instead of the strange and foreign acronyms that had marked their journey so far. One by one they counted them down. A hundred and thirty kilometres. A hundred and ten. Eighty. Under an hour to the city in normal traffic.

A town emerged from the shadows of the forest, not much more than a service station, bridge and hotel. The fuel at the station had been run dry and the doors were shuttered. A pair of old drinkers sat out on the hotel balcony, sipping draught and watching the traffic with a focused disdain.

They had no need to stop, so continued through the town and over its tall wooden bridge. As the buildings receded back into the forest, a series of blinking road lights appeared ahead of them.

Vivienne slowed and they passed a sign reading *Detour ahead.* The southbound traffic emerged from a side road in the forest, the highway closed and abandoned in the distance. They sat upright in the car but remained silent as Vivienne followed the signs onto the narrower road that skirted a power station. This continued for a time, traffic slow and headlights walled in by the towering forest, until another sign pointed them north again on a road that ran parallel to the highway. This road was wider, and the traffic gained speed in the lane across from them. Cars flashed by, knifing along just feet from the hulking trunks by the roadside. Elora watched them and wondered what had befallen the highway.

Twice Vivienne was forced onto the shoulder of the road by angry, speeding utilities. Elora noticed a shudder in her sister's legs that she hadn't seen before. She watched as it grew in intensity, then switched on a light and took out her roadmap.

'What are you doing?' asked Vivienne.

'We need to get off this road.'

Vivienne didn't argue, instead passing Elora her phone. For a moment Elora was caught out by this gesture – her sister's prize possession, given to her so freely. She opened up the map, but they were too far from a functioning mobile tower. Vivienne took it back and Elora returned to the folded roadmap.

She found the previous town after following their path from the mountains, then traced along the thin service roads they had been sent down by the detour. It seemed they would be running north for some time before another road could carry them back to the highway. She backtracked, searching west for other pathways through the forest. There were two roads large enough to make it onto the map. The first ended abruptly at a water body set deep into the forest. The second met up with another, thinner road heading north. If they followed this far enough it met a wider road snaking back eastward to a point where it reached a satellite suburb, then eventually the city.

Vivienne glanced at her, waiting. 'So?'

'There's a left turn somewhere ahead of us.'

'Does it go to the city?'

'Eventually.'

Elora could feel her sister's resistance – she'd taken the same path for years now, a rolling highway that had returned her to the city many times over. Forest receding into pole houses and terraced gardens. One final rise, then a sweeping, arresting view of the metropolis.

'Tell me when you think we're close,' said Vivienne.

Elora nodded and trained her eyes on the trees ahead. They flickered by rapidly, like cogs in a giant machine. Cars continued to hammer past, headlights blinding in the darkness. 'There,' said Elora, pointing ahead.

Vivienne braked hard, clamping down on the steering wheel to stop them from fishtailing out into the oncoming traffic. The forest parted to their left and a thin road emerged without a sign or name. They turned, overshooting the lanes, but the way was clear and empty.

A final ribbon of daylight greeted them from the west. Elora sat back and exhaled. A familiar orange hue found its way to her skin. How long had it been since she sat on her board amid this same light while her friends played music from the sand?

They turned with the sweep of the road and the cars behind them were swiftly stolen from view. Elora felt relief, but also realised that the forest had swallowed them completely now. They had joined with the trees and fauna in their private battle against Draconis.

The sun sank, and the road continued west toward the burnt orange clouds that remained in its wake. There were no farms or buildings. No signs indicating a town that may be hidden somewhere ahead. Elora glanced at her sister, who looked uneasy amid such wilderness, and found herself feeling oddly similar.

'How far until the north road?' asked Vivienne.

'A little further,' said Elora without confidence.

They could hear Draconis crackling in the sky above them, but the forest canopy maintained a dark and solid ceiling above them, only occasionally thinning to silhouette against the purple beyond. Elora caught shudders of movement within these silhouettes. She had never seen a bat and wondered whether Draconis had already drawn them from sleep.

'Shall I put some music back on?' asked Elora.

'Maybe we should wait,' said Vivienne.

Elora nodded and they sat driving silently, upright and still in the darkness.

'What will happen to your place in the city?' asked Elora after a while, not really curious but searching for a distraction.

'They'll rent it to someone else,' replied Vivienne, shifting uncomfortably.

Elora glanced at her. It was dim inside the car. Not yet dark enough for the dashboard to illuminate their features.

'Unless you want to stay there,' said Vivienne. 'There are still a few months on the lease.'

'What's it like?' asked Elora.

'Like home.'

'In Esperance?' she asked, confused.

Vivienne shook her head. 'It's our house, Elora. In Attadale. Where we grew up.'

Elora stared at her. 'You live in our house?'

'It came up for rent,' shrugged Vivienne.

'How long have you been living there?'

'A few years.'

'Do Mum and Dad know?'

Vivienne shrugged again, and Elora realised that they must. She felt naive and manipulated.

'I can't believe you,' she said.

Vivienne sighed. 'What does it matter, Elora? It's just a house. Mum and Dad sold it years ago.'

'Do you live there on your own?'

'Are you kidding? That would cost a fortune.'

'Is there someone in my room?'

Vivienne sat up and shook her head tiredly. Elora could see her willing the turnoff to manifest from the forest ahead.

'Is the treehouse still there?'

Vivienne didn't answer.

'And Mum's herb garden?'

'This is why we didn't tell you.'

'You don't think it's weird?'

'What?'

'Making a home with some random people in our old house.'

'They're not random.'

'Who are they?'

'They're housemates, Elora. Most people have them.'

Elora shook her head.

'Forget it,' said Vivienne. 'I'll break the lease. You'll be better off in the village anyway.'

'This is happening, Vivienne,' said Elora, waving her hand up to the sky. 'You can pretend all you like that it isn't, but Draconis happened. It's still happening. The world isn't going back to how it was before.'

'You don't know that.'

'Take a look around!' shouted Elora.

Vivienne laughed, bitter and tired. 'I always wondered whether you secretly liked what happened to us.'

Elora looked at her, coldly.

'I'm just saying, Draconis turned out pretty well for you. You had Mum and Dad. Your beautiful bedroom. All that surf. More friends than you ever did in the city.'

The sky rippled in their windows.

'Even the occasional meteor to light up the kangaroos when we were camping.'

'Wow,' said Elora, eventually.

There was a flash of colour and a shudder somewhere behind them. Elora dropped her map and willed Draconis upon them. For her rocks to pummel the Earth until she finally had no more.

A road sign appeared, green and striking amid the wilderness. They slowed and Vivienne took the turn to the north without consultation. The road widened and she increased their speed away from the chaos behind them.

Elora turned away and closed her eyes, staring into the void of her eyelids. When their journey had started she could do nothing but sleep. Now it felt impossible.

CHAPTER NINETEEN

Almost immediately the forest thinned from the road, then from the land rolling away beside it. In its place were plots of open ground. Most lay empty, but occasionally they made out the dim grey of a shed or water tank. Houses were less frequent. When Elora did catch a roofline in the distance, it appeared silent and lifeless. She wondered about the people who lived there. Were they out on the highway, heading south or east like the others? Or had they left long ago? She felt certain that they were no longer upon this land. The place had a stillness that seemed devoid of life. It had been hours – days – since they had seen a bird in the sky, and now even the insects appeared to have vanished. In a warm and still dusk, not a single mosquito rose to splatter their windscreen.

Elora saw craters in every direction, broken rings of smouldering earth that dotted the terrain like a strange, foreign language.

Her breath caught in her throat at the sight of them all. She wondered if it had been this way for miles and the forest had sheltered them from the true scale of this new wave. Whether the craters were a sign of what lay ahead of them: a city reeling and besieged. She looked up at the sky and traced the rocks as they scythed through the outer atmosphere. Earth was robust and tireless, burning rock after rock in pops of disco purple. Occasionally, in the deep stretch of the sky, a meteor continued on without explosion. Elora stared hard at these places, waiting for dust or smoke to manifest into the sky above them.

A glow appeared on the horizon to the north. It was wide and yellow, brighter than any light Elora had seen in the evening. She sat up in her chair and blinked moisture onto her stinging eyes.

'It's the city,' said Vivienne.

Elora ignored her, but surveyed the dome of light regardless. So close to them now, as if any one of these rises could be the last, sending them down from the hills and into the maelstrom.

Vivienne seemed to sense this now also. She was upright and focused at the wheel. The road was empty, and she pushed the car hard in the growing darkness. Their headlights drew strange shadows from the craters and the engine shattered the silence. They were lone travellers upon an abandoned moonscape.

Long minutes passed as they edged closer and closer. The land beside them began to brighten again with the glow of the city. Elora craned forward, trying to glimpse the lights and buildings that were surely imminent. She drew a breath in anticipation, then a meteor materialised directly above them.

The brightness was stark, then paralysing. Vivienne hesitated, unable to reconcile the fate that had finally befallen them – in this moment, but also ever since they had driven from their docile home town.

She stamped down on the brakes and the back of the car kicked out onto gravel, then over-corrected and it snaked back around, tilting and shuddering with the force. They covered their eyes and heads as the light seemed to magnify and engulf everything. Elora's eyelids turned translucent, and her pulse faltered under the weight of something giant and overwhelming. She was unaware that the car had stopped, nor that Vivienne was yanking her from the seat.

'Come on,' came a voice in her ear and a breath on her face.

She followed, eyes still closed but her shoes finding gravel.

One one hundred. Two one hundred.

A few steps and the ground turned to grass.

Three one hundred. Four one hundred.

Elora opened her eyes long enough to see clear terrain and the silhouette of her sister running toward the fabled glow of the city.

Five one hundred. Six …

A boom, immense and galactic, and the both of them were thrust to the ground.

Silence and the empty echo of a netherworld. Elora reached across to put a hand on her sister's leg. Vivienne twitched, then pulled herself up to her knees. They remained there just a moment, then were upright and sprinting once more.

They hammered through the grass for a house that lay a kilometre away at the edge of the forest. It looked tiny – like a doll's – from where they ran. The sky was open and raging overhead, rocks descending like a laser battle in a science fiction film. The ground sloped downward to the house, and it seemed to Elora as though they were running too fast. She felt out of control. The earth beneath them now was hard and dangerous. Shelves of ancient rock broke through the surface, and the soil was baked down from drought. Falling in this place would shred their skin and knock out their teeth. They would be left, fish twitching on a headland, for Draconis to drag away at her leisure.

Elora kept her eyes down and focused hard on the placement of each foot. The grass seemed to be thickening around her ankles. Tufts of weed whipped at her shins and knees. A fence manifested from the darkness. They pulled themselves over the wire and continued on to the house. Windows glinted back like teeth amid the bricks and timber. Elora registered then that they hadn't yet seen a crater on this eastern slope.

She was ahead of her sister, and slowed as they reached a driveway leading up to the verandah. Vivienne said something that was swallowed by another deep explosion from above. She didn't bother repeating it, just took Elora's arm and pulled them up onto the verandah. The front door was decorative and heavy, painted a deep green that sunk into the darkness like an inky portal. Vivienne tried the handle, then slammed her weight into the timber – nothing.

They traced along the outside, hugging the bricks and searching for another entry. The windows of the building were broad and thick, framed by timber and cut to withstand the brutal, shifting weather. Smashing this glass felt both risky and sacrilegious, so they continued to the southern side of the house where a garage stood open and abandoned by a woodpile and chicken coop. Out of the dark, Elora caught the skeleton of a Hills Hoist spinning eerily where there was no wind.

At the end of the southern wall was another door. Locked again, but smaller in size. They shouldered it together and at first there was nothing. Then a sharp and brittle snap – chicken bones in the mouth of a dog. They rammed it again and found themselves in a large country laundry. The smell inside was damp and floral, as if detergent had been spilled inside one of the many cupboards. Vivienne closed the door and propped it there with a box that lay open on the tiles. She tried the lights, but the power was out.

'Hello?' said Elora, loudly.

'God,' said Vivienne, jolting in surprise.

'What if someone's in here?'

'Nobody's in here, Elora. Look at the boxes.'

The room was strewn with packing boxes, some sealed and scrawled with labels. *Towels. Books. Jean's toys.* Others still open and waiting to be filled. With the garage just outside, the laundry had been the final staging point before loading things into the car.

They stepped through the jumbled mess of cardboard toward the other end of the room.

There hadn't been time to take them all, thought Elora. She stopped and looked at a box by the wall, struck by the label. 'They left without their photos.'

Vivienne followed her gaze, the two of them motionless until another meteor flashed and burned like a projector outside.

They rushed forward into the belly of the house, down a long hallway where the doors were closed and the only illumination came from a skylight flickering wickedly above. A shockwave arrived and the house groaned in protest. Elora heard a sickly tinkle that she knew was the sound of fracturing glass.

Vivienne led them out of this area and into a living space with couches, a fireplace, and windows to the east.

'Where are we going?' asked Elora.

'Basement,' said Vivienne, tracking through the living room and into a kitchen.

'What?'

'They might have a basement,' she repeated.

The windows pulsed and Elora caught a glimpse of the kitchen. Finger paintings on the fridge. Cans and water bottles on the benches. A bowl of decomposing fruit.

Vivienne had continued on into a pantry with just a solitary window in the far wall. She hesitated and Elora arrived beside her.

'Here,' said Elora, moving inside to shelter on the floor.

Vivienne stopped her, pulling Elora from the room like a wandering child. Elora felt a deep anger rising inside. She was tired of being dragged along by this constant, unwavering force. Tired of being treated as an anchor when her connection to this person was blood and nothing more. She felt cheated away from her town and friends and parents. From the chance to be with them now as Draconis finally showed her hand.

They burrowed through an office and another lounge room. Empty bookcases, floor rugs, and a television hovering above a collection of Lego. The building seemed to end with the arrival at another large fireplace. Vivienne spun around and spotted a door by a staircase running up to the loft. Elora pulled her arm free as Vivienne fiddled with the locks. The room pulsed with a deep flicker of purple. Manic shadows all around.

'Come on!' grunted Vivienne, frustrated by the door.

Finally it gave, and again she dragged her sister after her.

Immediately they were greeted by a hot flash of light. Blinding and hallucinatory, like all of the others.

Elora yanked back on her arm and freed herself from Vivienne. For a moment she stood alone, floating in this foreign space, eyes closed and surrendered to the wash of a great wave shifting above. It was a feeling that had once held terror but which she had grown to accept. *Time is different under water*, her father had once told her when she was learning to surf. *If you fight it or try to rush, your lungs will burn and every second will last an hour. But if you can surrender to the movement of the water, the ocean will bring you back to the surface.* Elora remembered feeling warm and foetal in these moments, sometimes opening her eyes to gaze through the soft and shifting water.

As she opened her eyes again now, Elora was met by a different kind of blueness. More than she should be able to see within a basement. Or any room.

The whole of Draconis was somehow above her once again, surging and fizzing like a swelling organism. Yet the meteors held an iridescence that seemed unusual. They were hazy and distant, as if she were in a dream.

Something brushed her arm and Elora looked down to find plants all around her. Ferns. Succulents. Kitchen herbs. New seedlings and the ancient growth of their genus. The tall figs adored by her mother. Each plant was heathy and wild, leaves vibrant and flowers dripping with life and pollen. All of them nurtured by the warmth of a great glass conservatory.

As the shockwave hit, Elora caught a glimpse of her sister, finally still, in the space ahead of her.

CHAPTER TWENTY

A week before the arrival of Draconis, when people were yet to know of her true nature, Vivienne took Elora out for an evening at the shopping complex. Elora had been many times during daylight with her parents and friends, but never at night when the corridors and food halls swelled with teenagers, and Vivienne brought home whispers of a world full of drama and mystery.

The invitation was casual, and Elora played along, masking her excitement as she chose her favourite outfit and carefully counted the selection of notes in her purse. She didn't yet have a bank account like her sister, instead trading up from small notes to large as the weeks passed and she diligently completed her household chores. Vivienne had a weekend job at a juice bar and seemed to buy things constantly. They appeared by their doorstep in boxes and soft padded bags. Elora would sometimes read the postage information and see that they had arrived from places like California or the United Kingdom. It amazed her that her sister had access to such faraway places.

Her mother popped her head through Elora's bedroom door. 'Make sure you have a proper dinner.'

'I will,' said Elora, excited.

Her mother lingered, watching Elora tie her hair in a pony, assess it in the mirror, then tie it up again. Elora hadn't registered her mother's lack of surprise about Vivienne's invitation. It spoke of prior knowledge, or perhaps even orchestration, yet Elora felt as though she was humbling her mother by providing the details of their upcoming outing.

'Do you know what you would like to buy?' asked Janine, kneeling down to help with her hair.

'All Stars like Vivienne's. But the light-blue colour.'

'Sounds cool,' smiled Janine, standing back and taking stock of her youngest daughter in a way that Elora caught her doing every so often.

'The bus is coming,' called Vivienne from another room.

Elora hopped down from her bed and swung the purse over her shoulder.

'Dad will pick you up outside Myer,' said Janine. 'Tell your sister to message him when you're getting tired.'

Elora agreed, and dashed out of the room so as not to keep Vivienne waiting.

It was a Thursday, and the highway by their house was heavy with homebound traffic. They waited at a bus stop by the chemist that sold bouquets in buckets and the dry cleaners where her father had a weekly order for his blue business shirts. These were still open, as were the ramble of shops surrounding their local supermarket. Elora looked out at the familiar places now transformed by the violet dusk and the lights glowing in their windows. The air smelt full and complicated: car fumes, dry cleaning chemicals, grass clipped in the nearby park. The perfume Vivienne wore outside of school. Elora hoped that by the end of the evening her clothes and hair might take on the smell of all of these things and more.

Buses shuddered past, heading west to Fremantle and east to the freeway. There were dozens of them, yet Vivienne picked one out with confidence and ushered Elora aboard. They were met by a scattering of faces buried in phones, some lost to earphones and others glancing their way before looking back out the windows or forward into nothingness. They found a seat together and Vivienne pointed out a few things by the roadside before settling back with her own phone. Elora stole looks at the other passengers and clutched her purse like her mother had shown her. The river appeared beside them, still and grey in the cold August evening. Across the water were the blinking lights of the western suburbs, and beyond these the ocean. They passed sports ovals, service stations, and Chinese restaurants where Elora caught a glimpse of the people dining inside. Before the freeway they turned from the traffic and climbed through a suburb nestled neatly above the river. Elora knew that she could see the city skyscrapers from this road – as she had done many times during daylight with her father after weekend soccer. She wanted to turn and look for them now, but felt a pressure to stay still and quiet amid the other passengers.

'What is it?' asked Vivienne, eyes on her phone.

'What?'

'Why are you fidgeting?'

'I wanted to see the city.'

'So do it already.'

Elora turned and craned her head above the seat, but they had crested the hill and the city had already been absorbed by the suburbs.

The bus pulled into a port beside the centre, and they departed amid a flurry of people moving in and out of the southern entrance. Vivienne led them inside, past homewares stores and the soap company where they often bought gifts for their mother. Elora was used to entering the centre from the underground carparks, and found herself immediately disoriented by the way Vivienne was weaving them through the busy corridors. She seemed to be on a schedule, so Elora ensured that she kept pace. She knew that the visit would involve shopping and food, maybe even some of Vivienne's friends, but had no idea how any of these things would unfold. The feeling brought a tightness to her stomach and amplified the fabled mystery of her sister. She caught herself staring at the serious figure walking beside her, her hair bouncing lightly with each step, hands stuffed purposefully into her bomber jacket, eyes that searched beyond the endless people streaming by.

'Here,' said Vivienne.

'What?' asked Elora, not sure where she should be looking.

'You can buy All Stars in Myer, but they only have a few colours.' Vivienne led them into a shoe store drenched with thumping bass. 'This place should have all of them.'

Elora nodded, happy and surprised that their first stop had been for her. Vivienne found a wall of the shoes at the back of the store. Colourful and spot-lit, like fish in an aquarium.

'Do you know your size?' she asked, sitting on a cube-shaped cushion.

'Six,' said Elora.

Vivienne flashed a brief smile that told her to go ahead and find a pair. Elora saw her colour and cut right away, but pretended to look a little longer while Vivienne sent messages on her phone. After a couple of minutes she selected a box from the stack by the wall and walked back over.

Vivienne finished her message then took the package from Elora and looked inside at the shoes. 'Light-blue size sixes?'

Elora nodded.

'Nice. Let's pay and head up to Myer. I forgot my mascara.'

They spent a while evading the immaculate sales assistants in the makeup section while Vivienne found and applied the mascara she wanted. Elora toyed with some products, sprayed perfume from beautiful bottles, watched her sister's fast but careful movements, and laughed when Vivienne offered to apply some to her eyelashes too. They browsed some jeans and jackets on their way through the store, but it didn't feel as though Vivienne was really looking.

'You're okay to eat later, yeah?' asked Vivienne as they left this wing of the centre and headed for another.

'Sure,' said Elora, as lightly as she could muster.

'I have some friends coming out of a movie. We can meet them in the foyer.'

Elora felt immediately nervous. Vivienne had friends over at their house sometimes. Even held a few sleepovers. But these visits had diminished lately, and Vivienne's life outside of home had taken on a mystery for both Elora and her parents. They now received only clipped and measured accounts at the dinner table, and Vivienne's phone thrummed with constant messaging from names they often weren't familiar with. To be out at night and actually seeing these faces felt like stepping into a secret society.

Vivienne diverted them to a supermarket where parents raced through the aisles for cooked chickens and bags of salad with children flagging from school, sports and errands. She bought some cans of soft drink, and Elora watched as her sister entered the checkout and confidently requested a lighter from a man who eyed her with a kind of weary contempt. They bagged the items and cut across the southern end of the centre where jewellery stores and newsagents made way for market stalls selling bread sticks, chicken schnitzels and loose-leaf tea. Beyond these was the bustle of a food hall; a waft of salty Chinese food and fries cooking in oil. Elora felt a pang of hunger, but ignored it as they emerged back outside and took a walkway across to the cinema. Cars dipped and flashed beneath them, and Elora caught the glow of the moon, calm and waning above the hills to the east.

Queues snaked away from the yellow glow of the cinema's long counter. There were couples Vivienne's age with hands around waists or tucked into the other's jeans, and groups of friends loading their arms with popcorn and ice creams. Elora also saw some older people, dressed differently again, arriving from work or dinner in their skirts and chinos. Two of them appeared to be meeting each other for the first time, phones in hand and an awkward distance between them as they grappled for conversation.

Vivienne pulled her away from these things and over to an arcade area by the entrance to the different cinemas. They took up seats in a racing console, but Vivienne pulled out her phone rather than inserting any money. 'You can play if you want,' she said absently.

Elora smiled and declined. The game was clunky and old, but she also sensed that to play was to distance herself from the maturity of this new world.

'Are Mum and Dad still making you wait until high school for a phone?' asked Vivienne, after a while of sitting there texting.

'Yeah. Dad has a spare one, but Mum says I can't have it.'

'He's probably wrecked it anyway. You should ask for a Galaxy.'

Elora committed this to memory as Vivienne received another message and turned to the foyer. A session had ended, and people were drifting out into the light. Vivienne stood and Elora followed her over to a group of around eight people her sister's age. They seemed dazed and sleepy, with creased hoodies and bags hanging loosely from their shoulders. Elora recognised a couple of the faces, but the others were new. Vivienne hugged some of them and said hello to others. She seemed suddenly lighter, feigning a dance to the dull foyer music and laughing at an image on someone's phone.

Eventually she broke away from the conversations and introduced her sister lingering awkwardly on the periphery. 'This is Elora.'

The others turned, smiling and waving without too much interest. Elora waved back and wondered whether she should move in closer to the group. There were girls and boys among them, and two couples that she could discern. She had heard her parents talking about Vivienne and a boyfriend recently, but couldn't tell whether he was present.

They trailed out of the cinema as a group and took some steps down from the walkway to a path beside the adjacent parkland. The centre was cut into one side of an escarpment, and Elora had once walked through the adjacent bushland with her mother. Vivienne and her friends made their way towards this same bushland, talking and laughing about things Elora didn't know much about.

At some stage Vivienne emerged at her side and handed her a soft drink from the selection they had bought earlier. 'There's a place up here where you can see the city. We're just going to sit there for a bit and have a drink.'

'Sure,' said Elora, a little too eager.

Vivienne smiled at her and skipped ahead to talk to a boy.

The bush was thick, swallowing the noise of the centre and humming softly with traffic from the highway below. Everyone had a phone in their hand, the screens like lanterns in the dark. They fanned out at a small clearing where a pair of benches peered out over the dappled lights of the city beyond the river. It was a rest stop for joggers, and had a bin full of sports drinks. Some of the friends sat, and others hovered by the benches sharing images on their phones. Vivienne gave the lighter to a girl who used it on a cigarette, blowing the smoke away from the others and down toward the highway. A couple kissed for a while on the far bench. Cans were opened and something poured inside from a flask. Vivienne caught her sister's eye at one stage, and Elora tried to convey a sense of cavalier that said she had no issue with this or anything else. As usual she couldn't tell whether Vivienne understood or cared. Instead her sister whispered something to a friend on the bench, who then ushered Elora over to sit beside her.

'Hey, I'm Skylar.'

'Hi,' said Elora.

'Have you seen this?' she asked, showing Elora a video on her phone of some people dancing in formation while graphics swirled all around them.

Elora laughed and shook her head.

Skylar showed her through a series of other clips while someone played music on their phone. A jogger emerged from the bush, startled by the activity and drawing cackled laughter from the group. Vivienne flitted from person to person, talking and smiling, her phone in one hand and drink in the other.

Elora felt warm and surrounded, even when Skylar pocketed her phone and leant away from her to talk with some others. After a while Elora stood up on the bench, then the armrest, to get a full view of the city. Lights reflected in the river and cars streamed over the freeway. There was some laughter, and she looked across to find one of Vivienne's friends also balancing on an armrest. He waved and drank from his can. Elora waved back. Vivienne smiled at her in a way she hadn't seen before.

They stayed up on the hill for more than an hour, and Elora found herself shivering beneath her thin sports coat. She was tired, and tried to keep herself from yawning as the people continued to drink and talk around her.

Finally they were standing and hugging and Vivienne was back at her side. 'We better get back. Sometimes Dad comes early to buy that gross tea for Mum.'

Elora smiled and pulled herself up off the bench, her legs stiff and cold. They waved goodbye to some of the friends who took another path down to the buses running along the highway. The remainder trailed back to the cinema with her and Vivienne, eventually drifting away without fuss until they were alone once again.

They wandered back across the walkway. The moon was gone now and the sky clustered with cloud.

'We probably still have time for McDonald's, if you want?'

'Okay,' smiled Elora.

Vivienne turned them towards the food court. She seemed oddly calm and relaxed, gazing in the windows at things, then up at the strange, decorative ceilings. Elora wondered whether it was the alcohol or just the absence of school or home. Or perhaps this was how her sister was when the world allowed for it.

Only a handful of people remained in the food court. Cleaners had moved in to wipe down tables and prepare the space for the following morning. Many of the vendors had closed already, but the larger chains were still glowing and ready as always.

Vivienne stood aside and gave Elora the novelty of ordering her own meal, then they took their trays over to a table tucked in beneath a row of fake palm trees. Elora devoured a burger while Vivienne ate her fries without much interest, twirling them in sauce and looking around at the people still in the complex.

'Sorry if you were bored,' said Vivienne.

Elora shook her head in earnest.

'Mum and Dad think it's a huge party here at night, but it's pretty tame.'

'It was fun,' said Elora.

Vivienne watched as Elora cycled through the food laid out in front of her. 'Are you still doing drama class after school?'

Elora shook her head. 'It's only in Term One.'

'Right,' said Vivienne.

'Swim club starts in Term Three.'

'Who's that friend of yours from swim club?' asked Vivienne. 'The girl with the accent?'

'Celeste.'

'Will she be in your class again?'

'Mum said they're moving back to France.'

Vivienne nodded, looking around with a hint of awkwardness. 'Things will be more fun soon,' she said, after a moment.

Elora looked at her, noticing the slight change in pitch.

'You'll start high school and meet heaps of new people. There are different subjects, and other kids who will be into the same stuff as you. You can take drama or coding or whatever. And Mum and Dad will leave you alone more, too.'

Elora nodded, trying hard to mirror the conviction and enthusiasm in her sister's gaze.

'So far we've only experienced this tiny piece of the Earth,' said Vivienne, pushing a crystal of salt along the table with her finger.

'But there are millions of other tiny pieces.' Vivienne gathered more crystals and began clustering them together in a complicated pattern. 'People are out in them right now. Hiking up mountains. Riding subways. Shovelling snow from their driveways. Shopping in centres like this, but with swimming pools, and stores we've never even seen before.'

Elora smiled and sipped the final, syrupy glob of her thick shake.

'The world feels huge and unreachable, but everything is connected. There's nowhere you can't touch.' Vivienne drew the last of the crystals together into a tight pile, then scattered them dramatically across the table, drawing another smile from Elora.

'Can I come shopping again one time?' asked Elora.

Vivienne smiled, leaning in toward her sister's earnest young face. 'Yes,' she replied, eyes wide and intense. 'We'll watch a scary movie. Try on a bunch of ball dresses. Make the gelato guy let us taste every single flavour.'

Elora laughed.

Vivienne sat back in her chair and checked the time. 'But right now Dad is sitting in the car listening to Bruce Springsteen and wondering where the hell we are.'

'Oh no,' said Elora, wide-eyed and laughing even more.

'Are you finished?' asked Vivienne.

Elora nodded, and they carried their trays over to a bin, sliding the rubbish inside and stacking them on a pile of others.

'Should we run?' asked Elora.

'Yes!' said Vivienne.

They set off down the emptying corridors, drawing glances from people closing counters or wheeling loaded trolleys out to their cars. Elora felt a wash of life and colour swirling past her as she ran. She felt at the centre of everything, as if these people and things had all come together in this very moment just to allow them to run right by. Her hair flicked at her shoulders and Vivienne's breath filled her ears. Suddenly they were back at the beach together as children. Waves fizzing and crashing at their feet. Gulls scattering as they ran and laughed for no reason they could remember. Their parents chased behind them and there was nothing ahead but the sand, water, and a sky so clear it could barely be looked upon.

Chapter Twenty-One

Elora felt the night upon her skin, a cool and acrid breeze drying the moisture that beaded on her face and arms. It seemed strange to be sweating now, many hours after the sun had disappeared to the west. If anything, Elora felt cold. A shiver had jolted her from sleep, and remained with her as she sat, ball-like, on the soil and concrete. Her panic was tucked away somewhere low and hazy, a whisper in a gathering crowd.

There was a stirring in the space ahead of her. Shoes on concrete. The tinkle of glass falling to the floor. Elora lifted her gaze and found her sister, wavering and bloody in the glow of Draconis. Like a foal just delivered into the world.

Elora gasped and pulled herself upright. Pressure engulfed her forehead, and she staggered blindly for a moment before steadying.

'Elora,' croaked Vivienne, suddenly beside her.

'You're bleeding,' replied Elora.

'I know.'

'But it's everywhere,' said Elora.

Vivienne lifted her arms and twirled them slowly in the broken light. They were slick with blood. It dripped from her fingers and pooled in tiny lakes upon the floor. Her face and neck were rich with a splatter that seemed to continue up into a greasy mat of hair. Amid the dark and red, Elora was taken by the starkness of her sister's eyes. They were luminous and bold. Then suddenly wide with worry. 'Turn around,' said Vivienne.

Elora obeyed, and felt a needle of pain in her back that she hadn't noticed until now. Vivienne lifted her shirt and surveyed the skin beneath.

'What is it?' asked Elora as the sky pulsed, frenzied and electric, to the north.

'Glass.'

Elora sniffed and felt tears dampening the crusty blood upon her face.

'It's okay,' said Vivienne. 'We need to get inside. Find a shower and some bandages.'

They left the conservatory – now a wooden skeleton thrust open to the night – shuffling back through the house as it sang with an eerie stridor. In the hall by a bedroom they found an ensuite with a window still intact. Elora ran the shower while Vivienne pulled blankets from the bed and piled them ready by the door. Their only light was Vivienne's phone, which she placed in the basin and directed at the mirror. They undressed in this dim halo and stepped together into the frigid water. It bit and stung, and neither would have remained were it not for the other.

Vivienne wiped the blood from Elora's neck and shoulders, turning her into the light to assess the damage below. In the mirror they watched as her skin sparkled with glass like sequins on a ballgown.

Vivienne inhaled and steadied her shivering hands. One by one she set about pinching out the shards. She wouldn't get them all, but she would try.

Elora became numb amid the pain and cold. Her eyes found the frame of the window, steadfast amid the sieging outside. Then the shadow of her sister, naked and imposing on the wall adjacent. Eventually the needles ceased, and Elora turned to find her sister, limp and exhausted, behind her. Elora took a sponge from around the tap and gently lifted Vivienne's arm into the water. Some of the blood had dried, and other patches still wept. Elora moved the sponge in slow circles, squeezing it clean then starting over. Vivienne's skin was littered with so many cuts they looked, to Elora, like the freckles of a child. She realised then how close they had been to the meteor, the shockwave so heavy it had all but consumed the glass.

As she finished one arm and started on the other, Elora caught her sister looking at her.

'Sorry,' said Vivienne, crying.

Elora tried a smile and focused on the sponge. Vivienne's arm was tembling in her grasp.

'We need to get out and warm up,' said Elora, suddenly urgent.

Vivienne was in shock. She too, most likely. Annabel had told her about a boy her father had treated in Albany. How there was a window of time where a body could begin to shut down. Where people would die even though they seemed okay.

They dried themselves with stale, crusty towels, then wrapped in the blankets from the bed. Vivienne stood rigid as Elora pulled jackets and socks from a stranger's wardrobe and dressed her sister, then herself. The window of this room was intact, but they huddled low on the opposite side of the room regardless. Elora bundled pillows from the bed and draped a heavy blanket across them. Vivienne switched her phone off and they sat there, breath ragged but slowing, like two children pulled from an icy ocean.

'It's not normally like this,' repeated Vivienne.

'I know,' said Elora, softly.

'Do you think Mum and Dad are still okay?' asked Vivienne.

'Yeah,' said Elora, strangely certain.

Vivienne dropped her head on Elora's shoulder, and something tectonic seemed to shift between them. The inexorable moment between siblings where age surrenders its relevance. Something so defining. So present. Gone in an instant, and then forever.

'I saved your bedroom,' said Vivienne.

'What?'

'At our house. I saved the room and kept up the lease in case you wanted to stay there.'

Elora took a shallow breath. Her brain couldn't process this information, nor how she felt about it. 'Let's try to sleep,' she said.

'Okay,' said Vivienne.

'We've been lucky, but we're almost there,' said Elora.

'Lucky?' murmured Vivienne.

'Yeah.'

Vivienne didn't respond. She shook once more, a jerking splutter that Elora knew marked the downward tunnel into sleep. She listened as her sister's breath flattened out against the angry rumble of the galaxy. They were alone, but somehow she knew there were many others huddled like this across the land.

She thought of Donnie and Jenna making their way north and east into the desert. Pulled over in a truck-stop where they sat by a fire, making dinner and listening to the music drifting out from Jenna's car. They were not yet in the desert, but already the land was stark and endless beneath the glow of Draconis. Headlights creeping the arrow-straight highway like insects crawling over something dark and monumental, Donnie watching them from the fireside, eyes wide and drinking in the action all around. Already he would have seen giant burning craters and hurtling convoys of the famed steel caravans. Haul trucks carrying kamacite to processing plants in the desert. A roadside dump of more mobile phones than he could have ever imagined. And Donnie would know, with a tingling certainty, that there would be other things to come. A lifetime of stories to return home with when the time was right.

Jenna would be feeling a strange glow of happiness beside him, free of the town and the shadow it had thrown across her family. Slowly and gently allowing herself to consider the possibility that her father was out there ahead of them. There were places they'd heard of where people had tunnelled beneath the earth to build homes without windows. Years ago, at the start of Draconis. Jenna had described them as great woven communities, places with their own customs and mythologies, founded by people who had tunnelled, blind with fear, and instead found something more. Something to hold tight to, irrespective of the whims of the universe. Perhaps they would find her father there among them. Or perhaps he was someplace else entirely. It was movement that was important to Jenna now. To be no longer waiting, suspended, no longer circling the streets of her hometown. She was finally on her way somewhere, and it hadn't yet come at the cost of Donnie.

Frances would not be with them, thought Elora. She would be at the salt lake by now. Somehow she was certain of this. The draw of this place – of the challenge it threw down – was simply too great for Frances to ignore. The salt lake finally offered Frances her chance to face off with Draconis in its full and dazzling horror. To prove to herself, irrefutably, that the universe outside of her mind had no bearing on the chaos within. Frances had been moving toward this moment for as long as Elora could remember. Refusing to hide behind shutters. Wandering the streets when the townsfolk were sheltering. Burning through psychologists who sought to draw even the slightest connection between her anxiety and the meteors hurtling through the galaxy.

Elora also knew there were other things that Frances didn't tell her. Dark things that she didn't tell anyone, but they were there behind her eyes when she surfaced from seclusion.

That she had set her best friend on this path was something that Elora couldn't reconcile. Frances would brush this off as inevitable – she would have found her way to this lake anyhow. But Elora was terrified of what the climax of Frances' battle with Draconis might bring. Of the defeat she could suffer, but also the victory. Of what it was that Frances actually sought from Draconis throughout all of these years. The thought made her shudder, and she drew her mind away. Instead she held on to a simple hope that Frances was warm and sheltered on this evening. That maybe she had found her way into their motel room and was resting in the same bed before heading out to the lake. Maybe the television was back on and she was laughing at the same terrible advertisements Elora had seen just a few nights earlier.

Her thoughts found their way to Hayden, travelling onward to the towns and cities in the south, through tiny farming outposts open and resolute against the swell of Draconis, into the bustle of a city perched watchfully on the slopes of two rolling headlands. Eating and drinking in an ancient hotel before heading upstairs to lay and listen as people fled or danced beneath the falling meteorites. Further and further from the irrepressible roll of the holding. Elora saw Hayden at a promontory at the edge of the great Southern Ocean, nowhere else for the ute to take him. She hoped he'd found something on the way to this place, something to confirm his life on the holding, or to point him somewhere else entirely.

When her thoughts eventually landed on her parents, Elora couldn't see them in their home. She wandered each room, finding empty teacups, and towels hanging dry in the bathrooms and laundry. The balcony was vacant, and above the town a sea breeze was shifting gently through the Norfolk pines. Everything was empty and still. Elora felt a whisper of panic, then thought perhaps it was mid-semester and her parents had left for the city, travelling up in her father's car to holiday by the ocean and visit her at the campus. She fought off an urgency to wake Vivienne and race onward so that her parents wouldn't arrive to find an empty room. This didn't make sense, yet Elora couldn't drag the logic from her mind to dismiss her parents' troubled faces in the hall of her dorm.

Annabel would find them, she reassured herself. The friend she had spoken so much about. Annabel would find her parents and usher them somewhere safe and warm where the three of them could wait for her until it was her turn to arrive.

* * *

They woke to the sound of a bird in the house. It was fluttering, confused, somewhere down the hall from where they lay. A manic flap of wings as it circled, then returned to a perch somewhere in the loft, then around again a moment later. The house had been breached. It wouldn't take long for the forest to find its way inside.

Elora rose first and shuffled over to look outside. Draconis was buffeting the sky with her needles, but for the moment the atmosphere was holding them at bay. The day was bright, sun already high above the trees to the east of them. Elora pulled her eyes away and sat on the bed. Her skin felt tight and raw like a sunburn. If she remained still, the throbbing was tolerable, but even small movements sent out hot spikes of pain.

They found shoes in the cupboard and crunched through the house on a bed of glass that was thick like gravel. The pantry was full, but they could only stomach a single tin of fruit and some paracetamol between them before heading outside in search of the car. The grass and weed that had run up to their knees now lay flattened like a carpet all around the house, and many of the nearby trees were also cut down. Those that remained upright had been shredded of foliage and stood, naked and exposed, to the piercing summer sun. There was a smell in the air like bushfire, but as far as Elora could see the forest was intact.

Alone on the road, in a halo of glass and rubble, was the car as they had left it. The windows were gone and the paintwork warped by heat into a murky rainbow. None of the tyres had survived, so they set about pulling their things from inside and working out what they could carry. Vivienne made a joke about her car rental record, but otherwise she was silent. For the first time in days, Elora couldn't see the urgency in her sister's shoulders. Her movements seemed tired and mechanical, as if fate had finally worn her down.

There was little to discuss in terms of their direction or plan. Reaching the city was the only option now – there they could find shelter and another car. Maybe even send word to their parents. They were too close now to pivot or alter their plans.

After changing into their own clothes and shoes, they set off, both overloaded with luggage but unwilling to abandon anything more. The housing estate ended not far from the car, with a sign advertising new lots and a tranquil rural lifestyle. It also indicated that they were just minutes from the city. It wasn't literal, but gave them both a small spark of energy.

Thick forest resumed on either side of the road. Elora was glad of this, despite the risk of falling trees. She felt less exposed beneath the canopy, more able to chase Draconis from her thoughts and focus on other things. She tried hard to do this and ignore the pain in her neck and shoulders. The bag on her back felt like sandpaper against the cuts and scratches. She also noticed a strange weakness in her legs, as if there was no longer a guarantee that they could hold the rest of her aloft.

No cars travelled this road, and the insects had returned to score the forest with a soft morning hum. The two of them stopped often, drinking water and gingerly dabbing their wounds with cotton balls from Vivienne's first aid kit. For a while Elora walked with her headphones on and her ears full of music, but she couldn't relax. She heard crackles and explosions in the songs where there were none, and caught strange looks from Vivienne as she winced and glanced upwards.

At midday they stopped by an old fallen log and both slumped down in exhaustion. The heat had penetrated into the canopy; the air felt thick and difficult to breathe. Elora remembered what Frances had said about the dinosaurs, how their planet had baked amid the heat of a burning atmosphere.

Once they'd eaten she lay on her stomach and took the fantasy novel from her backpack. The story had been nagging at her, somehow holding a place in a mind that was full of so many other things. She was eager to finish the final chapter and find out what it was that this old book was so desperate to tell her.

Vivienne glanced over and let out a small laugh at the sight of her sister.

'What?' said Elora.

'You look like you're in a park in Paris somewhere.'

'I can't lie on my back.'

Vivienne nodded, stretching her neck and repositioning herself on the log. 'What's with that book?'

'What do you mean?' asked Elora, looking at the cover.

'Isn't your bag heavy enough?'

'Oh. Yeah, it is.'

'So, is it your favourite book or something?'

'No. It's not even mine. I just took it from Dad before we left. For some reason it was sitting loose on the shelves.'

Vivienne watched her, waiting for more.

'I wanted something to read as we drove out of town. Thought I might get upset otherwise.'

'That makes sense.'

'Really?'

'Yeah.'

'You get upset leaving town?' asked Elora.

'Town. You guys.'

Elora nodded, trying to mask her surprise.

Vivienne looked away and sighed.

'Sorry,' said Elora, watching her.

Vivienne played with the bark of the tree for a while. She looked oddly young and fragile. 'You know who watches all of those boring renovation shows with Mum every night?'

Elora looked at her, confused.

'When you're out with your friends and Dad is downstairs,' said Vivienne. 'Mum and I got through three seasons this summer. A new record for us.'

'You just sit there watching renovation shows?'

'Pretty much. Sometimes we eat ice cream. Make a cheese board. Talk.'

Elora put the book aside and sat up. 'What do you talk about?'

'Everything,' she shrugged after a while.

Vivienne's eyes were welling so she stood up and readied her bags. Elora felt like an idiot. With every layer her sister revealed, the careful picture she had drawn of her became further and further removed.

She rose, and was about to take hold of her own bags when the sky crackled with a shuddering boom.

They froze, then sheltered frantically at the base of a tree. Seconds ticked by as they huddled there, covering their heads.

'I'm so over this,' said Vivienne.

Elora glanced up at the canopy. The sky was white-hot with sun, the kind of day that could mask a meteor until it exploded right above. 'Let's just go,' she said.

Vivienne looked at her as the sky creaked again. Surely the weight of Draconis would soon be too much.

'We don't know where any of these things are going to land,' Elora said. 'And I'm sick of running and hiding. Let's just get it over with.' She stood back up and winced as she pulled on her bag.

A moment later Vivienne joined her, and they shuffled back out onto the road. It was dappled with shade from the forest, interspersed with blinding ribbons of sunlight. Every few seconds these ribbons pulsed even brighter with the sharpness of a rock bursting in the atmosphere. An edgy and electric river, plunging down to a city caught somewhere below.

They found themselves moving quickly in spite of the heat and baggage, both of them willing the forest to finally give way to the concrete sprawl of the city. Twice Elora caught a flash of movement above them and they flinched as the canopy shuddered like splashing water.

There was debris on the road – branches, litter, a car tyre – but nothing to block their way. Elora shifted her bags from her back to carry them under her arms, then back again when this became too difficult. Her shirt was wet with perspiration, and her cuts had bled through on the shoulders.

The road began a sharp and snaking decline. Elora glanced up expectantly, but the trees remained thick and constant. Her ears popped, releasing a pressure that felt as though it had been pooling for weeks. The downward slope revealed more of the sky above the city. Hazy trails of smoke disturbed the blue in several sections to the east of them. She looked immediately west, hoping to catch a glimpse of the ocean or the clean air above, but saw neither. Just forest, then a wash of pale blue. Then whiteness and the fever of Draconis.

Vivienne gasped.

A pair of meteorites emerged from the sky and thundered into the forest behind them. Trees bent in unison and a cloud of dust engulfed the road. They hurried forward, coughing their way through the hot, murky air. Elora felt dizzy and removed from herself. She thought she could hear sirens wailing through the hills. Maybe they were fire trucks. She wanted to ask Vivienne, but she was suddenly lost from view.

Elora spun around and found her sister some way behind her. Vivienne looked breathless and haggard. She had a stoop that looked as though she might tumble forward under the weight of everything.

'We have to lose the bags,' croaked Vivienne.

Elora hesitated. Her mind leapt to her clothes, jewellery, books – the curated selection of everything she had brought from home. 'Okay,' she replied, reluctantly.

Vivienne trudged over to the side of the road and shoved her bags down by the base of a tree. 'Here,' she said, tucking them out of sight. 'We can come back for them.'

Elora followed, yet she knew somehow that they wouldn't come back. This journey had stripped her of almost everything – it felt bitter and right to be losing the rest now that they were finally on the edge of the city.

They continued on with just a backpack between them, lighter and faster within the mindless snake of the road. A property emerged from the trees, and for a moment they were stunned by the sight. A long, terraced garden and a red-brick house. Elora looked for others, assuming that they had reached the city proper.

Vivienne dismissed the house and kept moving, Elora now trailing behind her. The forest resumed almost immediately and still there was no sign of a suburb ahead.

Another turn in the road. Trees, and the smoulder of a crater beyond them.

Elora saw pulses everywhere, and wondered whether the phantom streaks had now decided to invade her daytime. She rubbed her eyes and focused hard on each step. *Keep upright. Move forward. Stay awake.*

Vivienne stopped walking. A shape, dark and oblong, was hovering directly above them. Elora tried to scream but nothing emerged from her lungs. She looked helplessly at her sister. Vivienne was motionless, and seemed almost calm in the shadow of this thing. Elora watched as she took out her phone and turned to smile at her. Broad and true, like a photo from their childhood.

'It's a comms balloon,' said Vivienne.

Elora stepped closer. She was breathless and wary, despite her sister's sudden ease.

'There must be a launch site somewhere in the hills.'

She gazed up at the shape. A shimmering, squid-like object, drifting bravely up into the mayhem.

'Look at the network it's pumping out,' said Vivienne, showing Elora her phone.

'Call Mum and Dad,' said Elora, immediately.

Vivienne dialled their mother. Then their father.

Nothing.

They stood in silence for a moment.

'It doesn't mean anything,' said Vivienne, her feet shuffling on the road. 'The towers are probably still down in Esperance.'

Elora tried to shift her thoughts back to the present. She watched as the balloon continued skyward.

'Won't it get hit by Draconis?'

'They're stratospheric.'

Elora looked at her.

'Low altitude,' said Vivienne. 'Like a plane, but with heaps less surface area.'

Elora nodded.

'The math on them avoiding strikes is super high. Or it was, before all of this started.'

They watched as the balloon grew smaller and drifted eastward on the breeze.

'Maybe this one will sail right by,' said Elora.

Vivienne smiled, her eyes fixed skyward, soft forest light picking up the gold hue of the hair plastered to her forehead.

'This is what you've been learning to build?' asked Elora.

'Not this one. But others.'

'Pretty cool,' said Elora.

Vivienne looked at her and they shared a smile.

Elora shifted the backpack, her shoulders on fire beneath. 'Does this mean we're close to the city?'

'We're here,' said Vivienne, as if it were obvious. 'Listen.'

Elora lifted her head. Beyond the insects and the nervous shuffle of the trees was a dense and foreign hum. Cars driving on a highway. Air conditioners shuddering against the heat. Sirens – clearer now – drifting throughout the hills like a sombre chorus. Elora felt a wash of relief. Not everyone had abandoned the metropolis.

Vivienne was tapping rapidly at her phone beside her. 'Shit,' she whispered.

'What?'

'Shit,' she repeated.

'Vivienne?'

'A plane went down on the way to Adelaide. They're closing the airport.'

'When?'

'I don't know,' said Vivienne, scanning for more information.

There was a pulse in the sky to the west of them and a rumble that sounded like terrain. They flinched and considered again whether they should be sheltering.

Vivienne pocketed the phone and looked around in frustration. 'God,' she said, tearing up.

Elora watched her, saw the exhaustion of her sister's fight against the universe, so literal now and escalating with every day and hour. 'You should go now. It might still be open,' said Elora.

Vivienne took a breath, keeping her eyes away from her sister. 'It's no use,' she said, quietly.

Elora took off her backpack and let the cooling air drift over her bloodied shoulders. She felt a strange calm resonating all around her, as if she had risen from an endless swirl of white water. It was still there, pulling and fizzing at her waist, but her feet were now steadfast in the sand. She pictured the rocks of Draconis becoming small and distant, just lights in the sky like the Geminids or Perseids.

'I read about that star in Draco,' she said, after a while. 'There was a magazine about it at the hostel.'

'Alruba,' murmured Vivienne.

Elora nodded. 'The foal being chased by wolves.'

Vivienne was silent and pensive. Her shoulders rounded and the fire gone from her eyes.

'You didn't tell me about all of the other stars in Draco,' said Elora.

Vivienne looked at her, confused. 'What other stars?'

'Beta. Gamma. Xi. Nu. There's a whole ring of suns up there.'

The balloon was now a spot of paint on the canvas of sky above them. It would soon reach altitude and attempt to stabilise, free of the chrysalis and ready to fulfil its destiny.

Elora turned and found her sister's gaze. 'People called them the Mother Camels.' She stood tall and strong amid the mayhem. 'They're coming to protect that foal. The fight for Draco isn't over.'

Chapter Twenty-Two

Elora sat on a bench above an intersection. Surrounding her was a narrow stretch of parkland that bridged a bank of shops and the concrete delta of highways and off-ramps below. There were thick gumtrees above. Their bark caught the last of the sun as it sunk into the haze to the west. A flock of birds, white like porcelain, erupted from the branches and fled madly to some other place. A shrill and ugly call, but Elora found herself unable to look away.

The birds drew a childhood memory. A picnic by the river somewhere. Her ball rolling down a long, grassy hill, past trees like these ones to water bright with yachts and sunshine. Elora racing to stop the ball before it reached the river, wind filling her ears and the colourful wash of other children blurred in her periphery. The grass felt cool and soft beneath her feet, her legs like springs that could thrust her for miles – even right over the river – if that was what she wanted. She came up alongside the ball and caught it nimbly in the final sweep of grass, then it was back up the slope to roll it down again. Her parents and Vivienne were up there beneath the shade of a flowering gum, food pushed aside and lazing with drinks amid a patchwork of other blankets and people. Elora waved and her parents waved back. Vivienne didn't respond, her attention absorbed by a manic swirl of birds above them: cockatoos engulfing tree after tree in a mess of white wings. Elora stopped and followed her sister's gaze. Her breathing slowed and the ball forgotten. The birds were shrieking and fleeing for no reason that she could determine. She looked back at Vivienne, then again to the birds. Such madness in the tranquillity. What did these birds know that nobody else could fathom?

An older man emerged from a walkway with a stout grey terrier and Elora was pulled from her reverie. She watched as the man shuffled across the park, head down and swift in spite of his age, no heed for the nose of the dog by his side. The sight felt surreal, as if she was viewing someone from another world. A moment later they disappeared down another walkway and Elora was alone once again.

She was slightly stunned by the ocean of movement below her. Cars converged on the suburb from every direction but the south, headlights blurring in the endless dusk, idling and waiting as the traffic lights cycled from red to green, then speeding off until they were halted by another. The way south was submerged by the red blur of taillights, but it was the other roads that stole Elora's attention. A web of highways joining suburbs, streets and homes. There were cars upon these roads also – fewer in number, but still telling and mysterious. Where were the friends and families of these people? What lives were they still living in this place?

The city she could see was distant and static, a blip of grey towers on a horizon blurred by smoke and heat. Its presence was reassuring to a point, but Elora still knew nothing of what had befallen this place since their journey had begun.

She opened the backpack and peered inside. Vivienne had left behind everything but her purse and jumper. 'Radical self-reliance,' she had joked, but Elora winced at the thought of her sister continuing on with so little, empty-handed and alone at the final leg of the journey. The airport was set into the swampy plains to the east of the city, along a highway running in the opposite direction to Elora's university, but what did any of that matter after the journey they had taken? Vivienne may have felt this too, but said she couldn't fly from a city while her sister waved from the terminal. Instead, they cleaned up in the bathroom of a convenience store and said their goodbyes on the pavement outside. Vivienne wept. Elora couldn't, not until a few minutes after, when she locked herself back in the bathroom and didn't emerge for almost an hour. She bought water and a chocolate bar from an attendant who appeared to have forgotten her earlier visit, then found the park and bench at the back of the store.

Elora leant back and swore – the fantasy novel wasn't inside the bag.

She considered returning to the forest road to find their luggage, but it would soon be dark, and she had promised Vivienne she would continue on to the university or find somewhere to sleep or shelter. For the entire time she had spent re-reading the novel, Elora had tried hard to forget the ending, but now she felt desperate to know every detail. The fate of the two young elves tasked with uncovering the magic to save their people, and the citadel, its walls besieged by demons and its monarchy now breached from within. She felt a deep fear for these characters, and had to remind herself that the many of them would survive.

A subtle tremor had taken up in her left hand and now spread to the right. She tucked them under her legs and tried hard not to break down completely at how alone she was in the world. This was her truth now, not the irrational panic of a school-leaver willing a bus to take her home from a party in the Wheatbelt. She had arrived in a city where the only soul she knew was boarding a plane to the other side of the country. Her friends were scattered or dead, her parents severed and gone. *And for what?* she thought. *To study at a university she hoped would still be standing? To learn an art that the world could no longer use?*

It was all but dark, yet Elora could barely pull herself from the bench. She considered huddling beneath the steel and closing her eyes on Draconis until something forced them open. *Did it really matter where she lay?*

Eventually she walked back to the shops, finding the shutters pulled and the carpark empty. It seemed early for this to be happening, and panic spiked in her abdomen. The city was already bunkering down for the evening. Lights off and shutters drawn. Lanes beginning to clear on the highways below.

Elora cursed herself for staying so long in the park, and headed swiftly for a cluster of larger buildings adjacent to the trees. There were empty car parks all around this structure, some tucked beneath the building and others stretching above. It was a shopping centre. She felt a murmur of familiarity and searched for an entrance. The building was silent and drawn. No light escaped from within, and Elora realised she was traversing car parks that lay empty and strewn with sand and debris. She wondered whether the centre had been closed a long time ago, rather than earlier that day.

Noises echoed out from the lower car parks: voices and laughter. Elora stayed out of sight and stopped to listen. People were sheltering down there, but they sounded rabid and hyper. Elora shuddered and gave up on the centre, circling the hulking eastern wing to a walkway that sloped down to a train station. The tracks were empty but she continued on regardless. Vivienne had explained the train lines to her more than once during their journey. A series of arteries that would all drain into the city if she stayed aboard long enough. From here she could trace the river and find her way to the university. *Buy a day ticket. Make sure you're on the city-bound platform. Don't stare at people.* It was obvious and patronising, but Elora now found herself clinging to Vivienne's advice like a mantra.

The platform was built in brick, but not without some grandeur as the northern walls rose into a series of high arches and eventually a tower housing a faded steel clock. There were lights on around the station but no people that Elora could see. She stayed back from the building, not wanting to venture into the darker areas beneath the arches. Litter was swirling about in the breeze, and it felt as though the station may have been full not long before she arrived.

A voice rang out and Elora froze.

It was loud and metallic. An announcement revealing the next service into the city: six a.m. the following morning.

The voice continued on with a message about service interruptions and new safety initiatives. Elora ignored these and retraced her steps out of the station and past the shopping centre. In the darkness the suburbs stood dim and pensive beneath a sky so purple and electric that it seemed to Elora to be drawn from one of Hayden's video games. Earth was now circling through a thick and frenzied universe. Elora could almost feel the struggle around her. The moment soon when her planet would be ground to a fatal halt. Suspended with Mars, Venus and all the others, like the mobiles they had once built in school.

She didn't know where to go next, so just returned to the stores by the park and sat, exhausted, in the recess of a shuttered door. The city felt foreign and impenetrable, as if it were under siege and unable – or perhaps unwilling – to shelter any more souls. Vivienne would be at the airport by now, maybe even boarding a plane away from this place. Elora could already feel the distance between them, a chasm she had ignored or embraced for all these years, but now felt desperate to bridge. She had seen how distance could turn into forever in this world.

She stood again and made herself finish the water in her bag. When this was done she moved to the edge of the park and assessed the highway Vivienne had taken. It snaked away to the east under a bank of towering streetlights. There were still cars travelling on the highway – not many, but maybe this meant the buses were still running also. If she could find the right one, maybe it could ferry her to the terminal in time to reach her sister. Elora squinted at the blackness and tried to plot a way down to the highway through the park and houses.

It was useless in the darkness. She swore and was considering setting off regardless when a light caught her eye, low in the sky above the eastern hills. Calm and rhythmic flashing that set it apart from Draconis. It was a plane, she realised, collapsing inward.

The light was stolen a second later by a meteor knifing through the distant northern sky before pulsing into oblivion. A hot breeze tickled Elora's fringe and some leaves skittered by her shoes. She stood there, frozen and alone in the darkness. When her eyes recovered, Elora could no longer make out the plane. She scanned frantically, looking for the flash of the tail or anything that appeared in contrast to Draconis. Her eyes were tired and confused. *Had she really seen it?* The sky seemed to be swelling once more.

Another pulse, closer this time. West of the suburb and just out to sea. Elora cowered as the sky boomed in protest and a hiss of foul wind ripped across the park.

'No!' she yelled, angry and desperate.

Lights dropped from the suburbs like dominoes. Shutters slammed down. Cars pulled off highways.

Elora ran from the park and past the shops at the crest of the rise. She was too high. Too exposed.

The third rock exploded low in the sky and knocked her from her feet. She skidded on gravel and took a handful into the skin of her palm. She rose again, crying now, and continued on down the nearest road. It dipped steeply into an intersection, then into a patch of forest spilling down from the hills above. Elora stumbled through the trees and caught sight of a light ahead of her, windows framing a warm and yellow glow. They seemed fake, but she headed their way regardless. Draconis drew shadows from trees like warped prison bars all around her. Between these a series of old wooden buildings began emerging from the darkness. Pitched roofs and raised porches. Rose gardens out the front of each.

It was a pioneer village.

Beyond the houses was a two-storey inn with a hint of light escaping from behind the shutters and doors. Elora would have sought shelter there were it not for the stupid glow of the building by its side – at least a dozen windows, wide open and throwing their golden light out into the trees. To add to this, there were party lights decorating the entrance. Elora slowed as if struck by a mirage.

A barn-like wooden building stood before her, emitting a warm hum of noise and light. It had an A-frame roof that had been restored with clean iron sheeting, but the rest of the building appeared to be vintage and original. Decorative timber gables stood above a wide and colourful verandah. The front doors were painted yellow and the posts and railings a deep auburn. The building was set atop a small incline, allowing for the rear to stretch downward with the land to form a tall space with a large opening, side-of-stage. Elora could see light escaping from this opening along with the bustle of actors and stagehands. A jolt of electricity danced across her skin.

She walked up the steps and into the light of a hanging paper lamp. The verandah was cut from jarrah, old and rich timber that felt sturdy beneath her feet. At one end were tables and chairs with candles and programs, at the other was a box-office booth with a calendar of upcoming shows. *Rent. Cats.* An original play titled *Hills on Fire.* The local high school's version of *Chicago.* Elora stood, slightly awestruck in the wonder of the place. Lights were dimming inside the building and she heard the shuffle of feet on floorboards.

'Are you okay there?'

She turned and found the source of the voice. A woman sat inside the booth with double plaits and a t-shirt like one of Vivienne's.

'Sorry,' said Elora, her voice weak and fragile. 'Are there any tickets left?'

'A few,' replied the woman, smiling.

Elora moved over to the booth.

'But what I meant was, are you *okay* there?' She tilted her head slightly, looking at Elora with a soft and patient gaze.

Elora dropped her bag from her shoulder and wiped a bloodied hand on her pants. Her legs throbbed and her back sparkled with pain at every movement. She nodded, but fat tears were dripping from her eyes.

The woman reached across the counter and took her hand. Elora let her, watching as the woman assessed her raw and angry skin. The woman placed a napkin over her palm, pressing lightly with her own to pull away the dirt. When this was done she replaced it with a fresh napkin, along with something cold from the freezer beneath the counter. Elora wrapped her fingers gingerly around the object. It was an ice cream, she realised. Chocolate coated in a squat and heavy cone. She hadn't seen one of these since she left the city as a child.

'You can eat it later if you like.'

Elora took a shallow breath and smiled. 'Sorry,' she replied. 'My sister just left on a plane, and I can't reach my parents in Esperance.'

The woman smiled, knowing and kind, as if she had heard many tales greater than this one.

'I've come all this way just to go to university, and it all feels so stupid,' said Elora.

'University sounds like the opposite of stupid.'

Elora tried a smile. The sky crackled and some trees shook in the thin forest above.

'What will you study?'

'Drama.'

'Of course,' smiled the woman.

She removed the ice cream and napkin, studying Elora's palm like a reader in the warm orange light.

'Right now the theatre needs us as much as we need the theatre.'

Elora did smile this time. She took another look inside. 'You don't shutter this building?'

'When the show begins. Draconis makes a mess of our lighting.'

Elora laughed and sniffed. 'What seats do you have?'

'Upper stalls. Best you can buy,' said the woman, passing her a ticket.

Elora took her purse from the bag and handed over some money. The woman passed her the change and Elora packed it away. 'My mum said I should see a play when I get to the city.'

'And here you are,' said the woman.

Elora smiled and turned to enter.

'Hold on,' said the woman, reaching across to pour a drink of some sort into a paper cup. 'Mulled wine. My recipe,' she smiled.

Elora took a sip, her senses engulfed by cinnamon and berries. It reminded her of Christmas Eve with her parents and Vivienne. A pine tree blinking and fragrant beside them. Presents like a sparkling moat below.

The wine seemed to slow her thoughts and breath. 'Thank you,' she said, as earnestly as she was able.

The woman smiled and nodded to the foyer.

Elora hesitated. 'You're not leaving the city?' she asked.

The woman laughed and shook her head.

'How come?' asked Elora.

The woman leant back in her chair, sipping some wine of her own. 'I have a sister in Canada,' she said after a while. 'Molly. She lives with her son and partner in a ski town outside of Vancouver. Draconis has made a mess of the slopes up there, so most people don't bother skiing anymore. The resorts cleared out. Molly lost her shifts in the bar. They spend most of their time renovating the house now.'

Elora listened, the sky forgotten above them.

'She sent me a photo a few weeks ago. Before our internet went down again. The three of them were out skiing. First time in almost a year, and they found a slope without a single crater. Just perfect powder for miles. There was nobody else out and the day was incredible. It's too bright for Draconis, and from up that high you can see right out to the water and the city.' She sighed, eyes lost in the middle distance. 'Anyway, they're standing at the top of the slope, all smiling and ready to go down. And in the background of the photo I notice there's a valley with a road trailing down to a property. Just one tiny road that winds and winds past a river like Molly described it. Nothing down there but water and trees. I looked at the photo closely, trying to make out the house at the end of this road. See how their place was coming together.' The woman finished the wine in her glass, then reached across to fill it with some more. 'But it was gone,' she said. She took a long draw on the wine. 'Instead there was a crater. Only one in the entire valley. It was black and new, but small. Not much bigger than a house.'

Elora stared at her.

'They didn't even know until the boy asked to see the photos on the way home.'

'That's awful,' whispered Elora, her hand over her mouth.

'Molly says it's just luck,' said the woman. 'Whatever that means.'

Elora lingered a moment, not knowing what to say. Eventually she shuffled beneath the weight of her bag, then headed for the foyer.

'Don't you want to know what's playing?' asked the woman.

Elora turned and hesitated, then shrugged.

The woman laughed, loud and alive, and she continued on into the darkness.

★ ★ ★

Elora sat central in the upper stalls amid the soft gather of voices. Not a full house, but still, there were others like her with their heads turned to a stage pooled in light. The curtains were drawn, and beyond them lay the thickness of the present, coiled and ready. Existing once only and then never again.

A lever sounded and the shutters came down on the windows. The theatre became darker again, the sickly purple of Draconis cut from their view. If the rocks came for them now it would be by tree or by stone. Yet Elora knew that wolves had no agency in this place of fiction and fantasy. They could breach every valley, planet and galaxy, but not every world.

Elora drank the wine and thought about Hayden and Frances and their dinosaurs. She too had begun to feel a strange kinship to these ancient custodians, their bones suspended in the earth beneath her, their ash thrust skyward to drift in the atmosphere forever. What did they think of life and fate? Of the hand that had been dealt to them? Of Draconis now seeking a new reckoning of her own?

The curtains opened, and Elora felt a searing and wicked anger at what had befallen her planet. This thing that sought to take back the gift it had delivered so long ago. To rupture their roads and shatter their homes. She had seen too many people scattered and diminished, their voices drowned out or taken up by fear.

Elora felt a sudden urgency to stand firm amid this barrage. To continue searching. Feeling. Reaching. To join her sister, and shout loudest into the universe as it finally turned their way.

ACKNOWLEDGEMENTS

Thanks to Kate Pickard and the team at UWAP, alongside the judges of the 2022 Dorothy Hewitt Award, for their belief in me as the recipient of such a respected award, and *Eta Draconis* as an entrant into this young and impressive canon.

Thanks to Sam Cooney for his time and expertise in editing this novel from a distance, but always with great personability and professionalism.

I would also like to thank Emma Jarvis for her careful eye and kind words at a time when the manuscript was yet to receive much of either. Big thanks to Mike Sharpe for also offering these things, as well as much guidance on topics such as physics, satellites, telecommunications, air travel and just the whole entire galaxy. For someone who 'isn't an expert', you certainly display a suspicious number of the traits. And to my good friend and colleague Amanda Betts, for her time, advice and belief for several years now – all so valued.

This novel was written in an isolation born out of geography, parenthood, work and a pandemic, and brief moments of solidarity from friends and colleagues were a welcome reminder that there was worth and potential in the undertaking. Thanks to Donna Mazza, Lewis Attey, Jesse Phillips, Marcella Polain, David Settelmaier and Lydia Edwards in this regard.

Thanks to my parents Pamela and John for their love, support and grounding. It's difficult to get carried away with anything when there are topics like vegetable manure and organic cleaning products to discuss. And to my sisters and their families, love to you all, as always.

Finally, to my wife Claire, and daughters Harriet and Vivian. Claire for hearing me say, many times over, that writing a book right now isn't possible, and supporting me to keep finding a way. Harriet and Vivian for always being their brilliant selves. The three of you are my universe, but also my motivation to continue exploring others. Thanks for yesterday, today and tomorrow.